IN THE HEAT OF THE NIGHT

"You can never be certain what other people are feeling or thinking unless they tell you," Shannon whispered.

Gareth looked down at the top of Shannon's shining head, the elusive sweet scent that always hung about her drifting up. He felt his body hardening despite all his good intentions.

"You are so right about that," he finally answered. "I have no idea what you're thinking now. Let alone feeling."

For a long time Shannon didn't move or say anything. Then she loosened her fingers and moved away from him.

"We weren't talking about me. I was trying to make you see you might be wrong about how your family feels." Shannon became aware all over again of how she was dressed. Or *undressed*. Of how she shouldn't be here. Under this tree with Gareth so close. So tempting.

"But I would like to know what you're thinking and feeling," Gareth said.

"No, you wouldn't." She started to rise, but he reached out and grasped her arm.

"Yes, I would. Don't go just yet."

You shouldn't be doing this, Shannon told herself, but nevertheless let Gareth pull her back down beside him. Somehow, they were closer than before. Somehow, she was touching him.

Even through her nightdress, she could feel his warmth seeping into her. Feel the sweet lassitude of those other two times they had been together stealing over her. Making her want to get closer. As close as it was possible to be. . . .

Books by Elizabeth Graham

SWEET ENCHANTMENT

COURTING EDEN

MY DARLING KATE

THE HEART'S HAVEN

Published by Zebra Books

THE HEART'S HAVEN

Elizabeth Graham

Zebra Books
Kensington Publishing Corp.
http://www.zebrabooks.com

ZEBRA BOOKS are published by

Kensington Publishing Corp.
850 Third Avenue
New York, NY 10022

First Printing: July, 1998
10 9 8 7 6 5 4 3 2 1

Printed in the United States of America

For my husband, Lewis.

For my children and grandchildren: Laura and Harry, Matthew, Harold, Jr., and Jennifer; Lewis, Jr., and Nancy, Jennifer, Amy, Ashley, and Ian; Robert; and Susan and Dan.

Thanks for your never-failing love and support.

For my editor, John Scognamiglio, who lets me write my kinds of books—and always likes them. Thank you!

Special thanks to Alice Newton, Page County, Virginia, librarian.

And to Debby J. Owens, Secretary/Treasurer of the Genealogical Society of Page County, Virginia, for her invaluable help with research for this book.

AUTHOR'S NOTE

The flood I've depicted in this book was an actual event, the Shenandoah River's worst flood in history. It took out every bridge and covered every bottom.

Several lives were lost and much property destroyed.

Chapter One

Virginia's Shenandoah Valley—1870

What was that just ahead alongside the road? That crumpled heap?

Coming closer, his stomach tightening in shock, Gareth Colby saw it was a man.

Unconscious or dead.

"Whoa!" He yanked hard on the reins, and the horse snorted and stopped, the old farm wagon coming to a creaking, lumbering halt.

Gareth got down from the plank seat and, favoring his left leg, limped to the figure, bending beside it.

It wasn't a man—only a boy.

He searched for a pulse in the thin wrist and, relieved, found one, fairly strong. Blood seeped into the dirt from a cut on the boy's forehead, where a large lump had formed.

The boy groaned and tried to sit up, his eyelids fluttering open enough to reveal a flash of brilliant blue irises.

"Just take it easy. What happened to you?"

The eyes widened, confusion filling them. Mutely, he shook his head.

Obviously the lad was still dazed. He shouldn't question him now.

And he couldn't leave him here.

Gareth helped him sit up. "Can you stand?"

The boy nodded and with Gareth's aid struggled to his feet.

Shakily, with Gareth still helping him, he walked the few feet to the wagon. Gareth boosted him into the back and eased him down onto the hard planks.

The lad's eyes closed again, and his slight body sagged.

Gareth stood frowning, looking down at the unconscious form. "Who are you, boy? How did you end up unconscious and bleeding beside the road?"

There was no answer. Gareth hadn't expected one.

"Hell, looks like I'll have to take you home with me."

Gareth took off his coarse jacket and folded it, placing it beneath the boy's head. The blood from the cut was congealing. He'd probably be all right until Gareth got home; then Gwenny could clean and bandage the wound.

Still frowning, Gareth got back onto the seat, picked up the reins and clucked to the patient horse. They plodded down the road, through the bright spring day, toward Gareth's farm not far from Luray, off the south fork of the Shenandoah River.

Every few minutes he looked back to see if his passenger was riding as comfortably as possible, his head still inadequately pillowed on the coat. A mile or so from the farm, Gareth's inquiring glance again met the boy's stare.

Gareth smiled, relieved the boy had regained consciousness. "How do you feel?" he asked.

The boy cautiously lifted his hand to touch the lump on the side of his head, then winced. His hand slipped around to his nape, where short, dark reddish-brown hair curled, and then he glanced down at himself, stretching out his legs, clad in stained trousers.

His blue glance again met Gareth's gray one, and surprise went through Gareth at the look of startled panic in the boy's eyes.

Without answering, he jerkily turned away and lay his head back down on the wagon bed.

Looking at the top of the curly head behind him, Gareth frowned. Whatever had happened to this lad, it was nothing good.

Gareth guided the horse the rest of the way home and up the long, tree-bordered lane. Some of the trees were missing now, since the war, used for firewood by passing Yankees. He tried not to think of how he used to love coming up the last little rise and seeing the beautiful house awaiting him.

Grimacing, he turned those thoughts off, fast, before bitterness could set in. He'd had enough of bitterness. Feeling sorry for himself.

They had lost a lot, including his father and two brothers, but were still better off than many. At least they had the farmhouse, which had been the family's first dwelling. Somehow, it had miraculously escaped the torch that had left the big house in cinders.

Molly patiently clip-clopped past the crumbling remains of his former home and on down the lane. Pulling up in front of an old stone house, kept in as good a repair as they could afford, he again stopped the horse, got down from the wagon seat and walked to the side.

A large, nondescript dog ambled up. Whining, he pushed his nose against Gareth's leg. Absently, Gareth patted the animal's head.

His young passenger was sitting, legs pulled up in front of him, thin arms wrapped around them. His head bent into his arms in a despairing hunch.

A twinge of compassion snaked through Gareth. He hated to see a young creature hurt, in pain.

The back door of the house opened, and three women spilled out, laughing and talking. Gareth's youngest sister, eighteen-year-old Clarine, every hair of her blond head carefully arranged in its usual ringlets, reached the wagon first. Her sky blue eyes widened with surprise. "Gareth, who's that?"

Gareth motioned for her to be quiet. "Lad, are you all right?" he asked.

The boy slowly lifted his head, staring at the women surrounding the wagon. That look of near panic was in his eyes again. He nodded. "Yes."

His voice was higher-pitched than Gareth had expected. He decreased his estimate of the boy's age.

"Can you tell us who you are and how you got hurt?" Gareth asked.

The boy's tongue flicked out and moistened his upper lip. He hesitated for a moment. "I—" came out the high near-squeak; then the next words were lower, "was working for a man. He hit me and I fell off his wagon. I guess he went off and left me."

He paused, then went on, slowly. "My name's Shannon . . . Brown."

"Oh, you poor boy!" Gareth's mother Maud said, her fluttery voice and washed-out blue eyes full of solicitude. "Come, let's get you inside and clean up that cut on your head. Do you need help?"

"I'm all right!" Young Shannon quickly got to his feet. He stood swaying for a moment, then moved to the back of the wagon, where he looked down at the ground uncertainly.

Gareth followed, the dog trailing him. The lad acted as if he'd never descended from a wagon before. "Here, let me help you down."

But before Gareth could lower the tailgate, Shannon turned and lifted one leg over the back, then the other, awkwardly sliding to the ground. He swayed again, quickly grabbing the wagon to steady himself.

Guinevere, Gareth's older sister, stepped forward.

"You can't manage by yourself," she said, her voice as brisk as the movements of her tall frame. Impatiently, she pushed back a lock of dark hair. Glancing over her shoulder, her hazel-eyed stare met her sister's.

"Come help me, Clare."

"All right, Gwenny," Clare said, moving forward with alacrity.

"I don't need any help!" Shannon protested, his voice rising again. He clamped his lips together and squared his shoulders, but he still swayed a little.

"Nonsense," Gwenny said, reaching his side. She lifted his arm, placing it around her strong shoulder. Clare, now on his other side, slid her shoulder under his left arm.

A smile hovered over Gareth's mouth as he watched them steer the boy up the steps, across the wide porch and into the kitchen.

Just as he'd anticipated, his female household had taken charge. He lifted a sack of cornmeal and opened the kitchen door.

"No, Duke," Gareth told the dog who was trying to sneak inside. The animal whined at this order, his eyes beseeching, then settled down outside the door.

Young Shannon sat in one of the kitchen chairs. Gwenny was filling a basin with water, while Gareth's mother rummaged in a cupboard for bandage cloth. Clare stood close beside the boy, her head tilted sideways, a coquettish smile on her pretty mouth.

Gareth shook his head. Trust Clare not to waste any time before flirting with any passably attractive male. And this was a good-looking boy. He had a straight, short nose, good, clear skin without a sign of burgeoning whiskers, a well-formed if slight body.

Grandma Lucy rocked her white cat before the hearth, her faded gray eyes looking on with interest.

"Gwenny, add some hot water from the kettle," she directed. "That boy's had enough of a shock. He doesn't need to be sponged down with cold water to boot."

His grandmother might be eighty-five, her health and sight failing, but her hearing was as sharp as a twenty-year-old's. She knew everything that had gone on outside.

Gwenny gave a long-suffering sigh. "Yes, Gramma," the girl said. "I will."

She wrung out the clean cloth in the basin of warm

water and wiped at the congealed blood on Shannon's forehead. The boy winced.

"I'm sorry if it hurts," Gwenny said, her voice concerned but firm. "But we must get this cleaned."

"I know," Shannon answered.

The boy's voice quivered, despite his valiant effort to keep it steady. They needed to get to the bottom of whatever had happened to him, but not right this minute.

Gareth realized his gaze still lingered on young Shannon, and an odd, uncomfortable feeling went through him.

He turned abruptly away.

"I'll go unload the wagon," he said to the room at large.

No one answered. They were all focused on this new arrival.

Still disturbed by his feelings of a moment ago, Gareth went back outside.

The young woman who had given her name as Shannon Brown watched him go, her mouth dry, fear making her knees tremble.

She didn't want to be left alone with all these women. This pretense would be even harder to maintain with members of her own sex.

And how did she know she had to sustain the disguise? That, too, was shrouded inside her fogged brain.

When she'd come to her senses in the back of the jolting wagon, she'd remembered nothing prior to that moment.

Numb with shock, she'd spent the rest of the trip straining to remember, but nothing came. Then the man who had rescued her had stopped the wagon outside the house, and the women had come out.

Fear had flashed over her.

You can't tell them you're a female. You can't tell them anything until you regain your memory. Your life could depend on that.

The warning had come from inside her mind, and she

didn't dare ignore it—or the fear. She had nothing else to rely on.

Why had "Shannon" popped into her mind when Gareth had asked her what she was called? Was it her true name? She felt sure the quickly tacked on surname of Brown wasn't.

Why had the story about the man with a wagon come so easily? Was that also true?

Oh, how she wished she knew!

She shivered in her shabby shirt. The ground alongside the road must have been cold. How long had she lain there before Gareth found her?

All the questions she'd asked herself since she regained consciousness tumbled through her mind again.

Who was she? Why had she been lying by the road, injured, her hair roughly chopped off, her breasts bound with strips of cloth, dressed in men's clothing?

A new wave of confusion and panic hit her. She desperately fought it down, so the people surrounding her wouldn't notice.

"There, I'm almost finished," Gwenny said in her firm, no-nonsense voice. She swabbed at the cut, and Shannon winced. "I'm sorry, but I'm being as gentle as I can."

"It's all right." Guilt that she wasn't being honest with these kind people went through her. Maybe that voice in her mind was wrong. What if she told them she wasn't a boy? Admitted she could remember nothing?

Trusted them.

No! You can't trust anyone now!

A vivid picture filled her mind's eye. A man, faceless and huge, in his hand a knife. The knife dripped blood, and the man wanted more blood on it.

Hers.

Shannon swallowed, a shudder rippling through her. Somehow, she felt sure that vision was no hallucination born of her injury. No, it was a warning, just like the other one.

She mustn't tell these people any of this; she couldn't

trust them to have her best interests at heart. They would take her to the nearest town. To the authorities, who would try to find out who she was, where she'd come from.

Yet, wasn't that what she urgently needed to know?

No! her mind screamed. *It isn't! What you need is to hide, protect yourself, until you remember.*

Because the faceless, terrifying man searched for her, eager to plunge his knife into her body. . . .

Again she shivered. Despite the fog that descended when she tried to remember, some instinct told her he searched for a girl.

She must be fleeing from him. That had to be why she'd cut her hair, put on male garments. And she could have no family, no friends, no one to turn to, or she wouldn't have run away . . . from where?

Where?

Her mind told her nothing more, and she fought her fear, trying to think what to do. She must somehow manage to stay here. She had no other place to go. No one to turn to.

The bleak thought filled her with despair again.

"All finished." Gwenny smiled and dropped the bloody cloth back in the basin. "It isn't too deep a cut. It just bled a lot."

Shannon's hand went to her head, feeling the outline of the large lump with the slashing cut across it.

"Don't touch it! I'll have to wash it all over again," Gwenny said sharply.

Shannon's hand dropped. "I was just wondering if it would leave a scar," she said, hearing the tremor in her voice.

The four women in the room stared at her in surprise. Shannon stared back, her fear and tension growing. Her gaze came to rest on the grandmother in the rocker, who had stopped the movement of her chair, her white brows raised. Why had her remark caused these astonished looks?

"Oh, I don't think so," Gwenny said dryly. "It would be a shame to spoil your good looks."

Comprehension flooded over Shannon, and she felt her face warming. She'd sounded like a vain boy indeed, worrying about a scar.

Or a *girl.*

Already she was making mistakes, she chided herself. She'd have to be more careful.

She forced her mouth into what she hoped was a disarming grin. "Yes, wouldn't it, now?" she said lightly, pitching her voice as low as possible.

The faces around her relaxed into various modes of smiles. Except for Gwenny's. She still gave Shannon a faintly disapproving look.

Shannon sensed a more intent stare and glanced over at the youngest of the women, the one Gareth had called Clare. A shock traveled down Shannon's nerve ends as her gaze collided with the girl's.

Clare's smile revealed a deep dimple at the left corner of her mouth, and her tilted head caused a blond curl to fall halfway across her fair cheek.

"It certainly would," Clare said demurely, her long lashes lowering, then sweeping back up again.

The girl was flirting with her.

As if things weren't complicated enough already. Shannon felt hysterical laughter bubbling up inside. Along with that feeling another one hit. Giddiness. She swayed in the chair, the room darkening around her.

"He's going to faint!" she heard Maud say from what seemed a great distance. "Catch him before he hits his head."

Desperately, Shannon fought the blackness. No! She couldn't lose consciousness again. She couldn't have these women lifting her, touching her. They would be sure to feel the bindings on her breasts, probably think they were more injuries, investigate—and discover her ruse.

She felt hands on her shoulders and drew a few deep breaths, and the darkness gradually cleared.

"The boy needs to rest," the grandmother said firmly. "Put him in a bed."

"We don't have any spare chambers," came the mother's fluttery voice. "I don't know where we can—"

"There's plenty of room in the attic," Gwenny said. "Can you walk, boy, or shall we get Gareth in to carry you?"

That suggestion dispelled the last of the darkness. Shannon's eyes shot open. "No! I'm all right. I can walk."

"I'm not so sure of that, but I don't want to take Gareth from the fields unless we have to. Let's get this bandage on, and I'll walk beside you as I did before."

A few moments later, that task accomplished, Shannon, gritting her teeth and holding her throbbing head as still as possible, slowly got up from the chair.

The plain, but comfortably furnished room tilted for a moment, then righted itself. She took a deep breath and put one foot in front of her, then the other.

Relief shot through her. As long as she kept her head from moving and took small steps, she'd be all right.

But Gwenny settled one of Shannon's arms on her shoulders and led her across the room to a door opening onto a set of steep back stairs, Clare following closely.

At the top of the stairs, a hall which seemed to go on forever stretched before them. Finally, at its end, they turned left and opened a door to yet another set of stairs.

The attic was divided into several small cubicles, some with doors, some without.

"Here we are," Gwenny said briskly, stopping before the first cubicle and opening the door.

One curtainless window filled the room with dim light. A wooden chest stood against a wall, a kitchen chair beside it. A small iron bedstead was against another wall, with only a bare mattress.

Nothing had ever looked so good to Shannon.

Gratefully, she sank down upon it.

"Go ahead and lie down, I'll bring you some bedding," Gwenny's brisk voice told her.

Shannon, her eyes already closing, nodded drowsily. She felt someone tugging at her feet.

"His boots are way too big," Clare said. "It's a wonder he can even walk in them. And just look at these dirty old trousers and shirt! Oh, he must have worked for a very mean man."

"We may not know the whole story. This boy could have run away from somewhere. Tomorrow, we'll have to find out everything. Come on, now. Let him rest."

"We *are* going to let him stay here, aren't we?" Clare's fading voice asked as the two left.

"I don't know if—"

The closing of the attic door cut off Gwenny's answer.

Of course they would let her stay here, Shannon tried to convince herself, fighting to remain awake, to try to remember, think what she could do.

Fear crept in again, making her heart thump against her rib cage.

They *had* to let her stay until she regained her memory, until she could put a face to that menacing man with the bloody knife.

Her head throbbed unmercifully. She must rest, sleep . . . she could fight it no longer.

But what had been the last of Gwenny's statement as she left?

If.

If what?

She could stay if Gareth approved?

He seemed to be the head of the household, so the final decision would have to be his.

Gareth. His gray eyes, his black hair, the way his hard-muscled arms had felt as he half lifted her into the wagon. The vibrating timbre of his deep voice. . . .

His voice had sounded odd as he left the house. It had changed, grown cool and remote.

Could she be the reason for the change? Had something about her disturbed him. . . ?

The blackness began to overtake her once more, her last thought tightening her stomach with renewed fear.

Would Gareth let her stay?

Chapter Two

A shaft of warm morning sunshine streaming through the small window woke Shannon. She lay for a moment, disoriented. Where was she? What was she doing in this bed?

She raised her hand to the bandage on her head, and some of yesterday's events came flooding back.

But nothing before she regained consciousness on Gareth's wagon.

It was as if her life just began at that moment.

Fear started her heart thumping, and she fought it down. She *hated* being afraid all the time. Surely that meant she wasn't naturally a fearful person.

What kind of a person was she?

She closed her eyes and tried to relax, tried to make her mind a blank, begging her memory to return.

The image of a smiling, sweet-faced woman filled her mind's eye. Shannon sucked in her breath. She knew this face! It was . . . she strained, trying to hold the image, but it faded.

The menacing faceless man, still holding the bloody knife, took the woman's place. Cold invaded her, pimpling her arms and drawing the hairs up on the back of her neck.

No! She wouldn't let these fears get the better of her. She *wouldn't!*

She cleared her mind of the dreadful picture, relieved she could manage to do it. It was better to remember nothing than recall that face.

She jerked herself upright, threw the quilt back, and swung her legs over the side of the narrow bed.

Her movements had been too sudden. Dizziness assailed her, and she felt as if her head were spinning in large, swinging circles.

She clenched her fists against the thin mattress. In a few moments the giddiness passed.

Looking down at herself, she saw her feet were bare, but she still wore yesterday's dirty shirt and trousers.

Someone had brought the quilt, but thank God no one had undressed her while she'd been in that heavy, dazed sleep.

How she hated these clothes! How she longed for a silk gown, smooth against her skin. . . .

A *silk* gown? Where had that thought come from? Was she accustomed to such clothing? Or had she just always longed for it? That was certainly more likely, considering her circumstances. Probably she *did* work for someone who mistreated her.

Maybe even the man with the knife.

Quickly she buried the thought. Maybe she was a housemaid, and as Gwenny had suggested last night she'd run away.

But in that case, what had caused the head injury? And why had that story about falling from a wagon come so easily to her mind? *Had* it actually happened?

Was the woman she'd glimpsed a relative? Her mother? Had she a family looking for her, after all? Another thought crowded in.

Perhaps a fiancé . . . or a husband?

You have no family—no husband or fiancé. No one who

searches for you . . . except the man with the knife . . . and maybe the sheriff.

She gasped at the final words. "What would the sheriff want with me? Have I done something wrong?" she asked aloud.

No. But that doesn't matter—you mustn't go to any authorities. You must wait.

The words in her mind were so clear, so firm. She couldn't dismiss them as only more evidence of her confused mental state. With nothing else to guide her, she had to believe them.

There was no one to help her.

She took a deep breath, tightened her mouth.

If she wanted to live, she had to help herself.

And that meant persuading this family to let her stay here where she felt a measure of safety until her memory returned.

Any way she could. Even if it meant continued withholding of the truth.

She felt a twinge of conscience. She didn't like playing this part with these people, who seemed decent, kind folk—but she must.

She had to convince them to let her stay.

She had to convince *Gareth* to let her stay.

Gareth, who disturbed her in some way.

And whom she disturbed, too.

She pushed that thought even deeper inside, and looked about her.

A pile of neatly folded clothes lay on the rickety wooden chair against the wall. On the floor below sat a pair of boots.

Carefully now, Shannon rose and walked the few feet and picked them up.

The garments were a worn but clean pair of dark trousers and a white cotton shirt, both smaller than the clothes she wore. A pair of brown knitted stockings, a coarse cotton undershirt and drawers completed the ensemble.

Someone had brought up a flowered china pitcher and

bowl and placed it on the chest. A chamber pot sat discreetly in a corner. Shannon eyed it, then decided to wait and find an outhouse.

After washing her face and hands she ran the small comb lying beside the bowl through her short locks.

Pulling one down enough to see that it was a dark reddish brown, she wished the room contained a mirror. She didn't even know the color of her eyes. She moved her fingers over the contours of her face. High cheekbones, small nose, firm chin and jawline.

Quickly, she got out of the dirty trousers, unbuttoned her shirt and slid it off her shoulders. Her hands froze as she glanced down at herself. Maybe the image of the silken gown wasn't so farfetched after all. Under the trousers she wore lace-trimmed silk drawers.

Whatever she'd been in her past life, it was no housemaid.

Fear built up in her again.

Firmly, she forced it down and slipped out of the undergarment, then unwound the binding strips. She gave the pretty thing a regretful glance.

There was no help for it. And at least this would feel better next to her skin.

She ripped the drawers down the middle, making a long garment with which she rebound her breasts, then reached for the clean clothes.

They smelled of fresh air and sunshine, and the shirt was loose enough to conceal her bindings. After tugging on the stockings, she slipped her feet into the boots. They were a bit too large, but not so much as the ones she'd worn yesterday.

She picked up the other trousers to fold, and something rolled out of a pocket onto the rough boards of the attic floor, the morning sun sparking a blue flash from it. Stunned, Shannon stared.

It was a sapphire pendant, surrounded by sparkling diamonds.

That she instantly recognized these stones was another

indication of the station in life from which she must have come.

Her heart pounding with excitement, she picked up the necklace, hoping its touch would make her remember something.

The beautiful stone, large and perfectly faceted, lay cold in her palm, its fine gold-mesh chain pooling under it. Shannon closed her eyes, and again the woman with the brown hair and sweet face smiled from her mind's eye.

And around the woman's neck was a pendant exactly like this one.

Shannon's breath came faster, her excitement increasing as she willed her memory to return, tell her who she really was, what had happened.

But as a few minutes ago, the image faded, fear replacing it. She knew what that feeling heralded. Before the other terrifying vision could appear, she blanked her mind.

This pendant held part of the answer to her forgotten life, she felt certain.

But it wouldn't reveal its secrets to her now.

She had to hide it somewhere. She couldn't risk having anyone in this family discover it on her person.

Considering the way she was dressed yesterday, and the story she'd told them, they would be sure to think she'd stolen the gem.

Was she a thief? Had she stolen the pendant from the woman in her vision? Oh, God, no, how could that be true?

Did I? she desperately asked her mind. *Is that why the sheriff might be looking for me?*

Her mind gave her no new reassurance that she'd done nothing wrong, but she must hang on to that belief. She must!

Until she regained her memory she must also keep the jewel hidden.

She again glanced around the small room. It was austerely furnished, four plain walls with no nooks or crannies for concealment. She jerked open the four drawers of the chest. All empty. She couldn't toss the jewel in there by itself.

She'd have to put it under the mattress until she found a better hiding place. And be sure she was the only one to make up the bed. She'd slept on a bare ticking. No one had wanted to disturb her, she supposed, but someone, probably that efficient older sister, would be certain to bring up clean sheets later.

Today, with no giddiness to excuse a stumbling gait, Shannon realized she would have to walk as a boy would—freer, easier than a girl or woman with long skirts and petticoats to hinder her.

As she left the ragged, dirty clothes on the chair, with the socks and boots on top, another thought occurred to her. Why would they give her these clothes to wear if they didn't intend to let her stay?

That cheered her a bit. She opened the door and walked into the narrow corridor. The other three cubicle doors still stood open as they had last night, revealing stored items and trunks.

"Trunks," she said aloud, then jumped at the sound of her voice.

Quickly she retrieved the pendant and walked across to the nearest cubicle. In the corner stood a trunk that not only held a thick layer of dust, but a spider busily built a web above it.

Biting her lip, Shannon knelt and tugged at the lid. To her relief it opened—but with a shriek of rusty hinges that made her wince.

The trunk was filled with papers, their dry, dusty smell tickling her nostrils. Holding back an incipient sneeze, Shannon shoved the pendant deep into a corner. The gemstone thudded against the bottom of the trunk, leaving no trace of its entry. She moved papers across to make sure, then lowered the lid again, just as the sneeze overcame her.

"Oh, lord!" She listened, but all was silent from below. Whooshing out her breath in relief, she got to her feet and turned to go.

Something flashed in a far corner. She tensed again, then looking closer, realized it was a mirror with a crack down its middle, propped against the wall.

A mirror.

She could look at herself, see if that brought back any memories.

Maybe it could even trigger the return of all her lost past.

Carefully she made her way to the corner, picked up the mirror, took her palm and wiped off some of the dust coating it, then brought it up and looked into its smeared, cracked surface.

As she already knew, reddish-brown hair curled around her face. Her features were as she'd thought from her scrutiny of them with her fingers. She had dark, arched eyebrows and deep blue eyes, fringed with thick black lashes.

She stared intently, willing a memory . . . something to enter her mind, but nothing came. No rush of recognition.

Nothing.

Bitter disappointment filled her. The girl in the mirror was just a girl in a mirror.

Swallowing hard, she replaced the mirror where she'd found it and left the cubicle. Quietly, practicing walking as she thought a boy would, she descended the attic stairs and came out into the hallway.

Silence still greeted her. Halfway down the second flight of stairs she heard a faint creak from beyond the door leading to the kitchen.

The grandmother's rocker, she guessed. She opened the stairway door and saw she was right. The old woman sat as she had last night, the large white cat on her lap, before the hearth. Only a small fire burned, since it was late spring.

Spring? Shannon stopped in her tracks. She'd remembered that fact, too. If she didn't push so hard, surely her memory would soon return. She had only to keep her disguise from being discovered until it did.

Only?

Shannon felt her lips turning up at the corners, although she was far from amused.

She glanced around the large room. Its walls were whitewashed, and cheerful, red-checked curtains hung at the sparkling windows through which early morning sun poured. The floor of wide pine boards was scrubbed white, with several bright braided rugs on it.

In addition to the fireplace, across the room was also an iron cookstove with its pipe attached to another chimney. A big sink, with a hand pump, stood along the same wall, a table beside it. Open shelves held dishes and glassware and pots and pans.

"And how are you feeling this morning, lad?" the old woman asked, her faded gray eyes shrewd as she looked at Shannon.

Uneasily, Shannon felt as if the old woman could see right through her masculine clothes, to the woman beneath. She took a deep breath, remembering to pitch her voice as low as possible before she answered.

"Much better, thank you. I slept well."

She heard herself and inwardly cringed.

Another thing she'd forgotten. They thought she was a poor boy, hired out to a mean master. But the kind of speech that came out of her mouth sounded cultured, educated.

She'd just been given another clue to her background. She wished she knew what to do with it.

"Did you now?" The grandmother tilted her head sideways.

Shannon swallowed, fearing the woman had taken notice of her speech.

"Head still hurts," Shannon said, as gruffly as she could manage. "But that'll be all right in time." She hoped that sounded more like a working boy's speech.

"No doubt it will. Everyone is outside doing the morning chores. They'll be in soon to get breakfast. Are you hungry?"

At the mention of food, Shannon's stomach rumbled loudly. She shrugged, embarrassed, as the other woman smiled.

"I guess you are. A growing lad like you should be, since you had no supper last night. Whereabouts did you work? One of the local farms?"

Shannon tensed. She had no idea where she was, or where she'd come from. She wet her lips nervously. "I—I'm . . ." Her voice trailed off. What should she say?

"That's all right, lad, you don't have to tell me if you don't want to. God knows, I've seen plenty of mean masters in my time."

The back door suddenly sprang open, and Clare entered, carrying a woven basket full of eggs. She stopped just inside the door, her eyes widening as she saw Shannon.

Then her face changed, a smile turning up the corners of her mouth. "Oh! You're awake. How are you feeling today?"

Shannon swallowed, avoiding the girl's eyes. "Better," she said again, as gruffly as she could.

"For heaven's sake, get out of the doorway," Gwenny's impatient voice said from behind Clare.

The other girl moved aside, and Gwenny came in, carrying a pail of milk. She shot a sharp glance at Shannon, then carried the pail across to the table and set it on top.

Turning, she surveyed Shannon thoroughly. "At least your clothes are clean now."

Before Shannon could think of a suitable reply, the door opened again, and the older woman who must be the mother entered.

And looming behind her was the man who had rescued her from the roadside. The man who would decide if she stayed or left.

Gareth.

A thrill shot through her as his name reverberated in her mind. Shannon looked at him, her breath caught in her throat.

The early morning sun caught blue-black glints in his

hair, but failed to warm his eyes, gray as winter storm clouds. He stared at her as appraisingly as the other two members of his family had.

He was tall and broad-shouldered, his muscled forearms revealed by the rolled-up sleeves of his white cotton shirt. His jaw was square, with a stubborn look to it. His face and neck and forearms were sun-bronzed.

He was extremely handsome.

Her stomach contracted.

In one blinding moment, Shannon realized how attracted she was to him.

No! she denied. She couldn't be. She didn't know him at all. This was only the second time she'd ever seen him.

Her pulse raced, and she knew that made no difference at all in her feelings.

But it made a lot of difference in her situation.

How could she stay here even if this seemingly nice family let her?

How could she keep her disguise from being discovered if every time she looked at this man she wanted to move to him, touch him? Press herself against his hard body? Kiss those firmly molded lips?

Shannon felt a hot blush suffuse her face and neck as these incredible thoughts tumbled through her mind. She turned her head away.

The movement left her staring at Clare again. The girl still gave her a flirting smile.

Oh, God! Was there ever such a muddle?

Chapter Three

Shannon didn't know how long the frozen tableau held, but suddenly she was conscious of another feeling. An urgent, not-to-be-denied need to empty her bladder.

"Excuse—" She bit off the "me," her blush deepening. Lowering her head, she walked rapidly across the room, the girls and then the man moving aside to let her pass through the still-open door.

On the back porch, she drew a deep breath of the fresh morning air, trying to calm herself.

She looked around, hoping to spy a privy.

The old farmhouse sat on a rise, surrounded by trees, outbuildings close by. A bulky mountain range loomed to the east.

A movement against her legs startled her. Looking down, she saw the dog she remembered from yesterday pushing itself against her legs, its liquid dark eyes gazing at her beseechingly, what seemed for all the world to be a grin stretching its mouth.

"Oh! Nice doggy," she said tentatively, then slowly reached down and fondled its floppy ears, rewarded by a widening of the grin and the sudden mad wagging of its long, shaggy tail. She liked dogs, but she wasn't used to them, she had a cat. . . .

Excitement filled her as she strained to remember more. *A cat.* Yes, she'd had one . . . gray? Tabby?

As before, the image faded, and a stab of discomfort in her lower abdomen reminded her of why she'd bolted from the room.

"Good boy." She removed her hand and walked off the porch, still searching as she approached a small building, which turned out to be a woodshed. The dog kept pace with her.

Finally, she spied the object of her search, half-hidden in a grove of trees. "You can't come in with me," she told the dog firmly.

A few minutes later, feeling much better, she left the building, to find the dog waiting.

A flash of consolation went through her. "At least you won't be asking me questions."

She glanced at the farmhouse. The back door was now closed, no one in sight. For a minute, she had a wild, crazy urge to start running and not stop until. . . .

Until what? She'd found another farmhouse at which to beg shelter? She couldn't run any longer?

Her throat closed in a spasm of half-remembered fear. She swallowed, fighting the feeling.

She might not be so lucky next time. No, she had to stay here as long as she could, until she remembered everything—if they would let her.

Somehow, she had to persuade them to let her.

Straightening, Shannon walked back toward the house, the dog at her heels, practicing her boyish stride in case anyone was looking out the window. Taking a deep breath, she opened the door and reentered the welcoming kitchen.

Her mouth watered involuntarily at the smell of frying bacon.

The grandmother still sat in her rocker before the hearth, the cat on her lap.

Blond Clare leaned over, dreamily stroking the animal, glancing up as Shannon closed the door. Her blue eyes brightened, and she gave Shannon another one of those flirty smiles.

Shannon quickly glanced toward the older sister. Gwenny stood at the stove, stirring something in an iron skillet, and didn't turn.

The middle-aged woman fluttered around the already-set table, moving a fork, straightening a plate. She smiled at Shannon, the smile somehow managing to look fluttery, too.

"There you are! We were getting worried about you."

"I'm all right," Shannon muttered, remembering to keep her voice low.

Gareth was nowhere in sight.

Disappointment mixed with relief shot through her. Maybe she'd have a few minutes' grace time to build her defenses, steel herself not to reveal how he affected her.

Time to convince her traitorous body that she felt no attraction to him.

She stood by the door, hesitating. Now what? *Try to make yourself useful.* "Can I help with the meal?" she finally asked.

At that, all eyes swung toward her, except the grandmother's and the somnolent cat's, and she realized, stricken, she'd blundered again.

"I—I did all kinds of things at the place where I worked." She hastily turned away from Gwenny's startled, suspicious glance.

"What you need to do right now is get yourself up to your bedchamber and wash." Gwenny's brisk voice held an undertone of suspicion that matched her previous glance.

"Uhh, yes, of—sure." Fighting the wave of red engulfing her face and neck, she hurried past the girl toward the narrow back stairs.

Halfway up, she stopped, leaning against the wall and taking deep breaths. "I'll never, ever be able to fool them," she whispered.

She wanted with all her heart to tell this family everything. What a relief that would be. To ask for their help . . . yes, she would do it!

She half turned to go back down, but something inside her mind shrieked at her to stop. She was being a fool. Appearances were deceiving, and she couldn't trust these people no matter how nice they seemed . . . look how she'd been fooled already. . . .

Her heart pounded. Her palms became clammy. Her feet wouldn't move to walk downstairs. She strained to complete the thought, to remember, *remember*. . . .

What? *What?*

No more mysterious messages came from her mind. She slumped against the wall, trying to calm herself. Finally, she straightened, firming her lips. She couldn't take the easy way. She had to be strong, strong enough to resist that urge to confess the truth.

She had to continue this charade. She had to believe that her mind was steering her right, that as it insisted, her very *life* could depend on keeping her silence.

Shannon went on past the first landing and up the steep attic stairs, relief hitting her as she opened the door to the tiny chamber she'd slept in the night before. She pushed the door closed and leaned against it, wishing desperately she could stay up here until her memory returned.

Until she had her life back again, filling up this frightening, empty void.

But she couldn't do that either.

She washed her hands again in the basin and smoothed back her hair, feeling how the ends turned up in curls from the dampness. That wasn't good, was it? It would make her look more like a girl, and soon someone might put all the pieces together, and. . . .

"Stop it!" she muttered, tight-lipped. "Everyone thinks you're a boy. No reason for them to try to put pieces together."

Besides, she thought, her mouth twisting, all the pieces weren't there. If they were, she'd put them together herself and be out of here, back in her real life.

Which might be worse than this limbo, she reminded herself.

Back outside the cubicle, she glanced into the one across from it, making sure the trunk she'd left the necklace in wasn't disturbed.

Everything looked the same. She went on to the landing, and as she opened the attic door, another door below opened. Gareth came out.

He glanced upward, his eyes meeting hers, and that overwhelming attraction hit her again. For long moments, she stood mesmerized, unable to move, to tear her gaze from his.

Finally, Gareth jerked his head around and hurried down the stairs, not looking back.

His movement broke the spell, and Shannon followed, her steps lagging, feeling her heart pounding in her chest as if she'd run a long distance. When she opened the stairway door, Gareth sat at the kitchen table, a cup lifted to his mouth.

"Come on in and sit down, lad," the grandmother commanded from her seat at the foot of the table.

Gwenny, putting a platter of bacon and eggs on the table, again didn't turn, but Shannon saw her shoulders tighten. The mother was already seated, too. She gave Shannon a diffident smile.

Gareth kept his eyes on his cup as Shannon slid into the chair between the two older women. Across from her Clare lowered her lashes and gave her a beguiling smile.

I will not blush, Shannon willed desperately. *I will not, will not!* At last her heartbeat slowed to normal, and her heated face cooled.

"Do have a biscuit," the mother murmured, handing her a plate heaped high.

Shannon's empty stomach rumbled again, and she had to restrain herself from taking two of the wonderful-smelling biscuits.

The table was covered with a cheerful red cloth. Although the cutlery was heavy and crude and the dishes old and chipped, a beautiful cut-glass bowl sat in the center, filled with . . . cooked apples?

After Gareth had helped himself to two eggs and three slices of bacon, Gwenny gave herself a smaller portion, then handed the platter to Shannon.

Again, Shannon fought the urge to pile her plate and took only one slice of bacon and one egg, then passed the platter on to the mother.

"That's not enough to feed a good-sized sparrow," the grandmother protested. "Take more. You're a growing lad."

Shannon shook her head. "It's plenty," she said in the low-pitched tone which always came out as a mutter.

"At least have some apples," Clare's lilting voice urged, pushing the bowl closer to her. "I prepared and cooked them. They're very good."

"Ha! If you call peeling half an apple, then disappearing outside while I finished the job, preparing and cooking, then, yes, you did." Gwenny's voice was so acerbic Shannon winced for Clare, even though the girl was driving her crazy.

Clare tossed her head of blond curls and pouted prettily. "Oh, Gwenny! Don't be such an old sourpuss. You know you sent me to fetch wood for the cookstove."

"And you spent a good long time doing so," Gwenny shot back, but her voice was less biting. Shannon realized she loved her sister, even while scolding her.

The rest of the meal passed mostly in silence while everyone ate with a good appetite. The food tasted wonderful, and she liked all of it.

Apparently, she wasn't picky about her food preferences.

Of course she wasn't. She'd always loved biscuits, and during the war she'd had to learn to eat anything that came their way or starve.

Her fork froze halfway to her mouth. The war. Yes, she remembered. . . .

Nothing. Her mind was blank. The pieces of memory

came when she wasn't straining. So she'd try not to force anything, let it come naturally.

She managed to keep from glancing in Gareth's direction, and congratulated herself the ordeal was nearly over.

"Pass the biscuits please," Gareth said suddenly.

Shannon's heart lurched as she saw the plate sat nearest to her. She handed it across, keeping her eyes lowered and making sure their hands couldn't possibly touch during the exchange.

What ails the boy? Gareth thought irritably, scooping up two more biscuits. He acted like he thought Gareth was some kind of ogre, ready to bite his head off.

Deliberately, Gareth ignored the odd feeling that had again assailed him when he took the plate and saw the boy's slender hand so close to his own. Not to mention those moments on the stairs when their glances had met. . . .

His jaw clenched.

The boy was a disturbing influence. Clare was making a fool of herself over him, among other things. For all they knew he could be a thief—or worse. As soon as this meal was over, they would find out where he came from and see about getting him back where he belonged.

Accordingly, a few minutes later, Gareth pushed his plate back and fixed Shannon with an unsmiling, straight look. "Lad, it's time you told us where you live. We need to get you back to your home."

The boy's face blanched as if Gareth had suggested drawing and quartering him. Gareth's irritation increased. He'd never in his life seen such a timid youngster.

Young Shannon's tongue flickered out, and he nervously licked his lips. A tingle traveled the length of Gareth's spine as he watched.

"I—" The boy's voice cracked, then continued, in a markedly lower-pitched tone. "I'm an orphan. I have no home or family. And I . . . don't remember the name of the family where I worked and lived."

Doggedly, Gareth forced himself to concentrate on the

boy's words instead of his face and the unbelievable bodily responses Gareth had been experiencing. "What do you mean, you don't remember?" he demanded.

Again, the boy's tongue flicked out. He shrugged slender shoulders. "My head still hurts," he said in that odd, growly voice. "I guess that's why . . . everything seems fuzzy."

"Gareth, for heaven's sake, leave the lad alone. Can't you see he's not himself yet? And what difference does it make if he can't remember where he worked? We certainly couldn't allow him to go back to a place where he was so mistreated."

Grandma Lucy's voice wasn't raised, but Gareth and everyone else in his family knew to argue with her was like trying to dent an oak tree with their hands.

Again, Gareth silently cursed, knowing where he'd gotten his own stubbornness. "We don't know anything about him," he countered. "Everything he's said could be a lie."

His mother drew in a shocked breath, Clare gave an indignant huff, and out of the corner of his eye he saw Gwenny's half nod of agreement.

Which for some reason irritated him even more, making him feel like the ogre the white-faced boy believed him to be.

Well, damn it, they *didn't* know anything about the lad! He very well *could* be some kind of a culprit. Even while the thought passed through Gareth's mind, he admitted he didn't believe it.

Still, something wasn't right here. He just wanted to get this . . . Shannon out of his house, out of his life.

"Are you running away from some mischief you've done?" Grandma Lucy asked, her gray eyes fixed steadily on the boy.

Quickly, he shook his head of dark, short-cropped hair. "No. I—I don't . . ." He faltered, then visibly swallowed. "I've done nothing wrong!"

Done nothing wrong.

The words rang strangely in Gareth's mind as he resolutely kept his stare straight on Shannon's long-lashed, blue eyes. Then he realized why.

The lad's words and intonation were too educated for a supposed farm boy.

"And I, for one, believe you," Grandma Lucy said. "You may stay here with us until you heal, as long as need be, and then we'll see."

Clare let out her held breath in relief, and Maud gave a noncommittal sigh. Gwenny emitted an unladylike snort.

"Gramma, Gareth is right. We *don't* know anything about—"

"That will be quite enough, Guinevere. Let's have no more talk about this. We will let it rest for now."

Grandma Lucy rose from the table and picked up her cane. Her back was bowed from rheumatism, but chin high, gray eyes snapping, her glance swept the table's other occupants.

Absurdly, Gareth felt as he had at eight years old, after being put firmly in his place by his grandmother. Even then, she'd been stronger than his mother.

Although, of course, Gramma Lucy acknowledged him as the head of his family. If he insisted, young Shannon would be sent away. He held his tongue and also rose.

More than once, his grandmother had been proven right in her hunches about people. He'd go along with her for now.

"All right, Gramma, have it your way," he said, forcing a false indulgent tone, as if he were humoring her.

She nodded, a hint of a twinkle in her gray eyes. "Thank you, Gareth."

Slowly, leaning on her cane, she walked to her rocker by the fire. It gave a protesting creak as she settled into it and picked up her cat from the hearth. Her misshapen hands stroked the animal.

Clare's lips curved in a satisfied smile, and Gwenny sniffed in disapproval. Turning to leave, Gareth gave their guest one more brief glance.

The boy sat rigidly, still white-faced, but relief had softened the taut features of his beautiful face. He looked as if he'd just been saved from the devil himself.

Beautiful face.

Gareth's mouth thinned, his jaw clamped tightly closed.

God, had he actually thought that?

He strode toward the back door and left the kitchen. He headed toward the barn, trying to force his damaged leg into the long strides he'd used before with such unthinking ease.

Gareth jerked open the door and grabbed a pitchfork leaning against the wall. Savagely, he attacked the dirty straw of an empty stall, feeling as if the foundations on which he'd built his life were crumbling beneath him.

Beautiful.

He'd actually thought that about the boy back in his family's kitchen! As if he were thinking about describing a lovely woman.

One he was attracted to. One he'd like to bed.

Chapter Four

Shannon noticed Gareth's change of expression as he hurriedly left the kitchen. Last night's fears of his wish to get her out of his house had been all too accurate.

Thank God for Grandma Lucy's intercession. And for Gareth's not pressing the issue—but only for now, she knew. The grandmother and Clare were the only two who truly wanted her to stay.

And Clare for the wrong reasons!

The mother went with whoever won the current argument, and Clare was too young to have any influence.

How much longer could the old woman hold out against Gareth and Gwenny's opposition?

At that thought, anxiety flared through Shannon again.

She pushed back her chair and quickly stacked plates and cutlery. She must prove she was useful, that she wouldn't be a liability to this hard-working household which, like most of the South since the war, had obviously fallen upon hard times.

The war. Yes, she remembered about that terrible time, about the South's final defeat. Something about a battle tried to form in her mind, but then faded away.

"Don't move around so fast, or you'll likely give yourself a recurrence of yesterday's dizziness."

Gwenny's firm tones contained a mixture of irritation and disbelief. This sister of Gareth's had a lot of his traits.

The ones Shannon feared.

"Yes," she mumbled, knowing Gwenny was right. The quick, sudden movements had made her head begin aching again.

"I'll go upstairs and tidy the bedrooms," the mother said. Plainly wanting to get out of the room before any more unpleasantness arose, she hurried to the back stairs.

"I'll help clear." Clare gave Shannon a radiant smile and moved around the table until she was so close her small hand brushed against Shannon's shirtsleeve.

"Clare," Gwenny said firmly, "get back around here. It doesn't take both of you to clear one side."

Her pretty mouth puckering in a pout, the skirt of her faded calico dress swishing, Clare did as her sister bade.

Shannon let out a sigh of relief, eliciting a sharp glance from Gwenny. Nothing much got past her, Shannon realized. She'd have to be careful.

Until *when?* How long would she have to keep this up? How long *could* she? How she hated this pretense!

She carried a stack of dishes to the worktable across the room. After pouring water from the steaming tea kettle into the dishpan, she pumped in cold water, then added a handful of soft soap and swished it around.

"For a lad, you surely do know your way around a kitchen," Gwenny said tartly, setting another stack of dishes onto the table.

"I'll dry," Clare said breathlessly, saving Shannon from answering. The girl plucked a towel from a hook and moved so close their sleeves again touched.

Her nerves tightening, Shannon tried to edge away.

Rescued from one pitfall, only to be plunged into another.

"Do this first, and be very careful." Gwenny handed her the cut-glass bowl.

Her hands soap-slippery, Shannon held her breath as she slid the bowl into the pan. Breaking what was obviously one of the few nice things the family had left would be a wonderful way to show how useful she was.

"That's Gramma Lucy's bowl—and it belonged to *her* grandmother," Clare volunteered, flashing her dimple at Shannon.

A silence fell. Clearly a reply was expected.

Shannon cleared her throat. "It's very, uh, it's fancy lookin'," she mumbled hoarsely.

"Would you like to hear the story of how we still have it?" Clare asked.

No, she wouldn't. She wanted to finish up and get out of here.

Her arms trembling with the weight of the heavy bowl, Shannon scrubbed the fruit residue away. She placed it in the rinsing pan, and Clare poured hot water from the kettle over it.

"Well, would you?" Clare's petulant voice demanded again.

"Leave the lad alone!" the old woman said from her rocker.

Clare tossed her head, the motion causing her blond curls to bounce around her face. "I'm not bothering him. It's a very interesting story."

"It's not." Gwenny's lips clamped shut. "It only reminds me of how much we've lost." She snatched another towel from the hook and dried the bowl herself, her movements swift and angry.

"Oh, Gwenny, don't start that. It's all over and done with."

"It will *never* be over and done with. I *hate* the Yankees for what they did to the Valley!"

"Bitterness won't change a thing, girl."

Her grandmother's measured words only inflamed Gwenny further. She flung down the towel and left the kitchen, the door slamming behind her.

Shannon tried to ignore everything going on around

her, tried to concentrate on behaving as a young man would do, in every movement, every word.

Clare tossed her head again, her fingers caressing the sparkling bowl. "Now that that old sourpuss has gone, I'm going to tell the story. *I* think it's very nice."

She glanced across the room to see if her grandmother would challenge her, but the old woman stared into the almost dead embers of the fireplace, her gnarled hands absently stroking the purring cat on her lap.

Out of the corner of her eye, Shannon saw Clare give her another dimpled smile.

"It happened when the war was nearly over. Gramma Lucy took the bowl to the mill to pay for a sack of flour. It was the last thing of value we had to barter with. But the miller wouldn't accept it. He gave it back to Gramma, and—"

Her voice paused dramatically, and Shannon glanced her way. Clare's head was tilted sideways, and she looked at Shannon from under her long lashes.

"He gave her the flour for nothing. And until the Yankees confiscated the mill, he gave us some every week."

Shannon quickly returned her attention to the dishpan.

Why did the story sound so familiar? Was this another clue? Was the miller a relative or perhaps a family friend?

No, she couldn't be from close by or these people would know her. She hadn't thought of that before. She must have gotten a ride in a buggy . . . or a wagon.

The feeling that the story she'd told these people was true grew stronger.

Another quick glance showed her Clare's pretty face now held an expectant look. "Uh . . . that was ni—good. Yes, he was a good man to do that."

The door opened and shut again, and Gwenny came back to the work area. Her face was closed as she gave Shannon a sharp glance. "Do you really not remember where you lived, or are you lying to us?"

Shannon turned back to her pan of dishes before Gwenny could see her face. "I'm not lying, I'm. . ."

Oh, God, once more she'd forgotten. Her voice sounded like an educated young woman's, not a roughly raised boy's.

Gwenny sniffed. "*I* think the whole thing is very odd. If you can remember your name and what happened to you, you should be able to remember the name of the family where you worked."

Dizziness assailed Shannon again. Gwenny was right. She'd made a mistake. Why hadn't she told them she remembered nothing about what had happened to her?

Because that would only lead to more problems. Desperately, she held on to the table's edge, willing the dizziness to pass, her head to stop swirling. "I . . ."

"Are you tormenting the lad again?" Grandma Lucy's voice cut through the fog.

"Gwenny, you are a beast! Oh, he's going to faint! Here, lean on me."

Shannon felt Clare's arm slide across her shoulder as the girl moved close against her. "I'm all right."

"For heaven's sake, find a chair for the boy," Lucy directed.

Gareth swung the door open, then stood transfixed in the doorway. His younger sister was carefully easing young Shannon into a chair, while Gwenny looked on, biting her lip.

Good God, was there ever going to be any peace in his household again?

The lad looked frail and sickly—his face as white as winter snow. His long lashes were closed over those startling blue eyes. . . .

Gareth came to himself, letting out a whoosh of breath. He shouldn't have allowed his grandmother to overrule him in this matter of allowing the boy to remain here.

And where would the lad go if you send him away? his mind asked. *He says he has no money, no home, no family. He can't even remember the name of the man who misused him.*

A strong desire for some spirits surged over Gareth. He wished he was a drinking man. If he were, he'd go back to the barn and get thoroughly besotted. Of course, that would be hard to do since the only liquor in the household was a small bottle of brandy and another of whiskey—both for medicinal purposes.

Before anyone noticed his presence, he eased back outside, closing the door quietly behind him.

Never mind the drink of water he'd been after. He'd go to the spring and get it. And then he'd work in the fields until he was too tired to think about anything.

Which of course, he had to do anyway. It was what he did every day. So they wouldn't starve. So if they were lucky, they could keep this farm.

He'd worked all his life, but not like he had these last five years since the Yankees had stripped the South of everything.

No, not quite everything.

He lifted his head, gazing toward Massanutten's dark shape.

The Valley people would never be stripped of their pride, their love for this special little piece of heaven they called home. Nor their willingness to work hard and endlessly in order to stay here.

He could be happy no place else on this wide green earth.

It was worth everything he and countless others had gone through, and would still go through for years to come.

"Another whiskey." Vance shoved the shot glass across the bar, the scowl on his face matching his rough actions.

Damn. He *had* to find the little bitch soon. Before she got over her fear of him and what he'd threatened her with and went to the authorities.

That couldn't be too much longer.

And before the nosy sheriff started wondering about a lot of things.

How in hell could she have just disappeared? Wearing

the damned necklace, too. Why hadn't he grabbed it while he had the chance?

His jaw tightened at those thoughts, and sweat sprang up on his forehead.

"Here you are." The bartender set the glass down a little harder than necessary, signaling his annoyance with Vance's manner.

Caution belatedly hit Vance. *Better ease off,* he told himself. *You don't want him remembering you later and how mad you were.* He forced a smile for the burly man across the bar.

"Nice little town you have. Wish I could stay longer. But I'm only here on business this time. I'm looking for a young woman."

Vance fumbled in his inside vest pocket and brought out a small photograph. "Don't suppose you happened to see anyone around these parts who looks like this?"

The bartender took the photograph and studied it, his face impassive. Finally, he handed it back. "Why you lookin' for her? She done somethin' wrong?"

Vance felt sweat on his palms now. He quickly shook his head. "No, no, nothing like that. You know how young females are. She just had a fight with her father and ran off."

Seeing the other man's eyes flicker, Vance winced inwardly. *Damn.* That was the wrong thing to say. Young women didn't run away from their homes—especially not decent young *Southern* women.

"You her kin, too?"

Vance lifted the shot glass to his mouth and swallowed the whiskey at one gulp, shuddering as the cheap liquor burned its way down his throat to his stomach. When he set the glass back down it slipped out of his sweat-damp grasp and turned over.

"Yes, of course. I'm her cousin."

The bartender studied the drops of amber liquid dribbling out onto the bar's polished wooden surface. He lifted his head, his dark eyes full of suspicion.

"Nope, ain't seen nobody looks like that. I wouldn't forget that purty face."

It was time to leave. This man *would* remember him and how nervous he'd acted. He didn't want the local sheriff to find out about his visit here.

Vance put enough coins on the bar to make the bartender's face light up, then left the shabby tavern.

Damn the bitch! When he did find her, he'd make her pay for these weeks of misery he'd put in.

He grinned and licked his lips, his eyes narrowing in anticipation.

As the bartender had said, she was a pretty piece. He'd itched to get underneath her skirts ever since he first saw her.

And before he killed her, he would.

The wooden pail was heavy. Shannon kept shifting it from hand to hand to ease its pulling weight on her shoulders and arms.

And to slow her progress toward the field where Gareth worked.

Duke trotted beside her, panting his eagerness for this outing. He'd taken a liking to her and followed her everywhere when she was outside.

Which hadn't been too often until now.

Two weeks had passed since she'd awakened in Gareth's wagon, with her memory gone.

Her head injury was healed, at least physically. The dizziness no longer assailed her without warning, although her muscles were still weak.

But her past was still blocked from her, hidden in the swirling cloud of fear that arose when she tried to remember. And something inside her still insisted she not reveal her disguise, her memory loss—or her fear of the knife-wielding man.

No one in the family had asked her again if she'd remembered the farm family she'd told them she'd worked for. Not even Gwenny or Gareth.

Instead, she'd been asked questions about her life before she'd had to work. Answers had come from somewhere in her mind—the ones that came easily without thought, she guessed might be true.

She supposed she'd woven a believable tapestry made up of part truth, part make-believe.

If she only knew which was which!

Her father was killed in the war, she'd said, and her mother died later. There was something hazy in her mind about maybe a brother killed, too, so she'd mentioned that.

When she'd said they had lived near Richmond until after the war, a memory flash surged through her mind.

A big brick house . . . a laughing, whiskered man who had played games with her, read to her. . . .

She'd tried to keep the picture, make it grow. But soon it had faded, and she'd felt that darkness pressing in her head that meant the terrible vision was next. She'd quickly blanked her mind and had gotten no more visions since.

This morning Gwenny had announced it was high time Shannon helped Gareth in the fields. After all, there were three women to manage the household chores and only Gareth and one of the sharecropper's sons to do the farm work.

Gwenny's words had sent a wave of relief through Shannon. To get out of the house and away from Clare's unwanted flirting would be wonderful.

But that was soon replaced by another kind of discomfort.

She and Gareth had managed to avoid each other these past weeks. It seemed by mutual consent and maneuvering they managed to never be alone together.

But for entirely different reasons.

It was obvious Gareth didn't like her—didn't completely believe her story or trust her.

She didn't want to be alone with him because her attraction toward him hadn't lessened a bit.

Her attention not on where she was walking, Shannon stumbled over a stone. At the sound, Gareth lifted his head and turned toward her, his hoe still in the rich brown earth.

Their eyes met, and as always her pulse quickened, no matter how much she fought it.

He'd taken off his shirt. She'd never seen him shirtless before. Sweat glistened on the curly black hair covering his muscled, tanned chest, and his equally muscled arms.

Her pulse quickened even more.

His jaw clenched, and his brows drew together. Clearly, he didn't welcome her presence.

"I've brought you water," she called. "It's a hot day."

Yes, it was, and that's why he'd removed his shirt. Cursing under his breath, Gareth reached for the discarded garment.

Why was the lad bringing the water he sorely wanted?

Gwenny, of course. She'd hinted for days it was time, past time, for young Shannon to help him in the fields. He'd put her off, but he'd known he couldn't do that for much longer.

And why, for God's sake, was he putting his shirt back on merely because this boy had come? Buttoning the shirt with angry fingers, he knew why and silently cursed again.

Because no matter how he tried to deny it, his feelings for Shannon Brown weren't those he should have for a young man.

Chapter Five

"Thanks," he said gruffly as Shannon reached him and set the pail at his feet.

Hearing the boy's quickened breathing, his scowl deepened.

Damnation! The lad couldn't even carry a half-full pail of water without strain. How on earth could he have done farm work?

Gareth dipped water from the pail, drank deeply, then dipped again. The lad still stood there with his head bent, obviously uncomfortable, too.

He'd make it easy.

"You can just leave the pail. I'll want more before dinnertime."

Shannon nodded, but made no move to leave. Finally, the boy raised his head, and the full force of his blue eyes hit Gareth, making something deep in his stomach clench.

"I, uh, I'm supposed to stay and help you," he said in that strange way of talking he had, starting out high-pitched and ending almost in a mutter.

Gareth let out an exasperated sigh.

Gwenny's idea, just as he'd thought. And he couldn't

send the lad back to the house. Do that and he'd have Gwenny herself, Shannon in tow, out here scolding him and insisting the boy stay and help.

A houseful of women was a sore trial for a man!

"All right," he said ungraciously. "Here, put the pail under that oak and we'll see what you can do."

Watching Shannon carry the pail to the tree, he noticed again the straining of the boy's muscles. Either he'd been injured worse than appeared, or everything he'd said was a lie and he'd never done farm work in his life.

Suspicion roiled in Gareth again. Something sure as hell didn't add up.

He watched as Shannon set the pail down, then turned and walked back toward him. The lad had a damned awkward walk, too, he noticed.

"What would you, uh, what you want me to do?"

That was another odd thing. The boy was always stopping in the middle of a sentence and then changing the way he said things.

A thought came to him. Shannon maybe hadn't done heavy work for a while. Or maybe he was just lazy.

Maybe the way to get rid of these troubling, unsuitable thoughts and feelings was to toughen up the boy, get him acting and looking like a young man should.

Gareth pointed to the end of the corn row. "Go get that hoe and start cutting weeds. Begin at the next row."

Feeling an unsettling mixture of relief and disappointment, Shannon nodded and walked off.

When her hand closed around the hoe handle, no half-remembered feeling of familiarity came to her.

Did that mean she'd never done this work before—adding another clue to her sparse list?

Did it mean her family were town dwellers—not plantation owners? Because if they were, she'd probably have done plenty of hoeing during the war.

Or did it merely indicate she'd just forgotten the skill, as she'd forgotten almost everything else from her previous life.

She stood for a few moments, taking deep breaths, then began hacking at the small green weeds around the corn plants.

A row away, Gareth stared in disbelief as the lad wielded the tool as awkwardly as he walked. Throwing down his own hoe, Gareth strode toward him.

"Here, let me show you how. I thought you said you'd done all kinds of farm work?"

Shannon's back jerked, and he dropped the hoe. Then he turned swiftly toward Gareth, a look of near-panic on his face.

Amazed, Gareth watched the boy battle his emotions until the look faded into his usual almost blank-faced expression.

"Guess I forgot how to do this, too," he offered, his voice shaky.

Had the boy told the truth after all? Had he been so badly mistreated that any sudden approach scared him to death? Compassion filled Gareth at this thought. Damn a bastard who would mistreat his workers like that! Especially a young lad.

"Never mind. We can remedy that." Gareth walked behind Shannon and put the hoe into the boy's hands. Shannon grasped it as ineptly as before, and Gareth placed his own hands over the lad's to show him the correct grip.

Shannon's heart thumped when Gareth's warm, strong hand covered her own. Oh, that felt so good, so wonderfully good! She savored the sensations for a few moments before her common sense kicked in.

She *couldn't* let him know how his touch affected her! He already considered her strange and disliked being near her. If he also thought she harbored unsuitable feelings for a member of the same sex. . . .

Taking a deep breath she willed her fingers to hold steady as Gareth guided them into the correct position.

"I—I believe I have it now," she said, forgetting to lower and roughen her voice.

To her ears it sounded exactly like what it was.

A young woman's voice, breathless at being touched by the man to whom she was so physically attracted she could think of little else in his presence.

Gareth stood so close she could feel his warm breath on her nape. She longed for his lips to caress that spot, too. He stood so close he touched her backside, causing even more delicious shudders to go through her body.

With the last remaining shreds of her sanity, she kept herself from pressing backward against him.

"Good."

Abruptly, he moved away, and her nerveless fingers once more dropped the hoe. Gareth's voice had sounded strangled.

Fear hit her. Had he noticed her slip?

She shot a quick glance at him. His jaw was clenched; he looked as if he was fighting a silent battle with himself.

Not the expression of a man who had realized that the boy his family had befriended was in reality a female.

Then what was wrong with him?

Another thought slipped into her mind and numbed it with shock.

Could Gareth be as attracted to her as she was to him?

That could explain why he'd tried to avoid her, why he'd wanted to send her away.

She was reacting as a normal female desiring a man. But if her suspicions were correct, Gareth must be undergoing the tortures of the damned believing his own desires were wrong!

Another, even worse thought hit her.

What if Gareth was the kind of man who *was* attracted to other men? And was fighting his attraction to her because of the circumstances?

He had to be at least thirty, and he wasn't married. Nor was there any evidence he was courting anyone.

Frantically, she pushed all these thoughts aside. She had to get to work. Bending to pick up the hoe, she realized the movement caused her trousers to tighten over her bottom. She hoped Gareth wasn't watching.

At the same time, she also hoped he was.

You idiot! You complete and utter fool! she chastised herself.

She drew in a deep breath, let it out, then took another. She placed her hands on the hoe as he'd shown her and carefully hacked at another weed.

In a moment, she felt rather than heard him moving away. Again relief filled her, mixed with a disappointment she couldn't deny.

It was torture being around him; but it was a sweet torture, and she needed, wanted it with an intensity that frightened her.

You are a fool, she told herself again, tightening her lips and concentrating on doing the job right, so that Gareth would have no further need to instruct her.

Yet at the same time, she wanted to call him back, tell him she didn't think she quite understood just how to do this after all.

Meanwhile Gareth, his mouth tighter than Shannon's, walked back to his own row.

What in hell is wrong with you? he savagely asked himself.

When he'd stood behind Shannon a few moments ago, placed his hands over the lad's, he'd had an almost uncontrollable urge to turn the boy around, enfold him in his arms and kiss him!

Never before in his life had he had such unnatural urges! How could this be happening now?

The weeds didn't have a chance today. Gareth grimly worked down the rows, moving as fast as he could, disregarding the sweat running in rivulets down his face, sticking his shirt to his back.

He tried to concentrate on his corn crop. They needed rain. If the drought continued, the harvest would be poor. His attempt to distract his thoughts didn't work—his mind was still where it didn't belong.

Only when he heard the bell clanging from the house, signaling dinner was ready, did he pause.

Pain shot through his back and his injured leg when he straightened, but he ignored it. This kind of physical pain was preferable to the kind he felt around the boy. Let it hurt—maybe it would take his mind off this impossible situation.

Shannon worked in the next row, bent over, face tight, as if he, too, was in the grip of powerful, unwelcome emotions.

Gareth sucked in his breath, the thought sending his overtaxed emotions into a spiraling whirlpool.

Oh, lord, not that!

Even worse, could the boy be aware of Gareth's feelings, and not sharing them, fear Gareth planned to try to . . . molest him? Could that account for the look of panic on his face when he hadn't heard Gareth approach him earlier today?

Could either of those suppositions be the reason the lad was making a point of avoiding him? Just as he was avoiding Shannon?

Gareth heaved an enormous sigh composed of frustration, anxiety, doubt—and also the ever-present desire he still felt.

God damn it all to hell! He was losing his mind. That was all there was to it.

One thing came clear of the muddle.

Either he or Shannon had to leave.

And since this was still his family's farm, at least for the moment, it would have to be the boy.

"It's dinnertime," he called, deliberately keeping his gaze from meeting the lad's. "You've done a good morning's work."

Straightening, Shannon winced as she, too, felt the pain of the bent position she'd been in for the last few hours.

Thank God this horrible morning was over! But there was still the afternoon to face. And tomorrow. How could she do it?

She also became aware of a new pain—in her palms. She'd been so emotionally upset, so doggedly intent on working so hard Gareth would have no cause to approach her again, she hadn't realized this unaccustomed work had raised blisters on her palms.

Big blisters, which had broken and were now oozing blood.

Gingerly she held the hoe as she approached Gareth, who was waiting for her. But not as if he wanted to. Just as if he knew it would be rude to go on to the house and not walk back with her.

He held the pail of water neither had made use of. Sudden intense thirst hit her.

"Could I—I need a drink," she said, lowering her tones into those untutored gruff ones that still sounded so odd to her ears, and not looking directly at him.

Gareth set the pail on the ground without a word.

Her thirst terrible now, Shannon gripped the dipper handle, wincing as it connected with her blisters. She drank thirstily, then refilled the dipper and emptied it again, handling the dipper carefully now.

Replacing the dipper in the pail, her glance collided with Gareth's. He was frowning as he almost always did in her presence, but his gaze was on her mangled hands.

"Why did you keep on working with your hands like that?" he demanded. "You surely didn't think you had to?"

She shrugged, trying to hide her hands. "It's nothing. I'll get used to it in a few days."

"Don't be such a damned fool."

Before she knew his intent and could back away, he'd picked up her hands and turned them over, palms up. He swore again.

"Get to the house and let Gwenny use some of Gramma Lucy's salve on these. Bad blisters can turn into blood poisoning."

Dismay went through her. No, she wasn't imagining it. His hands lingered on hers. He *was* attracted to her.

But in what way?

That thought was swallowed up in realizing his warm touch started all those hopeless feelings churning through her again.

Feelings that might not be hopeless if she knew who she was, and what had happened to make her flee.

Shannon simply couldn't make herself believe that Gareth was the kind of man who was attracted to other men.

Bleakness went through her. How awful it was to feel as if her life were lost. As if she weren't even a person.

She'd give *anything* to remember.

Anything!

She pushed at her mind, straining at that wall keeping the secrets of her past from her.

Something seemed to give a little, and a scene flashed before her mind's eye.

The same sweet-faced woman she'd glimpsed before, her face careworn now, wearing a faded cotton dress, held Shannon's hands in her own, then turned them over, grimacing at the palms, which were blistered and cut. Sadness went over the woman's face. She dipped her finger into a jar and smeared the contents on Shannon's sore palms.

Mama? Shannon silently asked, hope leaping into her heart. *Oh, Mama, is it really you?*

The scene blacked out as if a light had been turned off, replaced by the menacing faceless figure of the man holding his blood-dripping knife.

Shannon's knees gave way, and she swayed as fear rushed in to replace the momentary hope. Desperately, she searched for courage and strength. She wouldn't faint again, she just wouldn't.

Gareth swore again and released her hands, grabbing her shoulders.

What the hell had just happened there? The lad had acted possessed for a few moments, staring into space like he saw ghosts. Then his knees had buckled as if he was going to lose consciousness as he'd done several times before.

But that was weeks ago. And Gareth didn't believe in people being possessed, either.

Another thought struck him, accompanied by guilt.

He'd noticed how weak Shannon seemed just a few hours

ago. He shouldn't have let him work this long. The boy was no doubt exhausted.

It wouldn't happen again, he'd see to that.

But even with all that, as he'd thought from the beginning, something didn't add up.

Young Shannon wasn't telling everything he knew, and the sooner he was out of their lives and house, the better.

At that thought, which should have been welcoming, a strange feeling of loss assailed Gareth.

Also shame.

You can't send him away unless you find him another place to work.

And what about the fear he sensed in the lad? Maybe that was why he wasn't telling the whole truth.

Duke ambled over from where he'd spent the morning dozing under the oak, stretching and grinning at Shannon, who still looked like a sleepwalker awakening from a trance.

And what if the fear is connected with your own unnatural feelings for this lad?

All the more reason to get him away from here, Gareth answered grimly.

All the more reason.

Chapter Six

The apple blossoms were gone, the tender new leaves already formed, but the orchard was still a nice place.

Romantic, even. Clare was surprised Josh had suggested they meet there.

A month ago she would have felt this indicated he was becoming more like the gentlemen she daydreamed about. More like the kind of man she might eventually choose to honor with her promise to become his bride.

But not now. Not since Shannon Brown's unexpected arrival.

Remembering Shannon's deep blue eyes, his dark lashes and regular features, her heartbeat quickened. She closed her eyes to savor the image and feeling.

Of course, Shannon wasn't a gentleman, either, but he didn't seem like any of the farm workers she'd met. What was it that made him so different?

Opening her eyes, she was jolted by the sight of Josh striding toward her. Her daydream burst like a bubble, and she frowned.

A lock of Josh's dark blond hair fell over his forehead. His tall, lanky form was dressed, as usual, in worn homespun trousers and a faded cotton shirt. Even from this distance she could see his dark eyes flashing.

She shouldn't have agreed to meet him here. She knew why he wanted to see her. Not so they could be alone together like it used to be—before Shannon came.

No, he'd come into the kitchen yesterday when Shannon was helping with breakfast dishes and caught her standing too close to Shannon, looking at him and smiling.

Josh had left at once, but not before she'd seen the mixture of emotions on his face—confusion blended with anger.

Quickly, Clare sat down under an apple tree, arranging her skirts, tucking her feet under them and curving her lips in a fetching smile. There! Now he'd have to stoop down, too, not be towering over her.

Josh saw Clare's graceful movements as his long strides ate up the distance between them, and his angry heart softened. It was so hard to stay mad at her even though he knew he had just cause.

Or did he? His self-confidence, strong in other areas of his life, faltered. He tried to bolster it. Someday he'd have land, be a planter in his own right. Of that he was sure. Mr. Colby had promised Pa, and Pa in turn had promised Josh. He'd build a sturdy brick house—good enough for any woman. Good enough for Clare.

He reached the tree Clare sat under, looked down at her bewitchingly pretty face, her soft smile, and noted, as always, her unconscious air of gentility, and the bit of certainty he'd fetched up evaporated.

Josh knew he was smart and strong enough to accomplish all he dreamed of. Most of the time his confidence never faltered.

Only when he was in Clare's presence did he realize again the huge gap between them.

He was only a sharecropper's son.

The damned war had taken a lot away from the big planters, but it had taken even more from most of the small farmers.

It had taken everything away from his family.

He and his family appreciated Mr. Colby's kindness and generosity. Instead of the onerous terms many of the large plantation owners forced upon the small farmers in these hard days, Mr. Colby had been more than fair.

Pa could keep sixty percent of the crops he planted and harvested, doing with them what he wanted, instead of the lower percentages most often agreed upon.

At the end of five years, Pa could buy the two hundred acres made up of cleared land with some woods and a stream, and pay Mr. Colby by the season until it was all his. Pa, in turn, had promised Josh fifty of those acres on which to build his own homestead. His younger brother, Wiley, would get another fifty acres.

It was more than fair all the way around, and since everyone in his family was a hard worker, they should eventually prosper. Josh planned to own more than his fifty acres someday not too far off.

A *whole* lot more.

But that didn't change the fact that his family weren't of the gentility—and never would be. And Clare was—and always would be. No matter if she did live in an old stone house almost as shabby as the one his family occupied.

The Colby's present situation didn't change a thing. Something even more worrisome was knowing how much she craved pretty clothes, and a beautiful house again.

So why had she been making up to that boy who was staying at her house now? He was just a farm worker with no prospects, as far as Josh could see.

Josh's face darkened as he looked down at her.

Clare's smile became even more beguiling. She patted the grass alongside her. "Sit down, Josh, do. I can't bear it when you stand over me glowering like that."

Reluctantly, he lowered his long frame to the ground, taking care not to get too close, even though the fresh flowery scent that always seemed to hover around Clare was drawing him to move in as close as he could get.

"Isn't it lovely out here?" Clare took a deep breath of the fresh morning air, for all the world as if she hadn't any idea why he'd asked her to meet him.

She did, though. He knew her well enough by now to see through her little tricks, and most of the time he didn't let them get to him. But this time it was different.

"Why was—were you flirtin' with that boy your family took in?" he asked before her closeness made him lose all his righteous anger.

Clare's eyes widened as if she had no idea what he meant. He forced himself to keep the frown on his face, not let it soften into a smile. Her mouth puckered into a pout, and he had to fight the urge to lean over and kiss it.

"Why, Josh Archer! I wasn't flirting with Shannon. I was just being nice to him. The poor boy is an orphan! And he doesn't even remember who his mean old master was. Not that we'd let him go back there anyway, after the way he was treated."

Her soft voice was so convincing, for a moment Josh was almost swayed into believing her. Then, he took himself in hand. He shook his head.

"No, Clare, you were doin' more than that. And I want to know why. You promised me not a month ago that you'd be my girl. That you'd wait for me until I got my own land."

Clare's face turned red. She looked down and started twisting a lock of her blond hair around a finger.

Josh felt his resolve slipping. "Well, aren't you going to answer me?" he demanded.

She looked up, biting her lower lip. Finally, she shrugged. "I don't know why, Josh. Sometimes I just can't help flirting! Gwenny's told me stories of how it used to be. *All* the girls flirted and danced with all the boys, and everything was so much fun. Not like now!"

Clare felt a twinge of guilt, although what she'd said was the truth. It just wasn't the *whole* truth concerning her feelings for Shannon Brown. She didn't even know what the truth was herself. She just knew that being in the same room with Shannon excited her.

She glanced at Josh, forcing another smile.

Being with Josh used to excite her like that.

Was she just one of those heartless, fickle belles who didn't really care for anyone? Who only wanted admiration from every man or boy she met? Was she destined to spend her life driving men wild?

She toyed with that idea, finding it strangely attractive.

Josh let out a sigh as his expression gradually changed from anger back to the doting look he usually wore with her. His hand reached out, found hers and covered it.

"I know how hard it is for you to live like you have to now," he said, his voice softened, too.

Relief filled Clare. Although she found Shannon attractive, she didn't want to lose Josh.

At least not now.

Stuck here on this farm, only visiting neighbors once in a while, she *had* to do something to keep from dying of boredom.

Of course, she probably shouldn't have told Josh she'd be his girl and wait for him.

But that was after he'd given her such a sweet kiss she'd felt like swooning. At that moment she'd forgotten that he was just the son of their sharecropper, that he was far from being a landowner and might never be.

She'd just wanted more of those sweet kisses, to be held in his strong arms.

Clare gave him a sad smile as she turned her hand under his and returned his squeeze. "I'm sorry for complaining, Josh. I know your family lost more than ours. And so did a lot of others."

She smiled bravely, even as a small part of her was ashamed at her role-playing. But not ashamed enough to stop doing it, she knew in her heart.

Josh squeezed her hand again, then, instead of pulling her to him for another of those sweet kisses, he let go of her and stood.

He looked down at her for a moment, an odd look on his face as if he knew exactly what game she'd been playing, but was going to let her get away with it.

"I've got to go back to the fields. Goodbye, Clare. I do love you, you know."

He turned and strode away as rapidly as he'd come, leaving Clare staring after him, her heart beating a little faster.

His sincerely spoken words echoed in her ears. He did love her, she had no doubt.

But did she love him?

Her feelings even more confused than they had been before he arrived, Clare sighed, got up and walked back to the house.

"Come on, Rosie—quit dawdling—go to the barn! You'll get your grain."

Duke, alert to Shannon's irritated tones, darted to the recalcitrant cow's rear and barked, then shied away from her back hooves.

Just quick enough. Rosie raised one hoof, stained with the wild strawberries she'd walked through in the fields, and let fly.

In spite of her irritation and fatigue, Shannon had to smile at the sight of the bright red hoof. And the faithful dog, now her shadow.

There was so much about this place she loved.

The delicious strawberries which she picked every morning for their table—the promise of the raspberries and blackberries to come next month.

She'd be happy living here forever.

But of course she couldn't do that. Her mood darkened again.

Sugar made up for Rosie's slowness. Trotting ahead, eager for her evening grain and to be relieved of her swollen udder's rich milk, the other jersey was almost at the barn.

Shannon took a deep breath and let it out in a sigh. Since that disastrous day over a week ago when she'd helped Gareth hoe the corn, she'd spent no more time in the fields with him.

Scolding all the while, Gwenny had tended her blistered hands, but it had taken several days for them to heal.

Gareth had announced at the dinner table that he'd decided the lad would be of more help doing the morning and evening chores—leaving Gareth free to tend to the crops.

She felt Gareth's decision was based mostly on his reluctance to be alone with her. She still felt he was attracted to her and horrified at himself for these feelings.

Her own feelings weren't weakened by not being with him—would that they were!

Instantly, she denied that thought. What she really wished was that she had her memory back, that she could tell Gareth and his family everything.

She wished the man with the knife and her other fears were only unreal fancies. That her forgotten life contained no dark secrets.

And that she and Gareth could. . . .

Could what? Fall in love and marry and live happily ever after like the ending of a fairy tale?

She fought against the despair trying to cover her like a smothering cloak.

She *wouldn't* give in to it!

Resolutely, she forced her mind back to mundane thoughts.

She'd had to admit she didn't know how to milk, gaining another suspicious glance from Gareth. Josh, the nice-looking sharecropper's older son, had taught her, glowering all the while.

She'd been mystified at his surly manner until a few days ago when she'd been in the orchard, enjoying a short respite.

Not seeing her, Clare came and settled herself under a

tree. Shannon kept quiet. She had no desire to attract Clare's attention.

A few moments later Josh appeared, the same glower on his face as when he'd explained to Shannon the mysteries of getting a cow to let down her milk.

Caught, Shannon had no choice but to eavesdrop. Josh's accusations astounded her, as well as giving her the wild urge to burst into hysterical laughter.

Josh was a nice young man, ambitious, too. It was obvious Clare was toying with his feelings.

Clare was such a little fool!

It had rained last night, and a puddle glinted ahead of Shannon on the path. She skirted it, seeing her face in the wavy, reflecting water.

Her spirits fell even further at the glimpse of her curly reddish-brown hair, her blue eyes and regular features.

It had been nearly a month since she'd regained consciousness in Gareth's wagon. Little had changed.

She still could call to mind just a few fleeting images, only two strong enough to last. One the sweet-faced woman. The other the faceless man with the blood-covered knife.

Shannon's stomach clenched. She felt more sure all the time that she had no home or family left. No one to be distraught over her disappearance. No one to search for her.

Except for the man in her haunting visions.

And perhaps the authorities.

Why would the law want to find her? Surely, if she was a criminal, she'd remember something about the crime she'd committed, instead of only receiving those inner commands that she must keep the officials from finding her without giving her any reasons why.

Commands that were so strong she couldn't force herself to disobey them.

But yet she couldn't be sure that the terrifying vision was a real threat. Or that any of the warning thoughts cautioned her about true danger.

She couldn't be *sure* of *anything!*

Frustration filled her, and she fought it down, replacing it with determination. She had to try to find out something without endangering herself.

The next time Gareth went to Luray for supplies she'd go with him.

She tensed, waiting for her mind to object to this plan. Nothing happened. A spark of hope sprang to life inside her.

What reason could she give for going? She had no money to buy anything. Even if she figured out a reason for going to town, how could she get away from Gareth without rousing his suspicions? She couldn't go about the town asking questions openly. . . .

The hope sputtered and died. She'd never be able to manage it. Her lips tightened. She must try harder to remember, push herself, no matter how painful. Then another thought nudged at her.

What if her memory didn't return?

Ever.

Oh, God, no! She couldn't bear to live in this fearful limbo, not knowing who she was, what secrets from her past lay hidden, waiting to destroy her.

She forced the despairing thoughts away, following the cows and the dog, trying to make her mind a blank.

Both cows went into their stalls with no urging. Shannon gave them their grain, sat down on the milking stool, and pulled rich streams of milk into the pail.

Hearing a noise, she looked up to see Josh standing in the doorway, frowning at her.

Her stomach clenched again. Now what had she done to earn his disapproval? Somehow, she'd managed to mostly avoid Clare since she'd started the outside chores. So why. . . .

Then she remembered yesterday evening when she'd been feeding the big white hogs. After filling the troughs, she'd turned to find Clare almost at her elbow. Startled, she'd dropped the pail and retreated, but Clare had followed, until Shannon was against the pig-lot fence.

She'd heard a noise and looked up to see Josh's stiff and angry back disappearing around the corner of the barn.

Obviously he'd seen just enough to come to the wrong conclusions.

Wholly wrong conclusions.

Shannon turned back to her milking. Maybe if she ignored him, he'd go away.

But instead she heard his footsteps on the barn floor, and then she saw his feet, in his heavy work shoes, standing beside her.

"You leave Clare alone."

Shannon swallowed, her misery intensifying. How could she make him believe none of this was her doing?

She kept on pulling steadily at the cow's teat, but her nervous fingers must have pinched, for suddenly the cow kicked sideways, upsetting the pail, then connecting with Shannon's leg.

Shannon fell backward, landing in a puddle of milk.

Josh fell to his knees beside her, grabbing her by the shoulders, his frown even fiercer than before.

"Didn't you hear me? She's my girl!"

Hysterical laughter bubbled up inside her. If Josh only knew how far off the mark he was! How completely unfounded his suspicions.

"What's going on?" Gareth's angry, incredulous voice erupted into the barn.

Josh quickly scrambled up.

Shannon took a deep breath, then stood herself, wincing as a pain shot through her calf.

"I'm sorry, Mr. Colby," Josh said. "Rosie kicked Shannon, and I was just seeing if he was all right."

Gareth's gaze left Josh, turning to the overturned milk pail, to the milk trickling over the barn floor, then to Rosie, bawling now for someone to finish milking her.

Finally, it settled on Shannon.

His mouth tightened as he stared at her, and the expression in his eyes told her he still fought what he believed to be his unnatural attraction to another member of his sex.

"Go on and do your own chores, Josh," Gareth finally said. "I'll help finish the milking."

"All right, Mr. Colby."

Josh left the barn without looking at Shannon again.

She sighed inwardly.

How would she ever convince him she wasn't after Clare without revealing her true sex?

She realized that for now the best thing she could do was ignore Gareth and get on with her chores.

Shannon righted the pail, then sat down on the stool again. Her fingers were sticky with milk as she reached for the cow's teat, carefully this time, and pulled down on it in the squeezing motion that had to be done just right.

"I need to talk to you," Gareth said, his voice very close.

For the second time that evening, Shannon's fingers closed sharply on the cow's teat, and Rosie reacted as she had before. Shannon scrambled backward, but again, not fast enough. The cow's hoof connected with her other leg and missed the pail entirely.

Again, Shannon sprawled on the floor, looking up into a scowling male face looming over her.

"What in *hell* is wrong with you?" Gareth demanded. "Have you been in the household spirits?"

Everything suddenly caught up with Shannon.

The constant strain she endured from her masquerade as a boy and the fear that haunted every waking moment. Her leg throbbed where Rosie had kicked her. Her bottom was wet with the spilled milk and also ached from the fall.

"No, but if I knew where the spirits were, I would be," she blurted.

Then burst into tears.

The silence in the barn was so thick you could feel it, she thought a few moments later as she rubbed her eyes and glanced up at Gareth. His frown had faded, replaced by an indescribable expression, made up of several conflicting emotions.

Oh, God. No wonder.

Panic filled her. She had to get out of here, go somewhere until she calmed down. Quickly, she scrambled to her feet. Too quickly.

Her feet slipped in the spilled milk on the floor, and she started to fall again, her arms windmilling frantically.

But this time instead of hitting the floor, she collided with Gareth's solid chest. She felt him tense as his hands automatically came out to steady her.

And then she realized that somehow, in the melee, the strips of underwear binding her upper body had loosened and slipped down. Her unbound breasts were pressed tightly against Gareth's chest.

The masquerade was over—and relief swept over her.

She looked up at him and felt her lips curving in an idiotic grin.

"It's all right, Gareth. There's nothing wrong with you after all. I—I'm not a lad. I'm a lassie."

Chapter Seven

Gareth's mind tried to take in what his body already knew. His arms had instinctively gone around Shannon. Just as naturally, they tightened. He felt his body hardening, but now instead of dismayed shame, another feeling swept over him.

Profound relief.

Anger at Shannon's deception flared briefly, then was submerged by a stronger emotion, another blaze of desire.

Gradually, he became aware of other sensations besides the feel of a woman's soft breasts pressed close against him.

Shannon's slim back beneath his arms. A clean, sweet scent from her hair filling his nostrils.

Her face was still tilted up; her blue eyes, fringed with sooty lashes, still stared at him. Half-dried tears made tracks down her face toward the full-lipped pink mouth he'd long burned to kiss.

His eyes traced the contours of her mouth, and he felt her take a sharp little breath as if she'd felt that mental touch.

Gareth's hands moved up her back, underneath her

curly hair to the nape of her neck. He shivered at the feel of that tender flesh beneath his fingers.

He felt the tips of her breasts hardening against his chest, and he was lost. He lowered his head, while Shannon's strained upward. When his lips grazed hers, he drew in his breath. That first tentative touch flamed through him. And when she opened her mouth, inviting him, he couldn't have stopped kissing her if the barn had gone up in actual flames around them.

Her arms slid around his neck, and she pressed herself against him, further inflaming him. His tongue explored the soft sweetness of her mouth and found her own.

Dimly, he was aware of shuffling, impatient movement somewhere close by, but ignored it. He felt as if he'd never kissed another woman before, never held another one in his arms. . . .

A cow's annoyed bellow erupted into the silence, followed by a second one.

Shannon's mouth stilled under his; then her head jerked back. Her eyes wide with shock, her arms uncurled from his neck and pushed against his chest. "Let me go! Oh, let me go!"

Gareth released her and stepped back.

Rosie once more expressed her outrage at being left half-milked.

Gareth came back to himself with a snap.

My God, had he actually exchanged a passionate kiss with this waif whom he'd thought a boy only minutes before?

And wanted more than a kiss?

There was no doubt he would have had more if the damn cow hadn't brought them both back to reality.

"You have some explaining to do," Gareth said, his voice strained and tight.

Oh, yes, she certainly knew that! Shannon pushed down the near hysteria once more threatening to overcome her. She nodded. "Yes. But now I have to milk the cows."

"Damn the cows! I'll help, but first I want some answers."

How could this angry-faced, tight-voiced man be the

same one who had held her in his arms only moments ago, kissed her like she'd never before been kissed?

That thought brought her completely out of the half-swooning spell.

For all she knew, that *was* her first kiss.

Or maybe her hundredth!

"All right," she said, her voice shaking a little. "I'm sorry I pretended to be a boy, but there were good reasons."

Gareth gave an angry snort. "Then how about telling me what they were."

"I was afraid!"

"Of what? The mean master whose name you haven't been able to remember?"

Gareth's hard tones were filled with sarcasm. Shannon's desperation increased. He'd been suspicious of her from the beginning—what could she do now?

"I thought that story about not remembering the name of the family you worked for was a little too convenient. People don't lose their memories that easily."

Wild laughter pushed at her, demanding to be released. *Oh, yes people do,* she burned to tell him. *You don't know the half of it. I wish you did. Then maybe you'd understand.*

Her chaotic thoughts stilled. *Why not?* Why not tell him everything? The burden of this secret was weighing her down. And these kind, decent people should know the truth.

But would she be allowed to?

She held her breath, expecting that monitor in her mind to protest, to insist she not tell anyone anything. That she could trust no one—no one at all. But nothing came.

"Have you finally remembered? Can you give me the name of the family now?"

Before that inner guardian could stop her, she quickly said, "No—and . . . that's not all. I don't remember much of anything about myself or what happened to me before I woke up in your wagon."

She had his attention now. He stiffened, his stare intensifying.

"What are you talking about?"

"Just what I said!"

"You expect me to believe you remember nothing about your past life?"

"Yes!" She hoped the desperation she felt came through in her voice.

"Then everything you told us was a lie?"

She swallowed, hating his hard, disbelieving tones, knowing she couldn't blame him.

"No . . . I don't know. I—I've had some flashes of memory. They feel true."

"How can you expect me to believe anything you say now when you lied before?" he demanded.

She shook her head. "I guess I can't." She heard the wobble in her voice and tried to steady it. "But I swear I'm telling you the truth!"

Frowning, he said nothing for a few moments, as if considering her words, trying to decide if he believed her.

"I've heard of this kind of thing," he finally said, "but I never knew anyone it had happened to."

He gave her another piercing look. "If this is the truth, why didn't you tell us that first day?"

"Because I was afraid you'd send me away."

His stare deepened. "You thought we'd reject an injured, frightened, young woman who could remember nothing about her past?"

His voice was again thick with disbelief.

And put that way, her reasoning did sound ridiculous.

Her heart sank. There was no way she could explain those inner directives that were all she'd had to guide her.

Or the terrifying visions.

It was going to be hard enough to convince him she spoke the truth about her memory loss.

She took a deep breath. "I—I was hurt. I guess I wasn't thinking straight."

Oh, that was a strong defense!

His gray stare intensified. "That was weeks ago. You're

long over your injury. Are you telling me you still fear we'll kick you out of our house?"

She wet her lips. "I know how it must sound. But you don't understand what it's like not knowing where you came from, who you really are!"

To her ears, her words and tone rang with conviction. But maybe not to his. She held her breath waiting for his reaction.

"What flashes of memory have you had?" he finally asked. Some of the hardness had left his voice and his eyes.

Her tension eased a little. Had he decided to believe her? It seemed so—but she couldn't yet be sure.

"The things I've already told you and your family. That my name is Shannon and I'm an orphan. That my father died in the war and my mother afterward. That we lived near Richmond until after my father was killed."

"You don't remember why you disguised yourself as a boy? Why you were lying injured on the road when I found you? You made up the story about working for a cruel master on a farm and falling off his wagon?"

The questions were coming too fast. Shannon felt overwhelmed.

"I—I don't know. I think I was on a wagon . . . and . . ."

Without warning another of the flashes came.

Shannon stiffened, gasping in shock. "A man with a . . . canvas-covered wagon gave me a ride . . . told me to hide in the back . . . I found the men's clothes and put them on . . . cut my hair. The man . . ."

She put her hand to her mouth. "He . . . he tried to . . . attack me. I fought him and fell off onto the ground . . . and . . . that's all I remember until I woke up on your wagon."

He was frowning again. "Was that one of what you call your flashes?"

"Yes. Oh, they're so *real!* They must be true."

He shook his head, as if all this was beyond him. "As I said, I know nothing about any of this kind of thing."

One flash she hadn't mentioned. The man with the knife.

And she should. That might make him understand her fear since he'd just insisted his family would help and protect a defenseless female.

So wouldn't he be shocked and sympathetic if he believed her pursued by a man with a bloody knife?

Maybe he'd help her try to find out who the man was—discover if it *was* a true vision.

She swallowed a sudden lump. At last to be able to do something—not just wait.

Yes, she would tell him!

No! You can't! the voice in her mind awoke and commanded. *You had to reveal this much—but no more. He can't help you. No one can. You have to wait until you remember. . . .*

She couldn't wait! She couldn't go on like this! She opened her mouth to tell Gareth about the man.

Her throat tightened, and the words refused to come out. She tried to swallow and couldn't even do that. Her knees threatened to buckle. These physical reactions terrified her even more.

All right, she promised. *I won't tell him this! I won't tell any of them.*

The tightness in her throat eased. And some of the terror. She swallowed, then took a relieved breath.

Until her memory returned, she had to obey the voice in her mind. That had just been proved.

"I can't force you to believe me," she said, instead of the confession she burned to make. "But I'm telling you the truth."

He looked at her for agonizingly long moments as if weighing her words, deciding whether or not to accept them.

At last he gave a huffing sigh. "I've never heard a more far-fetched sounding story in my life. I may be a fool—but I'm going to accept your word."

Her knees almost buckled again—from relief this time. "Thank you," she said, her voice unsteady.

His face softened a little. "Now we've got to find out why you disguised yourself and what you're afraid of—why you ran away. I'll take you to the sheriff to see if he has a report of a young woman fitting your description missing from her home."

No! Again her mind protested. *Stop him.*

Fear rose anew in Shannon. "I don't want to do that. I—I'm sure I have no family left."

"You *can't* be sure if your memory is gone," he insisted. His face tightened again. "Are you still lying? Are you a thief or worse?"

"I'm no thief, or any kind of criminal. I can't prove it, but I—I just know I'm not."

But was she? As he'd just reminded her, she couldn't be sure of anything. What if her mind was lying to her to keep from facing awful facts?

"Then why don't you want to try to find out all you can?"

She'd stalled as long as she could. He wasn't going to accept more evasions. She had to answer him—if her mind would allow her.

"I don't know why, but something inside my mind insists that I can't," she said in a rush. "That I have to wait until my memory comes back."

New relief filled her. Her throat hadn't closed; no voice in her head had screamed at her to stop. Surely Gareth had heard the honesty in her words, her voice.

He again silently looked at her for more interminable moments, his gaze unblinking.

"I know it's asking a lot to expect you to trust me after what I did," she finally said. "But I *am* asking you. Please give me some time to remember before you do anything. Just let me stay here for a little while longer."

At last his facial muscles relaxed again. "All right. I'll go along with what you want—for a while. I won't take you to the sheriff. But maybe we should get you to a doctor."

She quickly shook her head. "I'm fine now, physically. I don't think a doctor can help this."

"You may be right. I don't know. And you don't know either."

She held her breath while she watched him debating with himself. Rosie again let out an indignant bellow, followed by Sugar.

His breath came out in a huff. "We'll let that go, too, for now, and see if your memory returns. These cows have to be milked. Maybe you'd better do Sugar. You haven't had much luck with Rosie tonight."

"All right." She hastened to her chore, not looking at him again.

No matter what he'd said, Gareth still had doubts about her. She'd only managed to gain a little time.

Unbidden, she again felt his strong arms around her, his hot mouth on her own, their bodies pressed tightly together.

Now that Gareth knew his desire for her was natural, now that he'd kissed her—what would happen? She'd offered no resistance to his embrace. Her mouth twisted.

Resistance? She'd been as eager as he.

Would he still want her to leave because of that physical attraction?

Or would he want her to stay because of it?

What future could there be between them until she regained her memory? Knew who she was. Found out if the man who haunted her was real.

And learned why he wanted to kill her.

Thank God rough boards separated the stalls, Gareth thought. He could hear sounds from the next one—Shannon soothing Sugar, the noise the milk made as it hit the empty pail.

But at least he didn't have to look at her.

He still could hardly take in how she'd hoodwinked him and his entire family for almost a month.

He grimaced. He'd thought the physical urges he'd felt

toward her were unnatural. Yet he'd still delayed trying to find another place for her to live.

He'd still burned to hold her, kiss her.

And the instant he'd discovered a woman hidden behind those men's clothes, he'd done just that, with no hesitation, no thought for what he was doing.

What a fool he'd been!

Gareth was grateful for this chore which gave him time to think, to decide what to do when they finished here and went back to the house.

Despite the girl's admission that she'd lied, somehow he believed she'd lost her memory as she claimed. He even believed she'd deceived them out of fear.

He could understand that. Could understand how lost and abandoned she must feel with most of her past wiped from her mind.

He winced. God, she must have been living in hell these past weeks.

No, that wasn't what bothered him.

What did was his instinctive feeling she still hid something. Her reasons for not wanting to go to the sheriff were weak at best.

Just a strong feeling she mustn't?

A voice in her mind, for God's sake.

Had she made that up because she was a thief—or worse? He realized his *own* feelings told him she wasn't.

Could he trust them any more than he could trust her?

Damn it—what a mess! He'd promised her he wouldn't take her to the sheriff. Hell, he'd have a hard time doing that anyway if she wasn't willing.

But he hadn't promised he'd not try to find out something on his own.

By the time they had finished the milking and the other barn chores, and were walking to the house together, Shannon insisting on carrying her pail of milk, he was no closer to sorting out his jumbled feelings.

He glanced over at her. She was a mess. The seat of her trousers was wet and stiff with spilled milk, and one knee was ripped. Her face was streaked with dirt, and she limped a little, favoring her right leg.

Just as he did. Only her injury was temporary, and would soon disappear. Not like his own permanent reminder of the war.

His reminder of the reason the only woman he'd ever cared for had rejected him.

Memories of that day when Dorinda had told him she couldn't marry him filled his mind. No, not couldn't. *Wouldn't.* She'd waited for him, but he'd seen her eyes widen in shock and something akin to revulsion when he'd limped across the room toward her.

He'd known Dorinda enjoyed beautiful, perfect things. But he hadn't imagined that her dislike of the defective could also apply to him. . . .

Although it had happened more than five years ago, the pain went through him again.

He tried to force his mind away from those thoughts and return it to the young woman walking beside him. Shannon was the only woman except Dorinda who had ever kissed him so passionately. . . .

Shannon—if that was her name—had lied to him. And Dorinda had proved to be shallow, devoid of real emotion and staying power.

His mouth twisted. She'd found what she sought. Laird Phillips, the eldest son of one of the county's most successful businessmen, who had come home with a broken arm after a few months of battle. He'd never gone back to the war.

And now, with the help of some Yankee dollars, his family's feed and grain business was thriving. They had expanded into the commercial fertilizers which everyone said was the coming thing.

Dorinda had married Laird only a month after she'd ended her engagement to Gareth. She now had two children, and lived in the Phillips mansion which had miraculously survived the purging the Valley had suffered during four years of hell.

Not paying attention to where he walked, Gareth's arm bumped against Shannon's.

She gave him a startled glance out of those eyes that had haunted his dreams for weeks and moved to the right.

"Sorry," he muttered, moving to the left. Now there was ample room between them. And a lot of good that did. The brief touch of his arm against hers had made a thrill of awareness go through him, effectively banishing Dorinda's image.

What in hell was he going to do about Shannon?

Gareth stepped in front of her to open the back door, holding it so she could go ahead of him. The kitchen full of his womenfolk glanced their way. Gareth groaned inwardly. Now it would start.

Grandma Lucy sat in her rocker by the cold hearth. Her gray eyes sharpened as she took in Shannon's bedraggled appearance.

Gwenny, lifting the steaming teakettle, frowned in disapproval. Not surprising. Gwenny had been frowning at Shannon ever since her arrival.

His mother, setting the table, looked a bit surprised, then went on placing knives and forks.

Clare was cutting a skillet of corn bread into triangles. Seeing Shannon, her eyes widened, and her mouth fell open. "What has happened to you?" she cried. "Are you hurt?"

Gareth shot a glance of his own at the . . . girl. Shock still went through him at this thought. Shock and relief. As well as other feelings he didn't want to deal with now.

Shannon took a deep breath and let it out. She visibly swallowed, then straightened her shoulders and firmed her chin.

Appreciation for her spunk dropped into his cauldron of mixed emotions. In spite of what she knew had to happen in the next few minutes, she wasn't cringing. He liked that.

He waited for her to say something, but she didn't. Finally, she glanced his way, her expression wary. She expected him to . . . what? Censure her before his entire family?

Gareth's mouth tightened. Of course she did, and no wonder. He couldn't do it, he realized. She'd suffered enough for one night.

He cleared his throat. "Gramma Lucy, Mama, Gwenny, Clare. I just found out a very surprising fact." He stopped and took a deep breath.

"Shannon is a woman."

Gareth swiftly glanced at them all. Grandma Lucy's mouth curved upward in a satisfied smile, and she nodded.

His mother looked up, a mildly surprised look on her face, smiled, then kept on laying flatware.

Gwenny's mouth clamped shut, and she set the kettle back on the stove lid with a resounding thump.

Clare's face paled, her mouth hung open. She dropped the plate of corn bread on the floor, shattering the china and scattering pieces of bread.

"I—I'm sorry," Shannon said. "I never meant to hurt any of you. You've been so kind to me."

Despite everything, relief went through her.

At least one good thing had come from this. She no longer had to try to talk like a farm boy. Or act like one.

"Oh! How *could* you do something so, so *despicable?* How could you humiliate me li—ike this?" Clare's last words ended in a sob. Picking up her skirts she ran to the back door, wrenched it open, and fled, leaving the door swinging open behind her.

Maud got up and closed it, then looked around at the room's remaining occupants. Finally, her glance returned to Shannon. "I'm sure you had a good reason for fooling us, didn't you, child?"

Surprise went through Shannon. She hadn't expected Maud to champion her. "Yes, I—I thought I did. I was afraid."

"Of course you were," Grandma Lucy's strong voice said. "I knew that the moment I saw you. You were scared to death."

She'd have to finish this. Gareth obviously was going to leave it to her. She might as well plunge right into the middle. "I was—am afraid because I've lost my memory. When I woke up in Gareth's wagon, I'd forgotten everything about my past."

Gwenny's mouth fell open. "Lost your memory? You don't even know who you are?" At Shannon's nod she continued. "Those things you told us about working for a cruel family weren't true?"

Shannon bit her lip. "I'm not sure—but I don't think so. I was afraid you'd make me leave if I told all of you the truth. I want so much to stay here until my memory comes back."

"And so you shall!" Grandma Lucy said.

"Whatever made you think we'd turn you out?" Maud asked.

The events of the last hour finally caught up with Shannon.

Both legs throbbed, as did her backside. She was sticky and wet and filthy. Her pants were torn. Both emotionally and physically, she felt awful. She desperately wanted to crawl up the stairs to her little attic room and into bed.

Instead, she had to go through no telling how much more of this before she could escape.

At least they wouldn't send her away—Gareth had promised she could stay. And so had Grandma Lucy. Maud also seemed sympathetic.

"I—I don't know," she finally said. "It seems foolish now."

She swayed on her feet, and her head swam dizzily. Oh, Lord, she was going to faint again. Well, at least this time it wouldn't be considered a sign of a weak lad, she thought wildly.

Just in time, Gareth thrust a chair under her.

Shannon sank gratefully onto it. "Thank you," she said, her voice as wobbly as her body.

Gwenny frowned down at her, her lips pursed. "What

on earth has happened to you? You look like something the cat dragged in."

Dully surprised, Shannon realized Gwenny's voice sounded exactly as it did when she scolded Clare for some infraction. Exasperated, but with an underlying fondness.

"I feel like it, too. Rosie kicked me twice. Do you suppose I could go to bed now and we can talk about all of this tomorrow?"

"I think that's best," Gwenny said briskly, going to the stove and lifting the steaming kettle. "You go on ahead and I'll follow with the kettle. You can't get under clean sheets with all that dirt on you. I'll bring the salve, too."

Her surprise growing, Shannon got to her feet. Maud hurried over and took her arm and put it around her shoulders. Shannon stiffened. This scene was like the one the first night she arrived. Too much so.

"Nothing that can't wait until morning," Grandma Lucy said from her rocker.

"I'll help you upstairs," Maud said.

"No, let me do that," Gareth said.

Maud gave him a surprised look, but moved back as he took her place beside Shannon.

Despite her fatigue, Shannon felt herself tensing even more. She didn't want Gareth to touch her again. Not now. Not until she had a chance to sort out her feelings.

"You can lean on me," Gareth said.

Their glances met, and in Gareth's gray eyes she saw all the confusion she felt herself. And the strong physical pull that drew them together even as they fought it with their minds.

She couldn't refuse to touch him. That would look very odd. But neither could she walk upstairs with him, her arm around his shoulder, feeling his strong muscles grow taut beneath her touch.

Panic made strength flow back into her body. She straightened her back, gave him a smile. "I'm all right now. I can walk by myself."

"Don't be foolish," he answered, but she saw the relief in his face.

"I'm *fine.*" she said firmly, and proved it by taking a couple of steady steps toward the stairs.

Memory swept over her—but not a flash of her old life this time. She and Gareth, locked in each other's arms, mouths and bodies pressed together. . . .

Her face warmed. These kind people wouldn't give her houseroom if they knew what had gone on in the barn this evening.

And if she and Gareth were alone together it would happen again. She was as sure of this as of her own name.

Shannon stifled the hysterical laugh pushing up from inside. Oh, that was funny! She *wasn't* sure of anything in her life . . . not even her name.

She fought against another thought forming in her mind, but lost.

Maybe she'd never get her memory back.

Then what?

Chapter Eight

" 'If you are not the heiress born,
And I,' said he, 'the lawful heir,
We two will wed to-morrow morn,
And you shall still be Lady Clare.' "

Reading the last words of Tennyson's poem, Shannon glanced at Clare, sitting as far away as possible.

"That was very nice," Maud said.

"Yes," Grandma Lucy echoed.

Gwenny nodded.

Shannon had deliberately selected Tennyson's happy-ending poem with the namesake heroine in the hope of softening Clare's attitude toward her.

During this past week, since that awful evening of revelations, Clare had avoided her, spoken only when it was absolutely necessary.

But not so the rest of the family. That next morning they had talked.

She'd told them about her memory flashes, and about her feeling she was truly an orphan, with no family left. No one had suggested going to the authorities. Greatly relieved, she'd sent Gareth a grateful glance and smile.

He'd returned her smile, but she'd seen something watchful in his expression.

It was clear he didn't completely believe her story. What he planned to do about it, if anything, wasn't.

All but Clare insisted she stay on as long as she wanted. Or until her memory returned.

The family could still use her help. Grandma Lucy needed a companion, someone to read to her, since her sight was going. Could she read? Gwenny had handed Shannon a book of poems, and Shannon, elated at this new discovery, read one with ease.

So Shannon could do that, efficient Gwenny declared, as well as help with household chores. Of course they couldn't pay her right now. . . .

Embarrassed, yet deeply relieved, Shannon waved away that consideration. How wonderful if that was all she had to worry about. She glanced at Gareth, who had remained silent during his womenfolks' talk.

Their eyes met. Remembering those moments in his arms the previous evening, a shiver went through her. His ruggedly handsome face held a musing look, as if perhaps he, too, remembered. Finally, he nodded, said if that was what they wanted, it was all right with him, and left for the fields.

Although she'd been relegated to women's work, she still insisted on milking the two cows. She liked the work, but there was another reason she couldn't deny to herself.

That would be the only time she'd have alone with Gareth, when he was mucking out the stalls.

Her vow never again to let that happen hadn't lasted the night. She'd awakened from a dream of being in his arms, held fast against him, lips pressed to lips. . . .

No, dangerous and foolish as it was, she couldn't stay away from him.

Gareth, however, had other ideas. The next day when he came into the barn and found her milking, he quickly left. A few minutes later Josh entered and said he'd be cleaning the stalls from now on.

He gave her an astonished look, then an embarrassed grin and said Gareth had told him about her memory loss. And that she was really a woman. He'd apologized for his accusations the day before.

She liked Josh. Now that he was no longer angry with her about her supposed interest in Clare, he was an agreeable companion. . . .

Shannon gave herself a mental shake, returning to the present.

She saw Gareth only at meals and in the evenings when the family sat together for a time. Like now.

Gareth hadn't listened to the poetry reading. Instead he seemed engrossed in a newspaper. Just the sight of his dark, bent head, his large, work-roughened hands that had touched her so tenderly, yet so passionately, sent a tremor through her.

Gareth, whose middle name was Lancelot. He hated it, Clare had confided. Shannon smiled. Somehow, overly romantic though it was, the name fit him.

She glanced at Clare again.

The girl was bent over her embroidery hoop. As if feeling Shannon's gaze on her, she looked up. The sullen mask was gone, her pretty face softened and dreamy.

"That was a lovely poem," she said, her voice soft and dreamy, too.

"I like it." Shannon let out a sigh of relief, hoping Clare was offering a lasting truce. It had been so unpleasant this past week.

Shannon now felt a gaze on her. Without looking, she knew it was Gareth. But of course she had to look. She turned her head so quickly she caught his expression before he could erase it.

She drew in her breath. His gray eyes were full of hunger. Heat radiated down her nerve endings, creating an answering fire from deep inside her.

Sharply, he turned away, laid the paper on the library table and stood. "Good night, all. I'm turning in."

"But it's still so early," Clare protested. "And Shannon has read only one poem."

Gareth was already halfway to the stairs. "It's been a long day," he said over his shoulder.

Shannon held herself very still, trying to calm her racing heart, the tumult of her feelings. She wanted nothing more than to also go to her room.

But, in spite of these women's kindness, she wasn't a family member, not even a friend. Her status was blurred between a companion and a hired girl.

Albeit an educated one, who could read poetry with the proper cadences and inflections.

And where had she learned that? From the sweet-voiced woman she felt had to have been her mother? From that kind, shadowy man she could never clearly see? Had she been tutored?

What?

She forced down her frustration. Pushing at her mind didn't work. Most often the memory flashes came unbidden, when she least expected them.

As did the menacing vision of the man with the knife.

Quickly, she blanked her mind of that thought, bringing it back to this cozy room, the lamplight spilling over the leather-bound book in her hand. As Clare had pointed out, she'd read only one poem. She owed them at least another half hour of reading.

Forty minutes later, holding a candle, she, too, climbed the stairs. On the lower landing, Gareth's door was closed. Was he already in bed?

Her face flamed as her mind's eye pictured his big body nude under the covers. Quickly, she hurried past and up the attic stairs. Pausing outside her own tiny chamber, she glanced across the narrow hall into the cubicle opposite.

As always, the trunk holding the sapphire and diamond pendant looked undisturbed.

She hadn't told Gareth or the family about it. She hadn't thought about it at first. Then, when she did, coldness hit her spine.

Despite his profession of belief in her story, and those moments he'd held her in his arms, she felt Gareth was barely convinced she wasn't a thief—or maybe worse. He still had doubts.

How would he react if she showed them the obviously valuable necklace? Told him she'd found it in the pocket of her man's trousers, described her memory flash of the woman wearing it? Her feeling that it truly belonged to her?

Would he believe her? Or drag her off to the nearest sheriff as he'd wanted to do anyway?

She couldn't risk that, not when just thinking about doing so brought paralyzing fear, that mind-voice forbidding her.

Why couldn't she remember? She hated this waiting! There must be something she could do to speed things up.

She felt a sudden urge to dig the pendant out of its hiding place. It was the only tangible object she had from her past. Maybe if she held it again, another bit of lost memory would come.

She listened for sounds from downstairs, heard the women talking in low voices. She'd wait a few minutes until everyone was in bed.

Half an hour later, she quietly opened her door again and listened. All was silent. Leaving her door ajar, she tiptoed across the hall and into the cubicle. She bent over the trunk and lifted its lid, wincing when the rusty hinges emitted a sharp squeak.

She'd forgotten that! Had anyone heard? She waited a few moments, rigidly holding herself still.

Finally, she relaxed and reached into the corner where she'd buried the pendant under the trunk's moldering papers. Her groping fingers touched the cold hardness of the stone and pulled it out.

She drew in her breath. In the candle's flickering light, the faceted gemstone glowed with deep blue fire. She squeezed her hand around it, closing her eyes, willing the stone to stir her memory, breach that wall as it had before.

The moments stretched out. Nothing happened. Disappointment washed over Shannon in a bitter flood. She opened her palm, uncovering the gem's brilliance.

She seemed to see something . . . some kind of scene that was drawing her into its depths. . . .

A big brick house sat amid wide green lawns. On the lawn stood the sweet-faced woman, holding out her arms to a laughing girl with mahogany hair and blue eyes who ran toward her. On the porch stood a boy of about fifteen with the same coloring.

Jeff. Her brother.

A hard fist closed around her heart, squeezing until she could hardly breathe. He'd been killed in the war, in one of the last battles. Her mother had grieved until the day she died. . . .

Died.

The hazy scene faded, and once more she held only a beautiful piece of jewelry. A despairing sob escaped her, then another.

She'd felt her mother must be dead, but still, she'd held a bit of hope that it might not be true, despite her mind's insistence she had no one left. Now, this hope was dead and buried, just as her mother was in the family cemetery . . . where?

What sounded like a door opening on the lower floor jerked her out of her reverie. Someone was up—had they heard her open the trunk . . . heard her cry out?

Shannon strained for other sounds, then heard a stair tread creak.

Her heart thudded. She dropped the pendant back into the trunk. It hit the bottom with a thunk and she winced. Quickly, she moved papers over it, closed the lid and got up, heading for her room.

In the doorway, she stopped, drawing in her breath.

Gareth stood on the top stair, holding a candle. "Are you all right?" he asked. "I heard noises."

She nodded. Had he seen her at the trunk? He must have. "Yes. I—I heard something, too. I guess it was a mouse in there." Pointing to the storeroom, she tried to look only mildly concerned.

He stared at her as the moments ticked by, then finally nodded. "Maybe so."

Did he believe her? She couldn't tell from his expression.

"I didn't see anything, so I guess it won't bother me. Good night," she said, and walked across to her open door, entered and closed it behind her.

Gareth watched her go, remembering how she'd looked crouched before the trunk, in that blue dress, her hair shining in the candlelight. Her head had been tilted forward, revealing a bit of her nape.

He clenched his fists, his body hardening as another memory assailed him. His hands caressing her soft skin, his mouth covering hers, his body pressed against her.

He shook his head to clear it of the disturbing recollections. He had other things to worry about. His mouth thinned. Shannon hadn't been looking for a mouse in that trunk.

She hadn't been *looking* for anything.

Halfway up the stairs, he'd heard an odd sound—a thud. No, she'd put something in that trunk—something hard. And she'd been nervous as hell about him finding that out.

Gareth walked across to the trunk and opened it, hearing the squeak that had alerted him earlier. He'd been wide awake, anyway, his thoughts on the evening just past, on Shannon's lovely voice reading the sentimental poem. . . .

The trunk was filled with papers and old letters. Puzzled, he stared at the jumble. Maybe he was mistaken. Maybe the thunking sound he'd heard came from something else not connected with Shannon.

No, it had to be, he decided, otherwise she wouldn't have worn that frightened look when she'd seen him, as if she'd been caught at something.

Gareth moved the papers around, realizing the trunk

wasn't packed solidly. He sifted through the top layer, with no results, then pushed the stacks aside to reach the bottom. His hand touched something hard and cold. He closed his fingers over the object and drew it to the top.

Astonished, he stared at the gemstone on its gold chain, shining in the light of his candle.

He didn't know all that much about jewelry, but he knew enough to be certain this was real. And valuable.

He was certain it didn't belong to any member of his family. This was an heirloom, something passed down from generation to generation.

And Shannon must have hidden it in this trunk. What was she doing with it?

All his earlier suspicions returned full force.

He'd sensed last week in the barn she hadn't told him everything. That something was still withheld, still bothering her.

Could this be it? Could she have stolen this jewel and run away? Donned men's clothing, cut her hair, accepted the ride on the wagon? This would explain why she was so alarmed at the idea of talking to the sheriff. . . .

Was her story about losing her memory a complete fabrication?

Something hard and cold hit his stomach. He didn't want to believe that. He wanted very much to accept her story at face value.

But he couldn't. He had to know. He closed his hand over the stone, shut the trunk, then rose. He walked to the cubicle doorway and stood looking at Shannon's closed door.

There was only one way to find out.

Chapter Nine

Very much doubting that Shannon would be asleep, Gareth pushed aside the vision his mind conjured up of her lying in bed, clad only in her nightdress.

He crossed to the door and rapped softly. It opened at once, as if she'd waited for his knock. She was still fully dressed.

He held out his hand and opened it, palm up, revealing the pendant. Her eyes widened, and he heard her sharp intake of breath.

"What are you doing with this?" he asked, hearing how brusque his voice sounded, knowing it was because he didn't want to feel these suspicions about her.

No, what he truly wanted to do was pull her into his arms and tell her she could confess anything to him.

She stepped backward. "Come inside. We don't want to wake the household."

Her voice had trembled. She didn't want anyone else to hear.

Were those the actions of an innocent woman?

Gareth followed her in and closed the door.

He shouldn't be alone in her bedchamber, but this was

no time to worry about propriety. He'd give her a chance to explain, not confront her with this before the whole family.

His mind told him he *should* be worrying, that part of his decision to talk to her alone was because he wanted to be near her.

They stood just inside the door, staring at each other.

"Do you think I stole this?" Shannon finally asked, her words clipped and tight.

"What do you expect me to think?" he answered just as tightly. "You hid it in the trunk, never mentioned it to us."

"I—should have told you," she finally said, and moved back a step.

She moistened her lips with her tongue, and despite the distrust and doubt, he felt a stab of desire hit him.

He wished it were *his* tongue touching her full pink lips, delving inside. . . .

Stop that, he told himself. "Can you convince me this belongs to you and you had a good reason for hiding it away?"

Her gaze met his steadily. "I don't know. I can try. I—I believe the pendant belonged to my mother. And she gave it to me before she . . . died."

The pain in her soft voice as she said the last words almost made him ashamed of himself.

Almost. "So you remember that? Clearly enough to be sure of it?"

She nodded. "Tonight, when I held the pendant in my hand, I had another flash of memory. I . . . saw my mother again. *Knew* she'd died."

Gareth's discomfort grew. He didn't want to do this, but he must, and not keep getting diverted because he was so attracted to her.

Not keep noticing how lovely she was.

Her short, curly hair looked odd now that she wore a dress. But very appealing. Her blue eyes had dark smudges under them, as if she'd not slept well for a long time.

They were almost the shade of the necklace. . . .

Get this over with.

"Then you've remembered that your family was well off?" he prodded.

"No . . . but . . . they must have been, at least at one time, to have owned this pendant. I saw the big brick house we lived in . . . but I think we lost it during the war . . . as we lost my father and brother . . ."

She paused a moment, her eyes darkening as if she'd thought of something that startled her. "Not my mother, though. She didn't die during the war. She . . ."

Her voice broke off. Tears welled in her eyes.

Sympathy twisted Gareth's gut. Again, as had happened last week in the barn, he found himself believing her.

But he still had to question her.

"Why did you hide the necklace in the trunk?"

She blinked back the tears. One slid down her cheek, and she wiped it away with a quick movement of her hand. "Because I was afraid! I was posing as a boy. I couldn't very well wear it around my neck, could I?"

Keep focused on what you have to find out, he told himself.

"You've been wearing dresses for over a week now," he reminded her, keeping his voice level, trying not to reveal the sympathy he felt.

"But I knew you didn't fully trust me. I feared you might drag me off to the sheriff if I showed you the stone."

Her mouth tightened. "Either you believe me now, believe this truly belongs to me, or you think I'm a thief."

She was right—she couldn't have known what he'd do. Did he know that even now?

But she could have trusted him.

Yes, as you trust women's motives so fully, his mind jeered at him.

He did believe she told the truth now. But trust was another thing altogether.

Are you sure you really believe her . . . you're not letting your body think for you? his mind asked.

No, he wasn't sure. He couldn't deny he desired her,

but he didn't think she lied, although there were still unanswered questions. "Why didn't you sell the jewel since you were penniless?"

"I don't know! I can't remember! Maybe because it's the only thing I have of my mother's—my family. Maybe I couldn't bear to sell it."

His heart contracted with sympathy. He trusted her story now, and he could understand her feelings. How would he feel in her circumstances?

Gareth moved a step closer. He again held out the pendant. "You don't have to hide this in the trunk any longer. Show it to the family tomorrow and let them find a safe place for it."

He paused, his gaze steadily on hers. "That is, if you trust us to keep it safely for you."

Her face reddened; then she took the necklace, closing her hand around it. "Of course I trust you. But where could a safer place be found than the trunk?"

"You don't want to tell anyone else in the family about it?"

She quickly shook her head. "That's not what I meant."

"Good. Our family isn't much for secrets. We like to keep things in the open."

That was true, but he didn't feel threatened by any secrets she still kept. Or was her possession of the valuable necklace the last one?

He'd gone to the sheriff a few days ago, asked if he'd heard anything about a young woman missing in the area. The sheriff, an old friend, had given him a curious look, but had said no.

That had greatly relieved Gareth's mind, while saddening him to think she had no one to care for her, to miss her. Maybe Shannon was still fearful only because she could remember so little about her past. Maybe her fear of danger associated with the authorities was based on uncertainty.

And he wouldn't go back to the sheriff and ask if any valuable jewels had been reported stolen. She couldn't be from right around here anyway, or they would know her and her family.

He didn't think Shannon was a thief. He didn't think he'd made a mistake in allowing her to stay.

What else could he have done? What else could any decent person have done?

Standing so close to her, breathing in her sweet, clean scent, he wondered if he was fooling himself. Had he agreed to her staying, told her he believed her explanation for having the necklace, only because he wanted to take her to bed?

Here they were, closed in her bedchamber, the rest of the household asleep. And she wanted him, too. Her eager response to his earlier kiss and embrace told him that.

What would she do if he reached for her, pulled her into his arms as he ached to do? Picked her up and carried her to the bed—and lay with her?

Her eyes widened as he stared at her, as if she could read his thoughts. She moved backward again, looking scared and small.

And very vulnerable.

Shame washed over him. She *was* vulnerable and under the protection of his household. And young. How old could she be—twenty at the most. He'd let things get out of control the other day, but he'd vowed it wouldn't happen again.

He'd stick with that vow if it killed him.

She was no young adventuress or trollop. He couldn't, *wouldn't,* take advantage of her physical attraction to him.

But knowing all that with his mind did nothing to cool the fire inside him, or stop him from clenching his hands at his sides to keep from pulling her into his arms, kissing her sweet full lips until she gasped for breath.

"Don't worry," he said, his warring feelings making his voice rough. "You will be safe in all ways here."

He turned and left the tiny room, knowing there was another reason he was leaving before he could give in to his temptation—and persuade her to succumb to her own.

He believed she posed no threat to his family, that was true. He could sleep soundly at night with her under their roof.

But as to harm to himself—to the part of him that still felt the injury Dorinda had inflicted—that was a different matter.

He'd vowed never to give his love to another woman, never leave himself open and vulnerable to that kind of hurt again.

He didn't really know this girl who so stirred his senses. Hell, she didn't even know herself! How could he even be considering making love to her?

Love. Now that was a fallacy if there ever was one. He wanted no more dealings with that kind of false emotion. He felt a deep affection for his family, of course. That was a natural feeling.

But what he wanted from a woman he could find at the nearest tavern. With no commitment asked or given. He hadn't been with a woman for a long time. That was the only reason he felt like this.

That problem could be easily remedied. With no worry about hurting anyone. Or getting hurt himself.

"Oo-hh. It's so beautiful!" Clare's fingers reverently touched the pendant. She glanced up at Shannon, a new respect in her eyes.

Shannon nodded, relief filling her that this was over. Gareth had believed her, and his family believed her, too. "It is."

Gwenny's brows were drawn together in thought. "Where did you say your family lived?" she asked. "I don't remember any Browns anywhere around here."

Shannon was startled at the question; then she understood. When this family had considered her a homeless waif, even after they knew she had some education, it hadn't mattered where her home had been. Probably even now, when her ownership of the pendant indicated her family had been of some substance, no one else but Gwenny really cared that much.

Gwenny was the most complex of the Colby women. She had strength of character like her grandmother, yet also had some of Clare's desire for nice things. But stronger than anything was her deep pride in the Valley and its people. Her sense of loss for the way of life the war had taken from them was greater than anyone else's.

Even Gareth's.

Just thinking about him brought Shannon's senses to life—all of her became more alive.

When he'd left last night, she'd lain awake until almost dawn, her feelings in turmoil. He'd wanted her—that had been obvious. And for a moment she'd been afraid.

She didn't know if Gareth's kiss that day in the barn had been her first one, or her dozenth, or even hundredth.

How could she even be certain no one had ever made love to her?

Just like almost everything else in her past, she couldn't—although in the deepest part of her, she *was* sure, just the same.

And she'd also known she didn't want her first experience to be in this attic bedroom, with a man who didn't fully trust her, no matter what he said.

She wanted it to be with her husband.

Thinking about last night again, her stomach clenched. Gareth was physically attracted to her, but she had no reason to believe he'd ever ask her to be his wife.

"Gwenny, I . . . don't think my last name is Brown. I can't even be sure Shannon is my given name, although it feels right to me."

Gwenny looked chagrined. "I'm sorry, Shannon. I keep forgetting that you've lost your memory. So you don't have any idea where you lived before?"

Shannon managed a smile. "No. But I don't think it was right around here. Or surely some things would seem familiar."

Gwenny's frown deepened. "You haven't been off our

property since Gareth brought you home. Maybe if we took you for a ride to Luray or somewhere else, you would recognize something."

For a moment, hope rose in Shannon as it had when *she'd* thought of this idea. Yes, if she could persuade them to take her to Luray . . . maybe she could find out something. . . .

No! her mind objected. *You need to stay right here. You can't take chances on anyone seeing you!*

As it had before, the hope died, frustration rising to take its place.

"Gwenny, for heaven's sake stop prattling," Grandma Lucy chided.

"I'm not prattling, Gramma," Gwenny said, in a tone of offended dignity. "I'm only trying to help Shannon regain her memory."

Clare looked up from her rapt contemplation of the pendant. "Could I try this on, just for a minute?" she asked.

Relief that the subject had been changed went through Shannon.

"Clare!" Gwenny reproved. "Mind your manners!"

"Why is that bad manners?" Clare asked, a rebellious glint in her eyes. "I only want to know what it feels like to have something this lovely around my neck. Sometimes I simply can't bear it that all our family treasures were stolen—or had to be sold!"

"Hush, you silly child!" Gwenny commanded, the pain of that loss revealed in the sudden tension of her features.

"Of course you may try it on," Shannon said quickly. "Here, let me fasten it for you."

She followed words with actions, and in a few moments the necklace lay upon the front of Clare's worn yellow gown.

Stroking the glittering ornament, Clare closed her eyes in bliss. "How wonderful it would be if the world was like it was before. When everyone wore beautiful clothes and had dances and balls and good times. I used to watch from upstairs, peeking through the banisters."

A memory flash hit Shannon without warning.

She saw herself crouching at the top of a long, curved stairway, chubby hands holding onto a white-painted railing, captivated by the music, the gracefully swirling dancers far below. . . .

The sweet-faced woman was one of them, laughing up at a tall man with mahogany-colored hair, who gazed at her in adoration. . . .

"Those days will never come again," Gwenny said. "And we have spent too much time this morning dawdling when we all have work to do."

She turned to Shannon, pain in the lines of her face. "We must find a safe place for your pendant. Clare, take it off."

"Oh, Gwenny, don't be such an old maid!" Clare protested. "Just because *you* aren't interested in beaux and beautiful jewels, you don't have to spoil things for everyone else."

Shannon heard Gwenny's sharp intake of breath.

"Girls, that will be enough," Maud said, mildly, before Gwenny could retort. "We mustn't squabble among ourselves."

Clare reluctantly slipped the pendant off and gave it back to Shannon. "I don't see why Shannon has to hide it away. If *I* had something that beautiful, I'd wear it all the time."

"It seems to me Shannon already had the necklace in the safest place," Grandma Lucy said. "Why don't you wrap it in a cloth and put it back in the attic trunk?"

"That's what I was thinking, too." Shannon gave her a wide smile, and the older woman returned it, a twinkle in her faded gray eyes.

"You ought to tell them about the man you think is after you—and wants to kill you."

Pulling rich streams of jersey milk into her pail, Shannon sighed. Josh's voice was very firm and sure. She wished she felt that certain about what they were discussing.

"I *can't,*" she said, not for the first time.

She still was amazed that her mind had allowed her, just this morning, to tell Josh about the man from her nightmare visions. "They'd insist on going to the sheriff. Gareth already wants to do that."

"That's what they *should* do. What *you* should do. No wonder you're afraid. Anybody would be. What if this man you see in your head finds you?"

A lump settled in her throat. "Don't you think I worry about that every moment?"

"Yes, and that's why you need to talk to the sheriff and try to find him before he finds you."

Josh's words were so reasonable. Exactly the words she'd hear from Gareth and his family. Sweat broke out on her forehead.

"I just *can't,* Josh. Don't you believe what I said? That something inside my mind stopped me from speaking when I tried to tell Gareth? I can't understand why I could tell you."

Josh let out an impatient sigh, then forcefully stuck his pitchfork into a pile of soiled straw. "Probably because I'll go along with what you want even if I think you're wrong—and Gareth wouldn't if you told him this. But what if your mind is playing tricks on you?"

"Don't you think I've asked myself that a hundred times?"

He was silent for a long time. Finally, she glanced over at him. He leaned on his pitchfork, gazing at her.

"If I was in your shoes, I might feel the same way. But how can you be sure there's a real man?"

Shannon sighed. "I can't tell you that. I just am. That awful picture is too real to be only something my mind conjured up."

The silence dragged out as Josh lifted and pitched refuse.

"You've got to try to find out if he's real," he finally said. "You can't just wait around, scared to death all the time."

Shannon pressed her lips together in frustration. "What would you suggest? Every time I even think about going, my mind forbids it. So I can't go into town with Gareth, go wandering off trying to find out things."

"No, but *I* could."

Shannon's hand froze on Rosie's teat. Why hadn't she thought of that? She turned toward Josh, her face alight with sudden hope.

"Could you do that, Josh? I feel so helpless and I *hate* feeling like that."

Without warning, her eyes filled with tears. She turned away, angrily determined not to let him see her cry. She'd done enough crying. She was sick of it.

She felt his hand on her shoulder, squeezing comfortingly.

"Don't cry, Shannon. Let's decide how we can do this." He crouched down beside her, his hand still on her shoulder.

"Yes." She smiled at him through her tears.

"Shannon, isn't it enough that you made an entire fool of me?" a shrill voice erupted into the quiet of the barn. "And I forgave you that! But this is beyond any hope of forgiveness!" Clare's voice broke dramatically on the last words.

Josh's hand dropped from Shannon's shoulder. He quickly stood and turned toward Clare. "This isn't . . . we weren't," he floundered.

Shannon closed her eyes, forcibly keeping herself from picking up the half-full pail of milk and throwing it across the room.

Did *everything* that happened in this barn have to turn into a farce, a comedy of errors?

Clare took a deep breath, drew herself up to her full five-foot-two height and marched across the barn floor.

"How could I possibly misunderstand anything? You had your arm around Shannon; you were holding her close."

Shannon carefully moved away from Rosie, wanting no repetition of what had happened in here before. She faced Clare, keeping her expression calm.

"Clare," she said, "Josh has no . . . romantic interest in me. We're just friends, and he was merely . . ." Her voice trailed off. She couldn't finish the sentence without exposing this secret between her and Josh.

The secret her mind wouldn't let her reveal to anyone else even if she wanted to.

Clare sniffed again, louder this time. "Merely what? Why would he have his arm about you if he *didn't* have a romantic interest in you?"

With a swish of skirts she turned toward Josh. "Have you nothing else to say for yourself? Are you going to break my heart and laugh at the pieces?"

Josh shot Shannon a questioning glance. She knew he was asking her if it was all right to tell Clare everything.

She couldn't let him do that. They couldn't tell Clare without telling the rest of the family. Without telling Gareth.

"You didn't let me finish a moment ago. I was feeling low about my memory loss, and Josh was only comforting me," Shannon said.

The girl tilted her chin higher. "Surely, you don't expect me to believe that!"

"Clare, you are being unreasonable," Josh said. "Nothing is going on. And you don't have any room to talk. What about the way you were flirting with Shannon when you thought she was a boy?"

Clare's face turned bright red. "Oh! You are not a gentleman, Joshua Archer, nor will you ever be one, to throw that up in my face!"

She spun around and ran for the door, her head down, sobbing as she fled.

And collided squarely with Gareth.

"What in hell is going on?" he demanded, catching her by the arms to keep her from falling.

"Wh-why don't you ask Josh and Shannon? I'm sure

they can tell you all about it," Clare said, her voice small and pitiful.

Gareth let go of her. Frowning, he looked across the expanse of the big room. Josh and Shannon stood side by side, with peculiar expressions on their faces.

"There is nothing at all going on, Mr. Colby," Josh said, as he'd told Clare a few moments ago. "Clare just made a mistake, and she thinks that—"

"Made a mistake?" Clare's tones changed to outrage. "What do you mean *I* made a mistake? I know what my eyes tell me! You were embracing this, this female who has no one and nothing and we took her in, and treated her like family!"

A white-hot spear of jealousy shot through Gareth. His jaw set. "Clare, that will be enough! Go back to the house and I'll sort this matter out."

"I don't *want* to go to the house! Josh is my beau. He's *more* than that, he's . . ."

Clare's blue eyes widened in shock, and she clamped her small hand to her mouth. She gave her older brother a guilty look.

"Go to the house," Gareth repeated. "I'll be up in a few minutes to talk to you."

Gareth marveled that his voice sounded so firm and controlled. God knew, he certainly didn't feel as if he had *anything* under control. Especially this damn situation, whatever it turned out to be.

"All right." Clare's tones were subdued now. She settled her skirts and pushed at her hair, then lifted her chin and disappeared out the door.

Gareth turned to the other two, his glance settling on Josh. "I'd like an explanation."

Josh swallowed, then pulled himself up straight and squared his shoulders.

"Yes, Mr. Colby. Shannon was feeling bad about losing her memory, and I just patted her like I would my sister. I love Clare, and I've asked her to be my wife when I can support a family."

Gareth let out his breath, realizing guiltily that Josh's explanation had made profound relief go through him, when he should be feeling anger and outrage toward this boy he'd trusted.

"Why have you done your courting of Clare behind our backs?" Gareth demanded, keeping his voice hard. "I thought you were an honorable young man."

Red appeared on Josh's cheekbones, but he still held his head high and looked Gareth in the eye.

"I *do* have honor, sir. There's been no courting, except for a . . . kiss or two. I have the highest respect for Clare and her family."

"Then why have you two been sneaking around?" Gareth asked again.

Josh's mouth firmed. Anger appeared in the set of his own jaw. "Because my family lost even more than yours. I knew that you and your family wouldn't welcome me as a suitor now."

He paused, then blurted out. "I love Clare and I couldn't help being with her. But we haven't done anything wrong."

Gareth sighed. He believed the boy spoke the truth and only a few kisses had been between them. But that changed nothing.

"Josh, you're right—you're in no position to marry Clare. I'm going to have to ask you on your word of honor to stop seeing her on the sly."

Gareth paused. He didn't know how the rest of his family would take this decision he'd just made, but they would have to accept it. As the eldest male, the *only* male, left in the Colby family, he had this right and duty.

"You may come to the house and sit with her on the porch in the evenings, under the eye of one of us. That is, when you can persuade her to talk to you again."

Josh's expression became almost comical in its astonishment and relief. A wide smile stretched his mouth. He crossed the distance to Gareth and held out his hand.

With no hesitation, Gareth extended his own.

"Thank you, Mr. Colby. I'm sorry for what's happened. It won't happen again."

Gareth smiled. "You're going to have your hands full with Clare. Guess you know that."

Josh nodded. "Yes, but we love each other and we'll be happy together."

"All right, that's settled. You and Shannon have chores to finish."

For the first time since he'd entered the barn, Gareth allowed his gaze to settle on Shannon. That guilty look he'd surprised on her face had gone, replaced by a blend of emotions he couldn't sort out any easier than he could separate the mix of feelings churning his insides.

But jealousy was one.

Gareth had to admit he'd felt a flash of that intense emotion a few moments ago.

He'd been jealous of this boy who wanted to marry his sister. A twenty-year-old. But that didn't matter. He wanted no other man near Shannon. No other man holding her, kissing her.

Damn the whole muddle! He was sick to death of muddles, and his family seemed to be constantly in them lately.

Ever since he'd carried Shannon Brown—or whatever her name turned out to be—to his wagon and brought her home with him.

Inwardly, he cursed himself for a fool. He didn't want Shannon for himself, but he wanted no one else to have her.

Turning to go, he made himself qualify those last thoughts.

He *did* want Shannon. He wanted her very much.

But he wasn't going to have her. Not now, not ever.

He'd never take any woman to wife.

Chapter Ten

Vance glanced around the smoky, ill-lit tavern. His over-full lips curled in disgust. Goddamn, but he was sick of this! Had none of these people ever heard of taking a bath? Or even washing once in a while?

He glanced down at his own worn, shabby clothes in equal aversion. He knew it was smart to dress like this, try to blend in with this crowd of peasants, so none of them would remember him later, but God how he hated it!

And after weeks of this, he still hadn't found a trace of the wench. How could a lone girl, one who had never fended for herself, vanish into thin air? It just wasn't possible.

Not for the first time, he wondered if she'd died somewhere. Crawled off into the woods and expired like an animal. Part of him believed that had happened, and was relieved.

Another part wanted her still alive.

He wanted the pendant she wore around her neck all the time. That thing was worth a pretty penny.

And he wasn't finished with her yet. Not by a long shot. His face tightened. He owed her for making him search like this. His hands itched to slap her around, pay her back for it, jerk that necklace off her white throat.

After that, he'd satisfy another, stronger itch.

His body hardened, and his tongue ran along his upper lip. He was going to enjoy that.

He could spare the time before he killed her.

"It is such a lovely evening." Maud, sitting by Shannon on the big back porch, looked up at the bright stars overhead, the almost full moon.

"Yes, it is." Shannon glanced across the porch to where Josh sat beside Clare, a foot of space separating them.

After Gareth left them alone in the barn yesterday, she and Josh had planned how he could try to find out something the next time he was in Luray with his father.

She felt a little better now. At least some kind of action would soon be put into motion.

Gwenny sat beside Grandma Lucy, who as usual had her white cat Emma on her lap.

Gareth sat by himself.

Although Shannon was careful not to glance toward him, she was so conscious of his presence a few feet away that she seemed to feel his every small movement in her own body. She should get up and go inside. But the thought of that tiny, almost airless room repelled her.

"I hope it rains tomorrow. The corn needs it bad," Josh said.

"Yes," Gareth agreed. "Everything does."

The silence stretched out.

Shannon glanced again at Josh and Clare. Clare's pert nose was tilted upward, her mouth primly pursed.

It was clear she wasn't going to make it easy on Josh. She wouldn't admit she'd made a mistake, or accept either Shannon's or Josh's explanations for what had happened yesterday in the barn.

Josh, dressed in clean clothes, his blond hair slicked

back, looked ill at ease. No wonder. This was his first time sitting with the Colbys as an equal.

Shannon hadn't been present yesterday when Gareth told his family he'd accepted Josh as Clare's suitor.

Looking around the porch, she decided no one was against that decision. Even Gwenny seemed reconciled to the idea.

Maybe—probably—they were all relieved, thinking Josh would settle the flighty girl down. Remembering the scene she'd witnessed in the orchard, Shannon wasn't so sure. Clare had quite a lot of maturing to do before she was ready for marriage.

Shannon sighed. She and Clare were back almost to where they had been after Clare found out Shannon was a female, with Clare hostile and angry toward her.

This morning Shannon had tried again to explain, coming as close to the truth as she could, but Clare had only given her a disbelieving look, sniffed and turned away.

This situation was awkward and uncomfortable. And Clare's words in the barn yesterday had been hurtful. They still stung when Shannon thought about them.

"Well, about bedtime for these old bones. Gwenny, will you walk with me?" Grandma Lucy stiffly rose, and so did Gwenny, watching to see the older woman's cane didn't slip.

"I'm going to bed, too." Maud got up and followed the others into the house.

Josh shot out of his chair as if he had a burr in his pants. "Guess I'd better be going along home."

He stood, looking down at Clare, who kept her profile turned away, her chin still tilted upward.

"Good night, all. Clare," he said.

"Good night, *Mr.* Archer." Clare kept her face turned away.

Josh walked away, embarrassment and dejection in the lines of his tall, gawky frame.

When he'd left the porch, Clare turned sharply and

watched him go, and Shannon saw her face soften into an expression of yearning regret.

"I'm going to bed, too. Might as well. There's certainly nothing else of interest to do around here." Her skirts flouncing, Clare also went inside.

Shannon realized she and Gareth were alone on the porch, under the bright night sky with its luminous stars and big, yellow moon.

Not that it mattered. Gareth was sitting clear across the porch from her. Even if he weren't, what difference would it make?

They had nothing to say to each other. She may as well go inside, too. With that thought in mind, she got up and headed for the door.

She had to pass close by Gareth to get inside. She felt herself tense as her skirts brushed him.

His black hair was tousled. The planes of his face looked taut and strained.

Shannon wanted badly to reach down and smooth that tightness away.

Did she cause some of that unease? Did he, like her, still play over in his mind the kiss they had shared? Did he, too, remember how wonderful it had felt to have their bodies pressed tightly together?

Did he, too, long for a repetition?

Don't be such a fool, she told herself. Gareth had shown no signs of any of that.

"Good night," she said, giving him a small smile, wondering if her expression revealed her thoughts.

He glanced up, his face clearing as if he'd returned from a far distance, from wherever his mind had been.

"Shannon, wait a minute, will you?"

At his words, her heart gave a hard thump inside her chest. What did he want with her? She wouldn't stay out here alone with him.

Yes, she would.

Blast her contradictory emotions!

"I'd like to talk with you."

Something in the tone of Gareth's voice made her wary. But she couldn't refuse his request without a good reason. The only one that came to mind was a headache. She didn't think she could convince him of that.

"All right," she finally said.

Gareth motioned at a chair beside him. "Sit down. We can't talk with you hovering over me like you're ready for flight."

Couldn't he see that was exactly how she felt?

Sitting again, she arranged her skirts around her. After the weeks of boys' clothing, skirts still felt strange. And awkward to do chores in. Men's trousers were much more practical.

Gareth gave her a straight, steady look. "I know I agreed that you could stay here for as long as you wanted."

Sudden tension hit her. What was he getting at? "Yes," she finally said. "And I very much appreciate it."

He frowned again, as if he wished she hadn't said that. "I'm not a man to renege on his word. But even you'll have to admit this isn't working out."

Shannon stared at him, shock going through her. She hadn't expected this. "Wh-what do you mean?"

He let out a huff of breath. "My household's been in a turmoil ever since I brought you home. One thing after another. Now you and Clare aren't getting along. *Again.*"

"I'm sorry, but I don't know what to do about that. I tried again this morning to explain to her, but she wouldn't listen."

"I can believe it. Clare is young and can be unreasonable, but the fact remains she's my sister and you're—"

Without warning, bleakness swept over her; tears welled in her eyes. "And I'm a nobody, who has no family, no one . . ."

Fiercely, she willed the tears to stay there, not fall.

Gareth's face changed, softened. "No, of course that's not what I meant. But I can't send my sister away. I think I should ask around, see if any of the families we know need someone to be a companion, help out a little."

Her heart froze into a cold, hard lump. He was going to send her away, as she'd feared all along. Send her to a strange household, away from the comfort and warmth of his close, loving family. Where she'd have no one.

No one, no one, no one. The words went through her mind like a church bell tolling a dirge.

Worst of all, she wouldn't have Gareth.

Abruptly, she stood.

Gareth stood, too. They were very close together. She smelled the earthy scent of the fields on his clothes, his skin. She saw a pulse jumping in his temple, his hands, clenched into fists, at his sides.

She wanted him to relax his hands, touch her face with them, her neck . . . and. . . .

"Of course, if you feel this way."

What he felt like was a louse.

"Dammit, I'm not going to throw you out the door! I wouldn't let you go to any household where they'd treat you badly."

She smiled at him, but he could see how forced it was. "I can't expect you and your family to take care of me."

He knew her stiff words hid fear. Whatever the secrets she still kept hidden, they made her want to stay here with a need that bordered on desperation.

"I'm not so sure of that. In some countries when someone saves another person's life, that person is responsible for the other forever."

Why in hell had he said that?

He'd been determined to have this out with her, once and for all, quietly and privately. When everyone left them alone, it seemed as if providence had set the stage and he'd better take advantage of the opportunity.

Instead, he'd scared her to death, made her cry, and now he was apologizing when what he'd said was plainly the sensible thing to do. No matter what his family thought.

She still stared at him, but her rigid posture seemed to relax a bit. Her tongue came out and ran along her lower lip. Dismayed, Gareth felt his body hardening.

Did she know what a provocative gesture that was?

No, of course she didn't or she wouldn't be doing it.

Gareth felt grateful it wasn't daytime. On the moon-shadowed porch she shouldn't be aware of his embarrassing condition. He hoped.

"What do you mean?" she finally asked, confusion in her light voice. "Are you inviting me to stay or telling me to go?"

That was a good question. He wished he knew the answer. But he'd started this and he had somehow to end it.

He couldn't take his gaze off her mouth. How soft it had felt beneath his own that day in the barn. Soft, and yet so alive and responsive. He remembered how her breasts had felt against his chest, her slim fingers twining in the hair on his nape.

"Shannon?"

His voice was a whispered rumble that rose goose bumps on her arms. And she knew what the one-word question meant.

Silently she moved into his arms, as if that were where she belonged. Hungrily, he found her mouth, and just as hungrily she opened to him and returned his kiss. She pressed herself against him, and his hands on her back slid farther down to her bottom, molding her lower body to his own.

Making her instantly aware how much he wanted her.

The kiss deepened, their bodies straining together as if rying to become one. Gareth sat down again, pulling her vith him, so she half sprawled across him on the wicker ettee.

Duke's sudden bark shattered the spell holding them n thrall. Shannon felt Gareth stiffen; then his hands and rms released her. She let her own arms drop from around is neck.

He moved away from her.

She moved away from him.

Gareth took a few deep breaths, feeling his heartbeat slow to normal. "I'm sorr—"

"Mr. Colby?" Josh's earnest young voice came from the yard. "I forgot I needed to talk to you about something."

Josh walked up the steps and stood a few feet away. He looked from Gareth to Shannon; then his expression changed, embarrassment coming over it.

Shannon closed her eyes, embarrassment flooding over her, too. How in the world would she ever be able to face Josh tomorrow in the barn? What would he think of her?

And what did Gareth mean, he was sorry? Sorry for what? Kissing her?

Her face flamed with more chagrin. Yes, that's what he meant. Kissing the homeless orphan wasn't something that he should be doing, that his family would want him to be doing.

"What is it, Josh?" Gareth's voice was almost normal, Shannon noted, but not quite. He still sounded a little shaken up.

"I forgot to ask if you wanted to start harvesting the wheat this week since we're having this terrible dry spell."

Gareth nodded. "Yes, we'd best be starting. We'd better do our upper fields first. Then we'll get to your family's."

"All right. We'll all be over first thing tomorrow."

Josh's gaze turned on Shannon again, his expression puzzled, as if he couldn't truly believe what his mind was telling him was true.

"Good night, Josh. Gareth." Shannon hurried inside the house. She walked to the kitchen, making for the stairs Maud stood by the table, an odd look on her face.

Shannon closed her eyes again, slowing her step. What did that look mean? Could Gareth's mother have also seen Shannon and Gareth in each other's arms?

"Good night, again," Shannon told Maud, forcing what she hoped would pass for a smile.

Maud plucked at Shannon's sleeve, and Shannon stopped.

"Will you please wait a minute?"

"Of course." Was Maud going to denounce her? Tell her to stay away from Gareth?

"We—we've all been so worried about Gareth since he came home from the war with his leg crippled. He's been so lonely, so alone, since Dorinda broke their engagement and married someone else. We feared he'd never look at another woman again."

No use trying to pretend she didn't know what Maud was getting at. But only kindness shone out of the other woman's face. Maud had seen them, and she was glad. Relief flooded over Shannon.

Gareth had been engaged? The woman had broken it off? What a fool she must have been.

A sudden suspicion came to Shannon. "Did all of you come inside so that—"

Maud gave her a smile. "Gareth never leaves the farm, except on business. Unless he has to, he hasn't talked to another woman in five years."

Five years. Since his fiancée had jilted him?

"But you don't know me," Shannon protested. "I—I don't even know myself. How could any of you want—"

"You're a good young woman, Shannon," Maud interrupted. "We can tell that. Many of the families in the South have fallen upon hard times since the war. Your family more than most, it seems, even if you can't remember everything about your past yet."

The front door opened and closed. Footsteps came down the hall toward the kitchen. Gareth stopped in the doorway, surprise in his face as he saw his mother and Shannon together.

"Good night," Shannon said to Maud. She turned and headed for the stairs, intent on reaching the sanctuary of her room before Gareth could overtake her.

Gareth watched her go, his frown back.

Dammit! What had happened on the porch? One minute he'd been talking sensibly to Shannon about her future and the next he was kissing her!

More than just kissing her. Holding her, loving her, never wanting to let her go.

And this not a day after he'd told himself he had no intention of getting involved with her in any way. Even now, his body still remembered the feel of her body's soft contours; his lips remembered the shape of hers.

His mind and body, all of him, urged him to follow her up those stairs to her attic room and make her his own.

Silently, he swore again. He hadn't felt this way about a woman since . . . since. . . . His jaw muscles clenched.

He'd *never* felt this way about a woman.

Even Dorinda. And he'd been so besotted with her he hadn't been able to eat or sleep for weeks.

Yes, so he had. He'd felt bewitched, not in his right mind. All he could think about was Dorinda's soft mouth and body pressed to his. . . .

His heat cooled as he remembered how it had been. He'd had no control of his emotions. He'd hated that even while unable to do anything about it.

And it hadn't meant a thing to Dorinda.

The bitch was passionate, but her fervor had gone when she saw him limp toward her down the lane. When she'd learned the full extent of his family's losses from the war.

He'd sworn then he'd never trust another woman, never let another female make a fool of him.

Yet here he was, well on the way to doing just that.

He could trust Shannon Brown no more than he could Dorinda. Less, maybe. At least he'd known Dorinda and her family all his life.

He knew nothing about Shannon. Nothing at all except what she'd told him.

And that was precious little. If she told the truth, she *knew* very little about her past and her family. Why had she run away, climbed in that wagon and dressed as a boy? Only fear could motivate such actions.

Deep fear.

And she was still afraid, as she'd told him. Her mind still insisted she stay hidden here, away from everyone.

Why? And was all of that true? Was any of it true?

"Gareth? Whatever is the matter with you?"

From what seemed a far distance he heard his mother's anxious voice, felt her light touch on his cheek. With an effort of will, he came out of his black mood.

"Nothing, Mama," he assured her. "I'm all right. Don't worry."

"Is it the taxes?" she persisted. "Are you still afraid we might not be able to pay them in the fall?"

Yes, he was concerned about that, and a dozen other things besides. But no use burdening her. Nothing she could do.

"The corn crop will be all right if it rains soon. We'll start harvesting the wheat this week. The hogs are doing well. Unless the Shenandoah floods out of its banks, we'll be fine."

He forced a smile to go with his last joking words and kissed her soft cheek, wishing that was all he had to worry about. "Now, go on up to bed. I'm right behind you."

She gave him a relieved smile in return and obediently did as he ordered, Gareth following.

Later, he'd remember that conversation and how he'd thought the idea of the river flooding the most remote worry they could have.

How wrong could a person be?

Chapter Eleven

"The storekeeper said the man was looking for a young woman with reddish brown hair and blue eyes. He was showing a picture around."

Shannon stared at Josh, cold rippling her spine, blending with the headache that had plagued her all day. "Did he say what the man looked like?"

Josh stuck his pitchfork tines into a pile of soiled straw. "Big, brown hair, dark eyes. Mr. Wister said he looked like somebody you wouldn't want to cross."

Disappointment joined the new fear Josh's discoveries had caused. The description didn't give a face to the terrifying man of her visions. Or spark her memory in any way.

But she owed Josh her gratitude for his efforts. "Thank you, Josh. I'm so glad you overheard him talking and didn't have to ask about new people being in town."

Josh nodded. "Me, too." He frowned at her. "But now you know there really is a man looking for you—maybe does mean you harm. You need to try again to tell the Colbys about your visions. Maybe now you could. You managed to tell me."

"Yes, because you're not insisting on going to the sheriff." Her mouth twisted. "Maybe I did something wrong and that's why the man is after me."

Josh shook his head. "I don't believe that for a minute. But what I found out didn't help. You still don't remember anything more."

Shannon managed a wan smile, wishing the headache would go away. "No."

Josh looked even more worried. "That's why you just *have* to try to tell Mr. Colby and his family about all this!"

Shannon turned away, back to milking Rosie. "Josh, let up, please."

"Mr. Colby will protect you. You know he will. Especially since . . ."

His voice trailed off. Shannon felt her face redden, and was glad Josh couldn't see it. She knew he was referring to that evening two weeks ago when he'd almost caught her and Gareth kissing and had guessed what he hadn't seen.

Josh hadn't brought it up, but it was time she tried to explain. Explain what? That once again she hadn't been able to resist falling into Gareth's arms? That afterward he'd told her he was sorry—and acted ashamed?

Her face reddened even more, but she carefully took her fingers off the cow's teats and turned back around. Just as she'd expected, Josh's expression was speculative.

"I don't *want* anyone to have to protect me! I'm tired of feeling helpless. And there's nothing between Gareth and me."

"I saw him kiss you. And anyone can see how he looks at you. Even Clare mentioned it."

Oh, why wouldn't her head stop aching? She couldn't think straight! And now her throat was getting sore and scratchy.

She decided to change the subject and ignore what he'd said. "I'm so glad Clare and you are getting along again."

Josh's nice face lit up. "Me, too." His expression once more sobered. "But that's not what we're talking about."

"I'm not talking about anything. I'm going to finish

milking this cow and go up to the house. I have a dreadful headache."

He looked even more worried. "I'll finish the milking if you don't feel good."

"No, you have your chores to do at home after you finish here. I'll be fine."

Josh's mouth firmed, and he strode over to her. He reached down and pulled her up off the milking stool. "You don't look fine. Go on up to the house."

With a force of will Shannon kept herself from swaying on her feet. She would not give in to this headache. She'd been sickly enough since she came here.

But the idea of going to her room and crawling into bed was so appealing. . . .

She gave Josh a weak smile. "All right, I think I will. Thanks, Josh."

"Get some rest." He paused, then went on. "What if *I* tell the Colbys about the man? *My* mind won't prevent that."

Shannon gave him a startled look. "I—I'd never thought of that."

"Well, think about it. We'll talk about it tomorrow when you feel better."

"All right. I will."

Shannon walked to the house, trying to forget that she now had proof some unknown man was stalking her.

And when he found her he would kill her.

Why couldn't she get that image out of her mind? Maybe, as she'd suggested to Josh, the man was an authority of some kind. Maybe she'd fled because of a crime she'd committed. Maybe she *had* stolen the sapphire and diamond pendant.

Maybe the bloody knife was the untrue part.

And all those other images were false memories her mind was conjuring up just to make her feel better?

No, she couldn't believe that. If that could be true, why didn't she have some feelings of guilt? Why was terror the only feeling connected with the man?

As the throbbing pain increased, she pushed the nagging thoughts aside. All she was doing was making herself feel worse and not helping matters a bit.

Maybe the thing to do was let Josh tell the family—tell Gareth.

She felt too bad to consider that now.

The evening was warm, and the back door still stood open. Gwenny turned from the stove and gave her a sharp look as she entered the kitchen.

"You look awful! Are you getting a fever, too?"

"Is someone sick?" she asked, her tongue feeling thick, her head feeling that way, too.

"You know Gramma stayed in her room today, and we thought it was just her rheumatism acting up. But I went up a little while ago, and she's burning with fever. Clare seems to be coming down with it, too. And I don't like the look of you."

Gwenny walked over and put her palm on Shannon's forehead. "You're hot as fire! Get on up to your chamber. I'll bring cold compresses and some herb tea. Do you need help?"

Shannon quickly shook her head. "No, I'll be fine. You have enough to do, Gwenny. Don't worry about me. Is Grandma Lucy very ill?"

Dully, Shannon realized what she'd called the older woman—who wasn't *her* grandmother. She was growing closer each day to this family.

Gwenny let out a sigh. "I'm afraid so. She's almost ninety and hasn't the strength she used to have. You look sick enough to fall down yourself. Go on upstairs!"

Shannon followed Gwenny's command, her head pounding so badly she had to hang on to the stair railing to keep her balance.

Once in her chamber, she slipped off her shoes and crawled under the sheets and was instantly asleep.

* * *

Shannon came slowly awake, wondering why she was in bed with her clothes still on. She sat up and swung her legs over the side of the bed, shaking her head to clear the fog.

She'd been sick . . . yesterday evening? Now she felt almost well, only remnants of her headache and sore throat lingering.

It must be late in the day, from the slant of the sun through her one small window.

Quickly, she made herself presentable, then went to the door and opened it.

The absolute silence of the house sent a chill of foreboding through her. She heard no voices from downstairs, no clattering of pans in the kitchen. Nothing.

What had Gwenny said yesterday evening? Shannon strained to remember. Grandma Lucy was very ill and Clare wasn't feeling well.

She hurried down the stairs into the kitchen. The room was empty, except for Grandma Lucy's cat, who twined around Shannon's ankles, mewing hungrily. Unwashed dishes were stacked on the table, and the fire in the cookstove was completely out.

Was *everyone* ill?

Duke scratched at the back door, whining. Shannon found some scraps and put them in his bowl on the porch, then gave some to Emma.

She hurried upstairs again and over to Grandma Lucy's door. It was ajar, and she opened it and went inside. Maud bent over the bed, putting cold compresses on the old woman's forehead.

"Oh, Maud! Is *everyone* ill?" Shannon asked.

Maud turned. Her face was pale, dark rings circled her eyes, but she gave Shannon a weary smile.

"I'm so glad you're up and about! Yes, everyone but me is down with this fever. Spring and summer fevers are worse than winter ones, but I haven't seen anything this bad in years."

Shannon walked to the bed, her heart sinking when she

got a good look at Grandma Lucy. The old woman's face was flushed with an unhealthy red; her closed eyes were sunken in her head. She lay very still and somehow seemed shrunken.

"I'm fine now. Everyone's sick, you say? Gareth, too?"

Maud nodded.

Alarm went through Shannon. How sick was he? "What can I do?"

Maud pushed her straggling gray hair off her forehead. "If you'd build up the fire again, dear, and put on the kettle for more tea. And maybe make some chicken soup?"

"Of course I will."

"Thank you, Shannon. You don't know what a relief it is that you're over your bout with the fever and here to help. I was at my wit's end."

"Is—how sick are the others?" she asked.

"Clare seems to have a light case, and Gwenny is pretty sick, but fighting it. If she could stay on her feet, she'd be up and helping. Gareth is the worst, next to Mama."

Fear shot through Shannon at her words. "I can't imagine Gareth sick."

Maud's tired gaze slid away. "Oh, he's so strong. I'm sure he'll be all right. Would you look in on him on your way downstairs?"

Shannon nodded and hurried out, her fear growing.

It was plain Maud wasn't at all sure her son would be all right.

Gareth's door was also ajar. Taking a deep breath, Shannon pushed it open and entered. Like his grandmother, Gareth lay in bed.

But unlike her, he wasn't still. He moved restlessly, his eyes closed, muttering under his breath. His nightshirt was hiked up to his thighs, and he'd kicked off his covers.

Shannon hurried to the bed and saw he was shaking with chills, his arms peppered with goose bumps. She pulled the covers up to his chin, carefully tucking his thrashing arms under them, then holding her own arm across his chest until he finally stilled.

She placed her palm on his forehead, scared but not surprised that it burned her skin. A basin filled with water, and with a cloth on its edge, sat on a nearby table. Her hands trembling, she soaked the cloth in the water, then wrung it out and spread it across his head.

Gareth muttered at the coldness, trying to jerk his head away. One hand shot out from under the covers and grabbed her hand. His eyelids fluttered open, and he stared at her from fever-bright eyes.

"Wh-at in hell are you doing in my bedchamber?" he muttered.

Although his hard grip hurt, Shannon felt a surge of delight from his touch. "You're ill. I'm helping take care of you."

Gareth shook his head, dislodging the cloth so that it fell across one eye, giving him a rakish look. "Not ill. I'm *never* ill. Go away."

His grip loosened on her hand, and Shannon drew it away, then moved the cloth up where it belonged.

"You are now," she told him, forcing briskness into her tone so he wouldn't hear her worry. "Go back to sleep. I'm going to make chicken soup. That will make you feel better."

His eyes closed again. His face sagged in weary lines. "Don' want any soup. Jus' want to sleep. Go away."

Shannon did, dejection added to her fear for him. Even when he was this sick, he knew he wanted no part of her. As he'd said last week, he *was* sorry he'd kissed her.

Of course he was. Otherwise he wouldn't have done everything he could to avoid her.

And this was no time to worry about her feelings, she chided herself. There was work to do.

Downstairs she quickly made up the fire and set the kettle to boil. Now for the chicken soup. She swallowed, dreading what she had to do next.

Halfway to the henhouse, she encountered a worried-looking Josh.

"Are you all right, Shannon?"

"Yes, but everyone else is sick with a fever. I've got to kill a chicken and make soup."

His worried expression deepened. "That's why the cows haven't been milked."

"Oh, lord, the cows!"

"I'll milk," Josh said quickly, then added, "Do you want me to kill a hen for you?"

Relief went through her. " If you don't mind."

He shrugged. "I'm used to it. Is Mr. Colby sick, too?"

Shannon nodded, her own worry back full force. "Yes, and he looks terrible! So does Grand—Miss Lucy."

Josh's young face reflected her concern. "Are you the only one out of bed?"

"No, Gareth's mother is, but she looks like she shouldn't be."

"I'll do all the outside chores," Josh assured her. "Wiley and Pa will help, too. Good thing we got all the wheat harvested. Go tend to the sick folk and I'll bring you the chicken."

Shannon gave him an anxious smile. "Thank you, Josh I don't know what we'd do without you."

"Maybe I should send Ma down to help," he said.

Shannon shook her head. "You'd better not. No use exposing her to the fever, too."

"I guess you're right, but if you and Mrs. Colby can't handle things, you have to let us help."

"I will. Now, I'd better get on back."

By the time she washed the dishes, the kettle was boiling. She made a pot of tea from the mint and sage and other dried herbs she found, and it wasn't until she'd carried the tray with the pot and the cups upstairs that she wondered how she'd known which herbs to use.

Another clue to the memories locked somewhere in her mind? Probably, but for the first time since she'd awakened in Gareth's jolting wagon, she had something more important to worry about than her unknown past.

Maud gave her a tired smile as Shannon set the tray on

a table. "Thank you, dear. I'm afraid all I can do now is try to spoon a little down Mama's throat."

Grandma Lucy looked no better than before. Maud looked worse. Shannon filled a cup with the strong mixture and handed it to Maud. "You'd better have some of this, too. I'll give the rest to the others. When I finish I'll take over here for a while and you must rest."

She glanced in at Gareth first. He seemed to be asleep, although his movements were still restless. She'd see to the others, then come back to him.

Clare was also asleep, her blond ringlets tangled and darkened with perspiration. Her forehead felt warm, but not dangerously hot, Shannon decided. She'd wait a bit to give her the tea, too.

Gwenny looked almost as bad as Gareth. She tossed restlessly, muttering to herself, her covers thrown back. Shannon's palm burned at its contact with Gwenny's forehead.

"Can you sit up a little? You need to drink some tea."

Gwenny's eyes opened, and she frowned at Shannon. "What are *you* doing here?" she demanded. "Why am I in bed? I'm supposed to be up taking care of Gramma Lucy and Gareth!"

Before Shannon could stop her, she jerked herself upright, then moved to the edge of the bed and stood.

She swayed, and Shannon caught her before she fell, easing her back down.

"You're ill, too," Shannon scolded. "You can't take care of anyone but yourself right now. Here, drink this tea. It will bring your fever down."

Gwenny's frown deepened, but she didn't try to get up again. "I don't want any tea! I hate those herbs. I'm fine."

In spite of her worry, Shannon had to smile. "You're as stubborn as your brother."

"How is Gareth? Gramma Lucy?"

Shannon hoped her forced smile looked reassuring. "They're doing all right. Now, drink this."

With ill grace, Gwenny allowed Shannon to steady her

cup while she drank most of the contents. Then, she pushed the cup away, making a face.

"Take it away. I can't stand the smell of it."

Shannon did, then straightened Gwenny's covers and placed a cold compress on her forehead.

Out in the hall again, she took a deep breath. Gareth next.

He was still sleeping restlessly and making unintelligible sounds. Shannon felt her tension increasing. When she removed the cloth on his head it was hot from his fever. She dropped it back into the basin, then turned to him again.

"Gareth, wake up and drink some tea," she told him as she had his sister a few minutes ago. His eyes stayed closed, and he kept on muttering and moving around.

Shannon swallowed, then took his shoulders in her hands and shook him gently. Even through his nightshirt, his flesh burned hers. Anxiety shot through her again. "Gareth, wake up!"

His eyes opened, and both his hands shot out and gripped her wrists. He glared at her. "What are you doing back here? I tol' you to leave me alone!"

Shannon's lips thinned. "And let you die, you hard-headed idiot! I won't go until you drink this tea."

Their gazes locked, and for a few moments, Gareth's eyes cleared. His gray eyes stared into hers as they had those times when he'd kissed her. When she'd kissed him back. When she'd never wanted to leave his arms.

His lips pulled upward into a tiny smile, and Shannon winced when she saw they were fever-cracked. The look left his eyes. He let go of her hand and, his jaw set, pulled himself up in the bed.

"Can I drink it myself or do you insist on spooning it down me?"

"That's up to you," she said, relieved her voice came out crisp, revealing none of the mixed emotions she felt. She handed him the tea.

His hands shook, his grasp so weak the cup wobbled,

spilling some of its contents on the quilt. With both her hands Shannon steadied his. While he sipped the liquid, she tried not to remember how his hands had drawn her close, inflamed her senses with their caressing touch.

At last he was finished. Shannon slipped her hands away, removed the cup and set it back on the tray. It clattered and tipped, revealing her own hands were none too steady.

"Is everyone sick?" he asked, his voice drifting off, his eyes closing again. He was asleep before she could find an evasive answer.

"Miss Shannon? I brought you the chicken."

Josh's voice from downstairs got her moving again. She hurried to the door and called back. "I'll be right down."

Shannon pulled Gareth's covers up again, careful not to touch him even if he was asleep, and placed the newly cooled cloth on his head.

She stood, looking down at him. He seemed to be sleeping easier now. His face was smoothed out, and he looked younger than she'd ever seen him. And those lines of worry around his mouth had eased. He couldn't be more than thirty.

Compassion hit her. Gareth had the care and well-being of this entire household on his shoulders. It was a heavy burden. Everyone expected him to be the steady rock that would never falter.

But he was only human—only a man. And now he was laid low like the rest of his family. Maybe for the first time since the other male members of his family had died, and he'd returned from the war, Gareth wasn't there for his family to lean on.

She swallowed a sudden lump in her throat, picked up the tray and went downstairs.

Josh had left the chicken, not only well plucked and cleaned, but also cut up, in a pan on the table. She heaved a grateful sigh and got the big soup pot down from the shelf.

There were onions in the garden, and she would make noodles. . . .

Noodles. She knew how to make noodles. In fact, she realized, deftly putting the soup together, although she'd done no cooking here, she seemed to know a lot about the art.

That had to mean she'd done quite a bit of it. *When? Where? For whom?* Her mother? The man who had been dancing with her mother when she'd watched from the stairs. . . .

Were any of these true memories? How could she be sure of anything?

Shannon shook her head, willing the thoughts away. She couldn't waste any time now on her lost past. She was needed here in this household.

Desperately needed.

And that felt good. Strength flooded over her.

She wouldn't let these kind people down.

Chapter Twelve

"Shannon, come here! I think Gramma Lucy is . . ."

Clare burst into sobs and buried her head in her hands.

Shannon dropped the cloth she was wringing out in the basin and turned quickly toward the bedside.

She drew in her breath as she saw the utter stillness of the older woman.

When she felt for a pulse and found none, her heart sank. She gently laid the old woman's thin hand back on her chest. Tears pricked her eyelids.

What had happened? Everyone had thought the older woman was a little better this morning. But the doctor had warned them that it was very doubtful she could pull through at her age.

Numbly, Shannon knelt before Clare and let the girl sob out her sorrow on her chest, glad that the two of them had made their peace. A sudden noise in the doorway brought her head up.

Gareth, still pale from his own bout of the fever, stood in the doorway. Grief made his face wild as he stared at his grandmother.

"Why didn't you call us? So we could be here . . . tell her goodbye?"

Shannon brushed away the tears on her face. "There wasn't time. I—it happened so suddenly. She seemed a little better. No one thought . . . "

He walked to the bedside and stood there. Shannon saw his chest heaving with his sorrow and felt an overwhelming need to comfort him.

She got to her feet. "Clare," she asked the girl, "will you go get Gwenny and your mother?"

Clare swallowed and nodded, then slipped out of the room.

"She went very peacefully," Shannon said softly, moving to stand close beside him. "I'm sure she had no pain at all."

Gareth lifted his head, tears making tracks down his face. "I loved her very much. We all did. She was the heart of this house."

"Yes," Shannon answered, realizing how true that was. Even at almost ninety, and infirm with age, Grandma Lucy's spirit had been indomitable. Shannon's hand gently touched Gareth's tear-wet cheek.

Their glances met, and to Shannon it seemed something moved between them. Something different from anything they had shared before. A connection of caring, of friendship, passed in that eye contact.

"You can't be gone, Mama!" Maud's tremulous voice cried from the doorway. Followed by Gwenny, she hurried over to her mother's bedside, and Shannon quickly moved aside.

Watching the wrenching scene from a few feet away, Shannon felt as if she were observing from a great distance, very much an outsider, even though she, too, had loved the old woman, as she might have loved her own grandmother.

When had her grandparents died? When she was a child? Had she ever known their love? Would she ever regain her lost life?

A sudden intense yearning filled her to be a part of a warm, loving family again.

To be a part of *this* family.

And how could that ever be?

"This is our cousin, Ellis, and his sons, Ames and Randall."

Gareth performed the introductions, wryly noting that Clare's eyes had widened and were fixed on Ames, the handsome younger son. Both men were good-looking, Gareth had to admit. He hadn't seen them since they were children.

None of this Maryland branch of the family had been here for years. They had apparently come in response to his mother's letter informing them of Grandma Lucy's death. Of course, they weren't able to come in time for the funeral, so why were they here now?

"Why don't we all go into the parlor?" Maud suggested, in her new, firmer voice.

Gareth still couldn't get used to the way his mother had changed since Grandma Lucy's death. Maud even put Gwenny in her place now, when she needed it, just as Grandma Lucy used to do.

Pain hit him anew when he thought of their loss. They had moved the old rocker that had sat by the kitchen hearth all these years, not able to stand to see it empty now. And Emma still searched in vain for her mistress.

"You have a beautiful place here," Ellis said, smiling around the circle of seated people. "Hard to keep up now, though, I imagine. What with taxes so high and labor costs even worse."

Gareth's jaw clenched. He didn't need to be reminded of these things. And he didn't like Ellis's smile, pleasant though it was.

"Yes, it hasn't been easy. But we're managing."

Just barely, but Gareth's pride kept him from adding that.

"Have you ever considered selling? From what I've been hearing, a lot of Virginians are doing that."

"Virginians, maybe. Not very many Valley people."

Randall, the older son, glanced at Gareth. "Why is that?"

"Because we couldn't live anywhere else," Gwenny put in, her voice heavy with finality. "The Valley is our home."

Gwenny had expressed his own sentiments exactly, Gareth thought, waiting for his mother and Clare to agree. But they didn't. Clare, he saw, was too busy making eyes at Ames, and his mother examined a picture on the wall in front of her as if she'd never seen it before.

"What about you, Miss Shannon? Do you, too, love the Shenandoah Valley? Or is your home elsewhere?"

Glancing at Randall, Gareth felt a jolt in his midsection. His cousin's hazel eyes, fixed on Shannon, held a gleam of interest. And not, Gareth felt sure, in what answer she might give him.

Shannon's face visibly paled as she stared back. Finally, she nodded. "Yes, I do love the Valley."

Gareth realized she'd ignored the other, decidedly awkward, question. None of these people needed to know about her amnesia. They wouldn't hear about it from him. Or his family, either, he felt sure.

When everyone had been sick with the fever, Shannon had taken hold and helped as if she were a family member. He didn't know exactly what had happened between them the day his grandmother died, but it had somehow changed things.

Added a new layer to his feelings for her.

Not that he now regarded her as a sister.

His mouth twisted. Hardly. His physical attraction to Shannon hadn't diminished, despite his determination to keep his distance from her.

And he didn't like the admiration he saw in Randall's eyes. He didn't like it a bit.

"Will you and your sons be able to stay for a while?" Maud politely asked.

Ellis gave her an affable smile. "As a matter of fact, we

will. We've decided to buy a farm in this area, and we want to look around a bit."

"We will be delighted to have you stay with us."

Gareth knew her courteous words hid her dismay. Clare and Gwenny would have to share a bedchamber, and Shannon would have to give up Grandma Lucy's, which she now occupied, in order to provide two rooms for the visitors. And cooking for guests would be an added burden—and expense.

He wasn't too happy about the idea of them staying on either. He hoped his affluent cousins realized he couldn't spare time to entertain guests.

These weren't the old days with plenty of workers in the fields and the plantation owners gentlemen of leisure. Not that the men in his family ever were. Gareth's father had taught Gareth and his sisters at early ages that working with your hands was an honorable occupation.

That had stood Gareth in good stead when the hard times came upon them—and stayed. Five years after the war things were somewhat better. At least Virginia was once again back in the union.

"Thank you. We will be honored to accept your kind invitation."

Gareth glanced at Shannon. Her color was back, but she still seemed ill at ease. Probably, Gareth decided, because Randall was still giving her admiring looks.

Another thought occurred to him. Maybe she liked—even reciprocated—Randall's admiration. Maybe her discomfort came from the fact Gareth was observing everything from only a few feet away.

Gareth fought a scowl trying to draw his brows together. He tried to be fair. He had no claim on her—nor ever planned to. It was none of his affair if she was attracted to another man.

In fact, that would be the best thing that could happen. Especially this young man, whose family was yet prosperous.

That thought made him feel no better—only worse. He

got to his feet. "Make yourselves at home, gentlemen. I must go back to the fields. I'll see you at dinnertime."

"Certainly. We don't want to keep you from your work," Randall put in.

Was there a slightly condescending note in his young cousin's voice? He'd probably never had to work with his hands in his entire life.

Gareth knew he was being unfair now. He felt Shannon's gaze and couldn't resist glancing at her. She gave him a small, stiff smile which did nothing to reassure him.

He turned away and headed outside, acutely conscious of how his worn working-man's clothes, his heavy old shoes, contrasted with the other men's fine clothing.

Damn it all! Was he a fool to doggedly hang on to this piece of ground that had been in his family for generations? To work like a dog, year after year, just to keep a roof over their heads, food on the table—and the tax collectors from taking the farm?

He could sell off some of the acreage and still stay here as others were doing—despite what he'd said a few minutes ago. He'd already bargained with the Archers for two hundred acres. He could sell more, ease some of the burden. . . .

No! He wouldn't, couldn't do that. If he had to give up this place, even a part of it, it would be like giving up his soul. He'd die, too, as surely as his father had done.

Shannon tiptoed down the attic stairs, holding her slippers in her hand. On the landing, she listened, thankful all was quiet. Everyone must be asleep. She hurried down the other set of stairs, crossed the silent, neat kitchen and eased open the back door, flinching when it creaked.

Outside, she breathed great gulps of the sweet, cool night air. Duke thumped his tail a few times, then went back to sleep. It was so good to be out of the overfull house!

The cousins were still here. Still occupying Grandma

Lucy's old bedchamber, which was now her own, relegating her back to the attic cubicle. Also Gwenny's chamber, creating a great deal of work for everyone.

And a great deal of upset. Maybe they didn't mean to create work or trouble, but they were used to servants, to a big house and plenty of good food. Of course, no one went hungry here, but the fare was plain and simple. She didn't like any of them.

And they wanted to buy the farm. She didn't want to think about that.

The moon was full, revealing the brooding hulk of Massanutten in the distance. She'd grown to love the mountain. Its benign presence seemed to watch over this part of the Valley like a living thing.

She put on her slippers and made her way to the apple orchard. This was one of her favorite places. She found her own special tree, ancient and gnarled, and settled herself on the sweet, soft grass beneath it.

Gareth, unable to sleep, heard the back door creak, and knew what that sound meant. Someone else was wakeful, was up and about. He rose and walked to the window overlooking the back.

The moonlight revealed a small, slight figure, dressed all in white, followed by Duke, slowly making its way toward the orchard.

Shannon.

Without letting himself think about what he was doing or why, he quickly slipped on his trousers and followed her.

The grass was damp and cool with dew under his bare feet, making him remember going barefoot as a boy over this same grass of his home place.

His face tightened. Which, during the last weeks, he'd discovered to his surprise and dismay wasn't as deeply loved by all the members of his family as he'd thought.

Damn Ellis Barton! Ellis and his family hadn't suffered the losses Gareth's family had. Damn Ellis's money and his benevolent goodwill.

And damn him for offering to buy the farm at a price that had Clare excited and begging him to accept. Even his mother hadn't come over strongly to Gareth's side as he'd expected. She'd remained neutral, staying out of the argument. Only Gwenny was as passionately against even discussing the idea as Gareth himself.

Gareth didn't want to be reminded that the taxes had been increased again. The wheat hadn't done well, because of the drought, and it was still over a month before the also puny corn crop would be harvested.

He wished Ellis and his sons would pack up and leave before they created any more chaos. Clare was bowled over by the younger son, Ames, responding to his open admiration with the most outrageous flirting Gareth had ever had the misfortune to witness. So far she'd managed to get away with it without Josh realizing what was going on.

Gareth felt like shaking some sense into the girl.

But how could he discourage her? If she was this fickle, he didn't wish her on a decent young man like Josh. She'd be better off marrying someone like Ames, who could give her all the fripperies she craved.

The older son, Randall, seemed to be dividing his admiration between Gwenny and Shannon. Gareth grimaced as a stone bruised his foot. At least Gwenny had enough common sense not to be flattered. She ignored Randall, and tried to avoid his presence.

Shannon. His face darkened. He didn't know what to think about her. He hadn't actually seen her flirting with Randall—but then Shannon wasn't the flirting type.

That didn't mean she wasn't interested in him, wasn't thinking about the kind of comfortable life the man could give her.

How could he blame her for that? *He'd* certainly done nothing to make her think those two times they had been in each other's arms meant anything to him.

He knew better, though. Try as he might to convince

himself otherwise, he still wanted her with a hunger that gave him no peace.

Stopping at the edge of the orchard, Gareth saw a glimmer of white ahead, under a tree. His heartbeat quickened.

For the first time since he'd left the house, he hesitated. Would Shannon welcome him? What had made him think she might? If he had any sense, he'd turn around and go back before she saw him.

Her head turned his way. He saw her stiffen and rise, as if fearful. Too late now. She'd seen him. He had to let her know who he was.

He walked toward her, steadily, and halfway there saw her stiff posture turn into another kind of wariness.

She recognized him, but that hadn't put her at ease. No wonder. On those other two occasions when they had been alone, it had led to more than either of them wanted.

No, he corrected himself. He'd *wanted* more from her. He'd wanted the ultimate giving. Was that true in her case? How could he be sure of her feelings? Both those other times, they had broken apart because of outside interruptions.

What would have happened if Rosie hadn't bawled . . . if Josh hadn't come back?

He stopped a few feet away from her and realized with small shock that she wore her nightdress. It was high-necked and long-sleeved, true, but still her nightdress.

Moonlight glimmering through the tree branches created patches of light and darkness, shadowed her eyes, made her hair shine.

"Wha-what are you doing here?"

Shannon heard the breathless quality in her voice and regretted it. She should have made her voice firm. She should have left at the first glimpse of him. Instead, she was standing here in her nightclothes, stammering like a schoolgirl.

"I could ask you the same thing."

"I couldn't sleep. And I love the orchard." At least her voice had lost that breathless quality.

"I was sleepless, too. I heard you open the back door. I saw you from my window and followed you."

If he'd planned to startle her, he couldn't have done a better job of it. He saw her breasts move as she drew in her breath and her eyes widened. She retreated a step, farther into the shadows of the tree branches.

"You shouldn't have done that," she told him, while her heart thumping in her chest told *her* how glad she was that he had.

He nodded. "Probably not. But I did. Are you going to make me leave?"

She forced a laugh. "How can I do that? This is *your* farm, your orchard, not mine."

She shouldn't have said that, she realized, because it made her homeless state, her lack of a family, knowledge of her past, all the things most people took for granted, come crashing down on her.

"But I am intruding on you, nonetheless."

He was giving her every chance to tell him to leave, and she knew she should do just that. But, God help her, she couldn't. She wanted too much for him to stay.

He was being very open and honest tonight. Why not be the same? Why not tell him how she felt? She knew why, because it might lead to the continuation of the last time they had held each other. It might lead to. . . .

"No, you're not intruding," she heard herself say. "I—I'd like for you to stay."

"Then stay I will." He smiled, then also moved under the shadows of the tree branches.

Sweet alarm went through her. It was as if they were closed inside a bower here, away from the outside world, in their own private universe.

"I can see why you like it here," he told her, settling down on the grass beneath the tree.

She stood for another moment, then sat down again, too, at a safe distance. "It's my favorite place on the farm. Of course, I like the river, too, and the fields, and . . ."

Her voice trailed off as she realized how much she was giving away.

"You love this place, don't you?"

His voice had softened, and some other quality had come into it—almost like relief. "Yes, I do. More than—"

Her voice broke off, and she swallowed. *More than what? Any other place she'd ever been,* she'd almost said. Wasn't that amusing, since she had almost no memories of any other place than this farm.

Bitterness and fear washed over her, and she frantically pushed them back. No! She wasn't going to ruin this special time here tonight with these fruitless thoughts.

"It's a beautiful farm," she finished, managing to keep her voice steady.

She heard his sharp intake of breath, then a sigh as he let it out.

"The most beautiful in the world to me. But not to everyone in my family, I'm afraid."

"What do you mean?" She was glad Gareth was keeping his distance, glad he hadn't taken her invitation to stay as another kind of invitation.

How you lie, she admitted.

"You know Ellis wants to buy the place."

"Yes, but I also know you won't sell."

He sighed again "Clare thinks we should. Mama doesn't seem to care one way or the other. Only Gwenny loves this place as I do. Maybe I'm only being selfish and stubborn. We could have a much better life if we sold."

Dismay shot through her. He sounded as if he might be considering selling. How could he do that?

"Better in what way?" she quickly countered.

"We'd have some money, a nicer home. Clare could have her pretty clothes; Mama and Gwenny wouldn't have to work so hard."

"Neither would you, but you don't care about that, do you?"

"No. I'd work until I drop in the fields to stay here. But we may not be able to much longer, anyway. Taxes were raised again this year. The barn and house need repair. This drought has hurt the crops, and you can never count on anything until they're safely harvested. I'd like to plant new apple orchards, too. And try some peaches. I'm sure those will be two of the most important crops here in the coming years. But there's no money to spare for that."

Shannon heard the near despair and defeat in his voice and couldn't stand it. She loved his strength, his determination. He couldn't lose those. He wouldn't be able to live.

She had to give him some kind of comfort, some kind of reassurance. She slid closer to him across the grass. In the dimness, she felt for his hands, found one and squeezed it.

His warmth moved up her arm, made a tremor go through her. Brought back memories of those other times. . . .

"Have you actually talked to your family about selling? Maybe they don't feel as you think." Her voice wasn't steady now.

Gareth sat very still for a moment after her slim fingers closed over his own. He didn't even want to breathe. He just wanted to savor this feeling.

But he couldn't do that. She wasn't trying to arouse him physically; she was just trying to comfort him. Was that true? Hell, he didn't know, but he'd try to control himself, follow her lead.

"I don't have to. I can see how they feel."

She gave a small laugh. "No, you can't. You can never be certain what other people are feeling or thinking unless they tell you."

He looked down at the top of her shining head, the elusive sweet scent that always hung about her drifting up to his nostrils. He felt his body hardening despite all his good intentions.

"You are so right about that," he finally answered. "I have no idea what you're thinking now. Let alone feeling."

Gareth marveled at his own words, his honesty. It wasn't like him to talk like this.

Her fingers stiffened against his own. For a long moment she didn't move or say anything. Then, she loosened her fingers and moved away from him.

"We weren't talking about me. I was trying to make you see you might be wrong about how your family feels."

Shannon became aware all over again of how she was dressed. Or *undressed.* Of how she shouldn't be here. Under this tree with Gareth so close. So tempting.

"But I would like to know what you're thinking and feeling."

"No, you wouldn't." She started to rise, but he reached out one big hand and grasped her arm.

"Yes, I would. Don't go just yet."

You shouldn't be doing this, Shannon told herself, but nevertheless let Gareth pull her back down beside him. Somehow, they were closer than before. Somehow, she was touching him.

Even through her nightdress, she could feel his warmth seeping into her. Feel the sweet lassitude of their previous encounters stealing over her. Making her want to get closer yet. As close as it was possible to be. . . .

A soft night breeze moved the leaves of the tree, and a moonbeam slipped through, lighting Gareth's face. She drew in her breath. His expression must mirror hers. That look of naked, undisguised wanting. . . .

She turned toward him. His arms folded around her, drawing her close. She slipped her arms around his neck, to bring him even nearer. Her face was against his chest, and she could feel his heartbeat thundering in her ears, echoing her own inner tumult.

In a few moments, this wasn't enough.

Hunger began to build inside her. She lifted her head, her neck curving backward, her lips apart.

Chapter Thirteen

An errant gleam of moonlight touched Shannon's throat with silver, made Gareth draw in his breath. Made his body harden even more. God, how he wanted her!

Tonight would not be like those other times—stolen kisses, shattered by interruptions. Tonight there was nothing to stop him from . . .

Taking Shannon.

A flare of heat ran along his nerve ends at that thought, subduing the sensible part of him that was trying to slow him down, make him see he shouldn't be out here. Shouldn't be holding this woman in his arms. It wasn't right.

The hell he shouldn't! It felt more right than anything he'd ever done.

Obeying the dictates of his body, his feelings, he placed his mouth on the white column of her throat, let his tongue make slow circles on her satin flesh, until he heard her low, desirous moan.

Satisfaction filled him at that small sound. His exploring tongue left her throat, found her ear and curled itself inside.

"Shannon," he whispered huskily.

His warm breath fell upon the moistness his tongue had created, making a delicious blend of sensation. Shannon heard herself moan again, felt herself writhe against the sweet grass beneath them.

She twisted herself in his embrace, so that her face was only an inch from his, their mouths nearly touching. She leaned toward him, and when his lips finally touched hers, she shuddered, opening her mouth, her tongue sliding between his parted lips until it found his own.

Against her, she felt his answering shudder and gloried in her power to arouse him.

Her voice of reason was buried deep inside, no longer accessible to her conscious mind—or feelings. This night was made for her and Gareth.

Gareth slowly but relentlessly pushed her backward until she lay full length on the grass and he was bent over her, his chest pressed tight against her breasts.

His lower body settled itself on hers. His thigh nudged her legs apart. Through the thin material of her nightdress she felt the hot, hard evidence of his desire against her most private place.

At last he broke the kiss and began lavishing kisses on her face, her closed eyelids, her neck. Reaching the barrier of her nightdress's buttoned collar, he impatiently fumbled with the fastenings.

Her fingers tangling with his own, she helped him. Finishing the last button, he pulled the garment apart, baring her beyond the waist.

"Beautiful, so beautiful," he murmured, his fingers tracing a path from her neck to her exposed navel, stopping just short of the nest of silken hair below.

Shudders even more delicious than the previous ones rippled through her. She strained upward, yearning for something she was sure she'd never before experienced but that her body clamored for. Something she knew would give her the ultimate pleasure.

"Not yet, sweetheart, not yet." Gareth's mouth followed

the course his hand had taken, slowly, slowly kissing his way down to her navel. He paused there, his tongue swirling inside.

He smiled as she gasped and involuntarily moved her hips upward, then continued his downward passage until he reached the barrier of her nightdress again. His tongue slid under the edge, just touching her woman's mound.

When she bucked against his mouth, just as slowly he slid his tongue out and traced his way back up to her breasts, where he continued his sensual teasing of her flesh.

"Gareth! Please, stop. I can't stand—"

"You want me to stop?" he whispered. If she said yes, he would die. He couldn't stand it. Already, he was nearly exploding.

"No! Yes, I mean. I don't know what I mean."

"I do," he whispered again. "Do you want me to stop this?" He circled one of her nipples, rewarded when it instantly hardened.

She moaned and writhed again. He did the same to the other nipple, glorying in its instant identical reaction.

Shannon's arms closed around his neck, drawing him to her. "I want you to stop. No, I want you to keep on and on," she said. "I want you to . . ." Her voice trailed off, and she pushed her body against his as tightly as she could.

Instinctively, Gareth's lower body pressed back against hers, his aroused manhood straining against the flimsy barrier of cloth separating his flesh from hers.

"We have too many clothes on." He moved away from her, quickly stripping himself of his trousers, his arousal increasing as he watched her pull her nightdress farther down her body, and slide it out from under her.

"Not anymore," she murmured. Smiling, she held out her arms to him.

Her body lay gloriously bare, glimmering in the fitful moonlight. Her breasts were rounded and thoroughly aroused; her long, slim legs were slightly apart, beckoning him to her.

Groaning, Gareth kicked his trousers free, and slid into her welcoming embrace. The first contact of their naked, fully aroused bodies drew gasps of pleasure from both of them. Gareth pulled her onto her side, gathering her as close as he could, his hand lowering to her bottom, pressing her forward, into his hard arousal.

They lay like that for long moments, savoring the touch of heated bare flesh on heated bare flesh, until that, too, was no longer enough to feed their growing hunger.

Gareth rolled her over onto her back and lay full upon her for another long moment. Finally, he raised his head and looked at her. "Are you ready, love?"

He saw her visibly swallow; then she nodded. "Yes, I'm ready. I want you so much!"

"As I want you." He lowered his head and kissed her long and deeply, his tongue's darting forays and retreats into her mouth previewing what was yet to come, making her writhe beneath him, moaning his name.

He felt her thighs move apart beneath him; then her body pressed upward. He could wait no longer—and neither could she.

He eased himself into her warm, slick tightness, until he felt the last barrier keeping them apart. "This will hurt for a moment," he told her.

Shannon nodded, her fear for the unknown that was coming momentarily sweeping over her. "I know," she finally said, wondering how she did. "It's all right."

With this reassurance, Gareth withdrew, then pressed inside her again, harder this time. She felt something give way, accompanied by a sharp pain. She gasped, her body stiffening. Gareth was now completely inside her, filling her in a way she'd never dreamed of before this moment.

"I'm sorry."

"Don't be. I'm fine," she said again. And she was, she realized. The pain had gone. She moved against Gareth, experimentally, rewarded by a wonderfully pleasurable feeling.

Gareth withdrew himself from her, leaving her bereft. "What? I said it was all right—"

He smiled down at her. "I know." He took her mouth and body at the same time, sending a spiraling pleasure through her.

"I never dreamed—"

Her words were stopped by his kisses, and then she no longer wanted to talk. Only move with Gareth and feel these wonderful sensations flooding her body.

They moved together as perfectly as if they had loved each other forever, and then together found the ultimate pleasure waiting for them, that bliss beyond all other delights.

Exhausted, Shannon lay in Gareth's arms, wanting to stay there forever, to never leave this perfect haven under the old apple tree. Her eyes closed, smiling, she listened to the rapid beat of his heart slow to normal.

She moved closer to him, hugged him. "I do love you so much," she whispered, smiling up at him. "So very, very much."

A breeze moved the tree branches, letting a bit of moonlight in.

Gareth wasn't smiling. He stared down at her, his gray eyes turning to that steely color she hated, his jaw tightening. He lifted her hands away from his shoulders, moved away from her, then got up and, his back turned, swiftly drew on his trousers.

For a moment, Shannon couldn't believe what he'd done. Then she did, and her body turned to ice. "What is the matter?" she managed to get out past her cold, stiff lips.

He didn't answer, just kept his back turned, fastening his trousers. Finally, he faced her. His eyes were still that cold steel, his jaw hard. How could this be the same man who had held her in his arms only minutes ago, kissed her, loved her until she'd thought she would die of sheer pleasure.

"I'm sorry I gave you the wrong . . . that I made you expect things I can never give."

In a flash, she understood. *Love.* She'd told him how much she loved him. Because she'd thought that he surely must love her since he'd so clearly enjoyed the lovemaking.

What a fool she'd been. He'd only *wanted* her. Hadn't he told her just that, *only* that, before he took her?

Her face flamed, the cold disappearing. At least she had her pride. He couldn't take that away from her, as he'd just taken her virginity. No, she had to be honest. He hadn't taken anything. She'd given it to him freely, joyously, willingly.

More fool she. Hadn't Gareth's mother told her just a few weeks ago he'd never looked at another woman after his fiancée had jilted him?

The only reason for that had to be because he was still in love with the fool of a woman.

What was her name? Maud had told her. It was . . .

"Dorinda. It's because of her, isn't it?" she asked, forgetting her pride, forgetting everything except that she had to know.

His jaw tightened. "How did you know about her?"

Shannon licked dry lips. "Your mother told me."

His jaw tightened even more. "It's none of her affair. It's no one's but mine. And I won't talk about her."

Hearing the pain in his voice, cold invaded her again. How could she fight something like this? Dorinda was married to someone else. Gareth could never have her. Yet he was still bound to her. He still loved her.

Desperately, she groped for the remnants of her pride, forcing her voice to come out steady and cold. "What makes you think that I expect anything from you? That I want to marry you?"

His face changed. His jaw loosened a bit, replaced by a frown. "You just said that . . . that you love me."

With an extreme effort of will, Shannon shrugged. "I guess I was just caught up in . . . the pleasure I was feeling."

His frown deepened. "I'm a good bit older than you

Shannon. I shouldn't have taken advantage of you. You are under my family's protection."

Shannon could feel her heart breaking inside her chest. The jagged pieces of it were jabbing into her sides, causing excruciating pain. "You took no advantage of me. I—I wanted this as much as you did."

Somehow, she managed another shrug, then reached for her discarded nightdress and quickly slipped it on. After she'd pulled it down around her again, she glanced over at him.

He still stood where he had before. Now a different expression was on his face. Confusion. Good. He didn't know what to make of her. But that wouldn't last. In a few moments, when he fully took in what she'd said, she wanted to be away from this place.

Away from him. Swiftly, she walked past him. He grabbed her sleeve.

"Wait, Shannon, we need to talk."

She pulled her sleeve loose. "No, we don't. Good night. Thank you for . . . pleasuring me so well."

Shannon hurried out of the orchard without looking back. The moon was high in the sky now, silvering the landscape, making it unearthly beautiful. She didn't want to see its mocking beauty.

At the house, Duke once more gave her a sleepy tail thump of greeting. "Good boy," she told him thickly, then opened the back door, waiting just inside to be sure all was still quiet.

Up in her room, she got out of the nightdress and kicked it into a corner. She pulled her other clean one out of the chest, poured water into the basin and washed herself.

The smear of crimson from between her legs made relief course through her. One thing tonight's events had proved—that spectral figure with the knife was no husband or lover.

Then the cold returned, worse than before.

Once Gareth recovered from her show of bravado, and started thinking about what had happened tonight, he'd realize that was all it was—a pitiful attempt to save her pride. He had ample proof she was no wanton.

That is, if he cared enough to think about it at all.

Slipping on her clean nightdress, she got between the sheets and lay rigidly.

She may as well face facts. Gareth had wanted her. He'd taken what she'd so eagerly offered him. Then he'd regained his conscience and apologized for what he hadn't intended to do.

But Gareth was no smooth-talking rake. He truly was sorry he'd given in to what he considered his baser impulses.

Because he didn't love her. He'd never love her.

He'd made that painfully clear with his alarmed reaction to her own impulsive declaration of love.

She'd behaved like a fool!

Shannon turned on her side and curled up into a ball, holding herself and letting the tears run down her face.

No matter how dangerous it was for her, she had to get out of here. There were other places she could stay and work. Gareth had already told her that.

Tomorrow she'd talk to Maud about it.

Another thought hit her roiling mind.

Randall. He'd shown some interest in her. As well as in Gwenny. But Gwenny let it be clearly known she had no interest in him.

Randall lived in Maryland. If she could somehow persuade him to marry her, take her away from here, she might be safe from the faceless man.

She swallowed a sour taste in her mouth and pushed away the crazy, desperate idea.

No, she couldn't do such a thing!

But there might be another choice. Maybe she could persuade Ellis to take her back with him. Maybe his family needed a companion/hired-girl combination. Or someone they knew did.

Anything was better than staying here and having to face

Gareth day after day, trying to keep him from seeing how much she loved him.

Anything? Even the man with the knife?

Her mouth tightened. Impotent anger filled her. She picked up her slipper and flung it against the wall, feeling no satisfaction at the dull thud.

If she'd thought things were bad before, now they were terrible beyond imagining. She couldn't stand the thought of staying on here—where at least she was physically safe for the time being.

Yet neither could she go, until she regained her memory, knew why the man was after her. Her throat closed.

Knew why he wanted to take her life.

Chapter Fourteen

"When you finish with these posters, come back here and I'll give you this." Vance held up a silver half dollar and watched the ragamuffin boy's eyes widen.

"Yes, sir! I'll give them out at the store and other places!" He took the half dozen pieces of paper from Vance.

Vance gave him a hard look. "Don't try any funny stuff. Like throwing them away. I'll know if you do."

The boy swallowed and quickly shook his head. "No, sir. Won't do nothin' like that. They'll go up right and proper."

Frowning, Vance watched him hurry away. Damn, he hated to advertise that he was hunting her. But he'd had no luck asking questions.

Now he'd put up these damned posters in every town within a fifty-mile radius. All he could do was wait to see if anything came of it.

Wait. He was damned sick of waiting! And this was risky as hell. If the local law in any of the towns saw his posters and started asking questions, he'd be in bad trouble.

Since he'd told them she was dead.

His frown deepened into a scowl. Goddamn but he wished that was true!

But if she wasn't dead, where in hell was she?

He wished she were here right now so he could get his hands on her. His fingers tingled as he pictured them around her throat, squeezing the life out of her. She deserved that, and more, for all the worry she'd caused him.

Of course, it was the knife she feared most. He licked his lips as he remembered the fear in her face when she'd run from the house before he could stop her.

If she was still alive, by the time he was done with her, she'd feel the blade of that knife.

As well as a few other things. His mouth twisted in a cruel smile as he thought of the other things he'd do before he finished with her.

"And you must be Miss Shannon Brown?" The young woman gave her a friendly smile, not quite able to hide the curious glance she gave to Shannon's short hair, now pinned into a small roll in back.

"Yes. How do you do, Miss Northrup?" Shannon responded politely, inwardly wincing at the "Brown." The more often she heard it, the more wrong it sounded. Shannon had been described as a distant visiting relative, just as she had been introduced to Ellis and his sons. Her amnesia hadn't been mentioned.

"Why, just fine. We're so glad to finally meet you."

Felicia Northrup, who looked like a somewhat older version of Clare, although they weren't related, beamed at Shannon and ushered her and the Colbys inside their big brick house, which had somehow withstood the ravages of the war.

Shannon wished she were back at the farm. She'd tried everything to keep from coming on this social call today, but nothing had worked. Of course she would come with them when they took their visiting cousins to meet their nearest neighbors, Maud had said. Gwenny concurred. Yes, they wouldn't think of leaving her behind.

Since it was Sunday and no one was working, even Gareth had come along. He didn't look any happier than Shannon felt, and he avoided meeting her glance, just as he had since that night in the orchard a week ago. Her face flamed as she remembered it, and she hoped no one noticed.

The next day she hadn't been able to carry out her desperate plan.

Her spirit had quailed at the thought of asking Ellis for work. And she also couldn't bear the thought of hurting Gareth's family, these good people who had taken her in and let her stay.

How could she explain her sudden desire to leave? Certainly, she couldn't tell them the true reason.

Maud and her daughters thought she was a suitable wife for Gareth. But they wouldn't think that if they knew what had happened in the orchard.

So, she'd said nothing, washed the grass stains out of her nightdress, and tried to avoid Gareth. That hadn't been hard, because obviously he had the same idea.

Her mouth tightened. Gareth would have no doubt been delighted if she'd announced her intention to leave. Hadn't he suggested that very thing right before everyone came down with the fever?

"Come along into the parlor," Felicia said. "I'm so sorry Mama has one of her sick headaches."

Shannon followed Clare into the room. Just inside the door, she stopped, staring at the spinet across the room. The beautiful instrument gleamed with wax and care.

With no warning, one of the unpredictable flashes of memory filled her mind. Her mother sat at a piano much like this, smiling at the young girl beside her.

Herself? No, this was someone else . . . her mother was giving this child a piano lesson. She gave them to several of the children in the town . . . it kept them in food and firewood . . . what town? Shannon strained to keep the vision from fading. . . .

That wasn't me, but I know how to play . . . She loved to play, and her mother praised her memory because she'd learned so many pieces by heart . . . oh, wasn't that funny? Her memory had been so good!

"Do sit here, Shannon." Felicia gestured at a striped settee.

The last wisps of the vision disappeared. Shannon came back to herself. No one was looking at her oddly, so she must not have made any peculiar faces or gestures.

She seated herself, and to her displeasure Randall sat down beside her. She wished he'd sat by Gwenny, who was across the room with her mother. Clare had managed to maneuver herself next to Ames and was simpering at him.

Gareth sat by himself, in a hard-backed chair that couldn't be any straighter than his spine. He glanced her way, and their eyes met. His gray eyes were dark and unreadable, his face impassive.

Shannon quickly lowered her gaze and turned to Randall.

"Has your father had any luck in finding a farm to buy?" she quickly asked the first thing that came to mind.

Randall gave her a surprised look. No wonder, his father had told them all just a day or so ago of his futile efforts.

"Why, no, Miss Shannon, he hasn't." He smiled. "I don't think he will. He likes Gareth's farm too well. He won't find another to equal it."

Something moved uneasily inside Shannon. She didn't like Randall's smile. It was too self-satisfied, as if he were sure his father would eventually be successful in his desire to acquire Gareth's farm.

Felicia brought in a teapot and poured the liquid into mismatched cups, which somehow made Shannon feel better. The Northrups may have saved their house, even a lot of their furniture, but they, too, had suffered losses. Just as the Colbys had.

She tensed before the thought was fully formed. Why should she feel like that? True, Gareth's family had taken her in, been extremely kind to her, but they weren't her family.

They could never be her family. Gareth had made that crystal clear.

Randall brought her a cup of tea and sat beside her again. "Father's sure he'll eventually wear Gareth down."

His smug tone and words confirmed Shannon's thoughts of a few moments ago.

Only a week ago, she'd have been positive he was wrong. Now, after what Gareth had told her in the orchard, she wasn't. It was quite possible, she realized, that Ellis could persuade Gareth to sell the land he loved more than his life.

Pain pierced her at this thought. Pain for Gareth, who deserved better. But many people in the South deserved better than they had gotten since the end of the war. Many people had lost their homes and left the places they had lived all their lives.

"I do wish Mama were able to be here," Felicia said. "And she could play for us. Clare, Gwenny, would you honor us with a few tunes? You know how I hate to play."

Shannon looked longingly at the beautiful instrument. Her fingers tingled to touch those ivory keys.

"So do I," Gwenny said briskly. She glanced at Clare, who was giggling at something Ames had said, and then her gaze fell on Shannon.

"Shannon, do you play as well as you read?"

Shannon started, realizing Gwenny must have noticed her yearning stare. "I—play some," she answered.

"Good!" Felicia said. "Please play for us, won't you?"

Why not? In addition to satisfying her longing, the act might trigger something else in her mind. Might reveal more of her past to her.

"I'd like to," she said simply, smiling at Felicia.

Shannon moved to the piano and seated herself on the stool, Felicia following.

"Do you play from memory?" Felicia asked. "I'm sure I could find some music, some hymnbooks, perhaps."

From memory. Shannon's stomach twisted. Could she? Or was that knowledge wiped from her mind, too?

She lowered her hands to the keys, and a flood of emotion filled her. Her fingers began to move across the keyboard, and the sweet, haunting strains of a Chopin nocturne filled the room.

She sat at a piano, playing this very same piece. Her mother was in the room, which was a music room in a very nice house, and so were two other men. . . .

Frustration filled her as her mind went blank, causing her fingers to falter. But in a moment, she continued, flawlessly playing the piece until the end.

"That was wonderful! Do play more," Felicia said.

"Yes, do, Shannon," Maud echoed. "Why, we had no idea you could play this well."

Nor had he, Gareth thought, his gaze on Shannon's slim back. What other talents did this young woman have they knew nothing about?

She has a delightful talent at lovemaking, his mind mocked. *But of course you do know all about that.*

His jaw tightened. It was all he could do to keep from bolting out of the chair, out of the room.

He'd let his body's desires create one hell of a mess.

And it was all his fault. He couldn't blame Shannon, willing though she'd been. Their hunger was mutual—but he shouldn't have given in to it.

He should have had more self-control. Hell, he shouldn't have followed her out to the orchard! None of this would have happened if he'd stayed in his bedchamber.

And for those few minutes of passion, he might well have gotten her with child.

It was a lot more than just a few minutes of passion, his mind taunted. *What happened that night was something you'd never experienced before. Or ever expected to. That you didn't even know existed.*

Be that as it may, it didn't alter the situation. He'd made love with a young woman who was in a very vulnerable position. Who was probably also an orphan, in his family's care.

Who had afterward told him how much she loved him.

He winced inwardly, guiltily, at that memory.

Afterward, *he'd* had the unmitigated gall to tell *her* he could never marry her. To leave her believing he was still in love with Dorinda.

Maybe he'd half believed that himself, once. But no longer. His aversion to marriage still remained, but it wasn't due to any lingering desire for his former fiancée.

He had nothing to offer Shannon, except their farm. Which might not be theirs too much longer if taxes kept increasing and crops failed once too often. Maybe this year, even.

And his own self. His lips curled in derision. *He* was no prize for any woman! Especially one like Shannon.

He glanced at her slender back again. She held her shapely head high. She was beautiful, accomplished. Eventually, she'd regain her memory.

True, it appeared she'd been reduced to poverty by the war, but so had most of the South. So had Dorinda. That hadn't kept her from finding a man with far better prospects than Gareth. A man with two whole, strong legs.

"Do play just one more!" Felicia urged.

Shannon turned and stood, smiling at the roomful of people. "I think that's quite enough."

Her glance met Gareth's, and he saw her smile falter, pain coming into her eyes. She quickly walked back to her seat next to Randall.

Gareth swore silently. He hadn't wanted to hurt her! That hadn't been in any of his plans.

Plans? his mind mocked again. *What plans? The only thing in your mind was satisfying your lust. Now what do you intend to do?*

Nothing. He intended to do nothing—but wait. He swore again. He was a man of action. He hated waiting. If Shannon were to be with child, then of course, he'd do the honorable thing and marry her.

Did he intend to ignore her for weeks? If she was with child, did he expect her to come to him, begging for marriage?

And have every busybody in the Valley counting the months until the baby arrived? Giving her knowing looks, gossiping behind her back?

He clenched his hands, revolted at that idea. Hell, no, he couldn't, wouldn't do that!

So what was left? He knew the answer. He had to marry this woman he'd bedded on that sweet orchard grass, the woman whose welcoming arms had given him a glimpse of heaven.

He glanced across the room again. Randall had his head close to hers, smiling and saying something to her, and she smiled back at him. A streak of jealousy went through Gareth.

She seemed to have lost her pain very quickly. Maybe she was seriously interested in Randall. If she were, if she married Randall, she'd be much better off than if she married Gareth.

Even if she's carrying your babe in her belly? his mind queried.

Randall lifted his head and glanced across the room, toward Gwenny. He gave her the same kind of smile he'd just bestowed on Shannon. Gwenny ignored him.

Gareth got to his feet. "We must be going. Sunday or not, there are the evening chores to do."

Randall was a male version of Clare. Unreliable as the weather. He'd see the man in hell before he'd let him near Gwenny.

Or near Shannon. A man like Randall would give her nothing but misery. But the bastard was already near her. Too damned near. There was only one way to keep him away: tell her he was willing to marry her himself.

He could give her steadfast faithfulness. That wasn't much, but it was all he had to offer. And he would. This very day. He glanced at Randall again, who once more had his head close to Shannon.

He'd better, before the bastard put ideas into her head.

Chapter Fifteen

Where was Josh? He was usually here before now. Shannon moved the stool over and started milking Rosie. She tried not to think of Gareth and how he'd looked in the Northrups' parlor that afternoon.

It was no use, though.

He'd been so cool and remote, as if he were a million miles away. Paying her no attention whatever. All that made no difference.

She still wanted him. She still *loved* him.

Why was she such a fool to keep on loving a man who wanted nothing to do with her?

Who deeply regretted giving in to his lust for her.

She heard a noise at the door. Good. Josh had finally gotten here. "I'm halfway through Rosie, Josh, where have you been? I wanted to talk to you about—"

"It's not Josh," Gareth's deep voice cut in from behind her. "Now, be careful, don't—"

Shannon's body froze, but this time she had presence of mind enough not to give the cow's teat too hard a squeeze.

She slowly turned toward him. "Don't worry," she said

crisply, determined to appear detached and emotionless just as he had earlier today. "I'm not always an idiot."

"I never thought you were."

His voice wasn't warm, but neither was it frosty like her own. Why was he here?

"What did you want to talk to Josh about?"

She swallowed. So he'd caught those last words. Another few moments and he'd have heard enough that she'd have to tell him about the man she feared.

No, she corrected herself, she'd have had to try to explain why she *couldn't* tell him.

But he hadn't heard more. And she wouldn't. She intended to talk to Gareth Colby as little as possible.

After all, he'd told her in the most brutally frank way just how inconsequential she was to him.

She shrugged. "Nothing important."

Damn it all! Gareth swore silently, his good intentions to stay calm and reasonable already about to desert him.

Was this female put on earth solely to cause him grief?

Here he was, ready to offer her his hand and name, and she'd gone cool and aloof. And she'd sounded pleased, ready to confide, when she'd thought he was Josh.

Not that he still had doubts about anything between her and Josh, but why did she want to talk to the young man, and why wouldn't she tell Gareth what it was all about?

Her hair had come unpinned, was curling around her ears, giving her a delightfully disheveled look, reminding him of that night in the orchard when she'd lain in his arms, become his own.

He pushed that thought away. He didn't want her to be his. He didn't want any woman to be.

But he'd take full responsibility for her, for his own actions.

"We need to talk about something that *is* important," he said.

He heard her sigh, saw her breast rise and fall under the too-tight bodice of Clare's old blue gown. His mind pictured her breasts bared to his gaze, his touch, as they had been that night. His heart leaped. His body tightened.

"I must finish the milking."

"I'll help, after I clean the stalls."

He made quick work of that chore, pushing away scenes his mind kept presenting him: He and Shannon bedded down in a clean stall. He and Shannon bedded down in a *bed*.

Gareth seated himself beside the other jersey, and in a few minutes, both were finished.

Shannon glanced over at Gareth as he rose from the stool and lifted his pail of milk. His face was set in firm lines. He looked determined, fixed on whatever he wanted to talk about.

Her stomach tightened. What could that be? Was he again going to suggest it would be better if she were to leave, find another place to live?

Probably.

Undoubtedly.

Her stomach tightened more. It was obvious how uncomfortable he was with her now. Of course, he'd always been ill at ease with her except for the brief period after Grandma Lucy's death, when they had been friends.

That fledgling friendship had been damaged by the arrival of Ellis and his sons. And destroyed by what had happened in the orchard. Now, Gareth was even more withdrawn. More hard and unhappy-appearing.

Shannon rose from her own stool and carried her milk pail to the corner where Gareth had set his. She took a deep breath and let it out, trying to dissolve some of her tension. Obviously, Gareth was finding it difficult to start the conversation he'd said he wanted.

All right, then. She'd do it. Get it over with.

"I've been thinking about what you said a while back. And I've decided you were right." She lifted her chin a little, straightened her shoulders.

Gareth stared at her. "Right about what?"

"About me finding another place to work—and live."

Pain shot through her. This was so hard! How could she bear it?

He took a step nearer to her. "What on earth are you talking about?"

She moved back a step. "Just what I said. I—it would be better for everyone if I left here."

"Like hell it would! Have you lost your mind?" He walked forward and grasped her shoulders.

"Yes, Gareth," she shot back, "that's exactly what's happened. I've lost my mind. I've mislaid my entire past."

Despite her snippy words and tone, she couldn't deny his hands warmed her body, made her remember things she didn't want to recall.

"Yet you want to leave here? You didn't before."

You imbecile! she screamed at him inwardly. *You hadn't made love to me before, either! Then rejected me in that cruel manner.*

"It would be the most sensible thing." In spite of her determination to see this through calmly, her voice trembled.

"Sensible? How can you possibly believe that?" He scowled at her, his eyes darkened now, the steeliness lost in another emotion.

She couldn't think straight with him touching her like that. "Please let go of me," she said primly, managing to keep her voice firm this time.

"No. You'd probably run away."

"What if I did? What would you care? You'd be rid of me then. Wasn't that what you were getting ready to suggest—that it's high time I left here?"

He gave her a tiny shake, as if irritated beyond measure. "You couldn't be more wrong. I was going to tell you we have to get married. Right away."

Disbelieving shock trembled through her body. She felt her eyes widen, her mouth drop open. "What did you say?"

"I'm only a foot away. You heard me. We need to get married."

"What do you mean, we *need* to get married?"

"Just what I said. You—we . . . "

For the first time his voice faltered. His hands dropped.

"You could very well be with child. If so, I'm responsible. I wouldn't let you suffer the consequences of that alone."

Her shock grew, hardened into mixed pain and incredulity. She'd never thought of that. She was a much bigger fool than she'd believed. How could she not have considered that possibility?

Gareth was offering her what her heart wanted more than anything. To be his wife. To belong to him.

The pain grew, threatening to overwhelm her.

No, he wasn't offering that at all. He was merely offering her his name, his protection. His heart still belonged to Dorinda.

She couldn't marry him, live with him, knowing he didn't love her. That he'd only married her out of obligation.

She'd blundered into this family's life and caused them nothing but trouble. She couldn't blame Gareth for making love to her. She'd been totally willing and eager.

If she married him, stayed here forever, more trouble could come. The man with the knife could find her before she found her memory. He might not only hurt her, but someone in the family.

And she couldn't be sure she hadn't done something wrong. The law might be after her, no matter how much she tried to deny it, how many times her mind insisted that wasn't true.

She had to get away from here, far enough away no harm could come to this family who now felt like her own. They *weren't* her own, and she couldn't endanger them.

"I—I don't want to marry you. And you've already told me that you don't want to marry me. Or anyone."

Except the one woman he couldn't have.

"We're not talking about what we *want*," Gareth said. "But what we have to do."

Heaviness filled her. If she'd had any doubts about how

he truly felt, he'd just dispelled them. "Why do we have to?" she countered.

He shook his head in vexation, and a lock of his black hair fell over his forehead. Impatiently, he swept it back. "You know why."

"We—we were only together one time. It's very unlikely that . . ." She couldn't finish, couldn't accept this possibility.

"Are you willing to take the chance that even now you may be carrying a child?"

Not a child. Your child, Gareth. Pain twisted her insides. She lifted her chin a little higher.

"Yes. I want to leave here. I'd appreciate it if you'd ask your cousin Ellis if he could offer me employment when he returns home. Or perhaps some of his acquaintances might be able to."

His scowl deepened. "I'll do nothing of the kind. That's not the right way to handle this."

"There is no right way," she told him.

Because you don't love me. Because you don't really know me. Because I don't know myself.

He gave a gusty sigh, and some of the hardness left his face. "That's true. I should never have let this happen. But I did, and now I insist on being responsible for any consequences."

Shannon forced a smile onto her face. "It's very doubtful there will be any consequences. If so, then I will tell you."

"Then you will *marry* me," he said flatly.

"We shall worry about that when and if we have to."

Long before that, she would be out of here. Of course, with Gareth's opposition, her idea about working for his cousin's family was no longer an option.

Only one solution remained.

She had to leave as she'd arrived, dressed in the men's clothes, her newly growing hair again cropped short. Josh would help her. She had no money, but she had the pendant.

Pain hit her anew at the thought of selling the only thing

she had from her past life. But she'd have to. There was no choice.

Gareth huffed out his breath again. "You are the most stubborn female I've ever encountered. I don't like this."

Shannon shrugged. "Neither do I—but it's better than wedding a man who only wants to do the right thing."

She stepped forward, to walk around him, to get out of the barn, but his hand shot out and grasped her arm, halting her escape.

"Wait. You can't leave like this."

Her features were set as she turned toward him. "Let go of me."

Even as she demanded this, she knew she wanted just the opposite. She wanted Gareth to pull her into his arms and hold her tight against his chest.

He looked down into her upraised face. "Shannon," he finally said, his softened, longing tone echoing those other times he'd held her, weakening her resolve.

Her lips parted involuntarily, and she heard his indrawn breath. His hand tightened on her arm, then moved upward, curving around her neck, holding her fast, while his head lowered to hers.

Not that he had to hold her.

No, as always, her will was dissolving, her body making its clamorous needs known. And she was listening to it.

She shuddered when their mouths touched, when Gareth kissed the corner of her mouth, her chin, her cheeks, then returned to take her lips in a long, drugging kiss.

Shannon pressed herself against him, her arms going around his chest, holding to him as to a lifeline.

She loved this man with every fiber of her being, with every breath she took. . . .

And he didn't love her. Not at all. He only wanted her physically.

Cold swept over her, chilling the hot desire that had held her in its grip. She dropped her hands and stepped back, pulling herself out of his grasp.

"Leave me alone! Please, just leave me alone!"

She turned, picked up her skirts, and ran out of the barn.

Gareth watched her go, his heartbeat gradually slowing to normal.

Hell. He'd made a mess of this.

What had he expected? Had anything gone the way it should, as he'd anticipated, since Shannon's stormy arrival here all those weeks ago?

He picked up the milk pails and left the barn. Shannon was nowhere in sight. What was he going to do now? Wait? Do nothing but wait?

He swore again. No, he hadn't the patience for that. He'd think of something.

Clare twirled and dipped on the orchard grass, holding out her skirts, smiling up at an imaginary partner, watching the afternoon sun shoot glints off the sapphire and diamond pendant around her neck.

Her hand came up; her fingers caressed the jewel.

She closed her eyes. To be in a real ballroom, circling the floor on the arm of a handsome man, wearing a beautiful ball gown and this dazzling necklace, would be wonderful. Would the man be Ames?

She considered. True, he was handsome and rich. But he seemed so young. He wasn't very interesting to talk to, either. She sighed. She guessed she couldn't have everything. She'd have to be satisfied with just part of all she wanted.

"What are you doing?"

Josh's unexpected voice shattered the spell she'd woven. She stopped twirling, and her eyes popped open. She swallowed, her hand curving around the necklace, trying to cover it.

He wore his old work clothes, sweat-stained and soiled. His face looked tired—and also angry. "What are you doing here?" she evaded. "Aren't you supposed to be working?"

His mouth tightened even more. "Of course I'm supposed to be working—every daylight hour. Not like some people I know who don't have to work for a living."

Clare lifted her chin. "If you're referring to Ames, then go ahead and say so."

"Yes, I'm 'referring' to Ames. Clare, I'm tired of all this. I've been patient, but a man can be patient only so long. Ever since those people came, I haven't had a minute with you."

She pouted prettily, relieved he hadn't noticed the pendant. "I can hardly be rude to our guests, can I? Especially when they're family."

"Not close. They haven't visited for years."

Clare shrugged. "It really makes no difference. They're still guests. I have to be polite—help entertain them."

"Mr. Colby wishes they'd leave. He's tired of them trying to talk him into selling the farm."

"I wish he would sell it! Maybe we could finally live decently again. All everyone does now is work all the time and do without and try to make ends meet. *I'm* tired of that!"

Josh's mouth turned down. "It doesn't seem to me as if *you* work all the time. Not any more than you have to."

Her mouth hung open. Forgetting the pendant, she pointed her finger at him. "You are just the most hateful thing, Josh Archer! I work lots—"

Her voice broke off as she saw him stare at her neck. She quickly covered the pendant again, guilt filling her face.

"That belongs to Shannon. Why are you wearing it?"

"Because I want to!" she said defiantly, lifting her chin higher. "Because I'm so sick of never having anything nice of my own!"

"You better take that off and get it back to the house. You know Shannon loves that more than anything. She told me so."

"Just why is she telling you all these things? Why are you acting all high and mighty about Ames when you and

Shannon spend an hour together in the barn every day. *Alone.*"

Josh let out an impatient sigh. "Don't start that again. You know better than to pretend to be jealous of Shannon. You know you like her and you don't believe what you're saying."

He had her there. Clare shrugged again, trying hard to keep the advantage. "Just the same, there's no reason to act like you're doing about Ames."

"I'm finished with your games. You promised you'd wait for me, be my wife someday. You didn't take that promise seriously. I don't think you'll ever take anything seriously. I release you from the promise."

Josh turned and left, leaving Clare openmouthed and disbelieving, her pride stung.

And something deeper than pride began to hurt.

"I hope I'm not interrupting anything."

In the space of a few moments, Clare was again so startled by a man's voice close to her she nearly jumped out of her skin. She whirled.

Ames stood a few feet away, the half-mocking smile he wore so often on his mouth.

"Why did you sneak up on me?" she demanded, her hand once again rising to cover the sapphire.

"Did you want me to whistle or yell or something? Walking through the orchard doesn't make much noise."

His gaze was on her hand, and she knew he'd seen the stone. She tossed her head.

"Well, it's certainly rude to eavesdrop on people." She wondered how much of her and Josh's conversation he'd overheard.

"You and the hired boy were talking loud enough I didn't have to eavesdrop."

"Josh isn't a hired boy! He and his father and brother work the land they'll own someday." She was surprised to hear herself defending Josh after the way he'd just talked to her.

"Close enough. Was what he said the truth? Did you actually promise to marry him?"

Clare felt her face redden at his derisive tone. Josh had said horrible, hurtful things to her and then told her he released her from her promise.

She didn't owe him anything.

"No, of course I didn't. He—he just misunderstood some things, I guess."

Ames walked closer. His hand came out and touched her arm. "I'm certainly glad to hear that. I think you know I'm beginning to care for you. I hoped that you felt the same toward me."

His voice was soft and low, his touch warm. But his gaze wasn't on hers.

It was fixed on her hand covering the necklace.

Without quite knowing why, Clare felt uneasy. She had a sudden urge to run back to the house and replace Shannon's pendant in the trunk where it belonged before she found out it was gone.

Of course Shannon never wore the jewel, and if she took it out and looked at it, it was after everyone was in bed at night.

Clare moved back a step, and Ames's hand dropped from her arm. "I—it's much too soon for us to be thinking about such things," she said primly.

"No, it isn't. You know we'll be leaving in another week or so. Just as soon as Papa concludes his business here. Your brother is about ready to discuss selling this place, you know. If we were to . . ."

His voice broke off, and he gave her a meltingly significant look. "You may not ever have to leave your home, Clare. Papa will tear down the old house and build a magnificent new structure. A mansion."

A mansion. Something cold struck Clare in the pit of her stomach. The old house gone forever. A beautiful new one in its place. Living in it with this . . . boy. Enjoying all the things she'd longed for all these years.

She swallowed and backed away. Everything was happening too fast. She couldn't deal with it now. She had to get back to the house.

"I have to go. I promised Gwenny I'd help with supper. I need to peel potatoes and go gather the eggs."

"You're far too pretty to spend your time and ruin your lovely hands doing such work," Ames said, moving toward her again.

Clare suddenly became aware that they were alone together in the big orchard, out of sight of everyone. Out of sound, too.

If she should scream, no one would hear her. . . .

"I have to *go,*" she said again.

She picked up her skirts and almost ran out of the orchard, hearing Ames's faint mocking laughter behind her. She tried to tell herself she was being silly, that Ames would never dream of doing anything that she didn't want him to do, but it made no difference.

She kept on running until the house was in sight. Relief filled her when she saw it, followed a moment later by alarm.

Shannon hurried toward the house, as if she were running away from someone. Just as Clare had been running, deny it as she might.

Clare stopped before Shannon could see her. She quickly unfastened the pendant and slipped it into a side pocket of her gown.

Shame washed over her. She should never have taken the jewel. What if Shannon decided she wanted to get the pendant out of the trunk?

"Of course she won't," she told herself out loud to keep her courage up. "Not now."

But she didn't want to talk to the other woman, so she waited until Shannon was in the house before she continued on her way. She'd hurry upstairs and put the jewel back in the trunk.

Ames was close behind her and he came into the empty kitchen moments after she did. She hurried on up to the attic, slipped into the cubicle, lifted the lid of the old trunk and carefully rewrapped the jewel before sliding it down to the bottom.

Turning to go, she thought she heard a noise on the stairs, and when she whirled, she caught a glimpse of Ames's dark head disappearing from view.

She frowned, an uneasy feeling hitting her. Why had he followed her up here?

And why didn't he want her to see that he had?

Chapter Sixteen

As Shannon entered the parlor, Clare glanced up from her needlework and smiled. But she didn't quite look herself, Shannon thought.

Shannon took a deep breath and held it for a few moments before letting it out. How could she do this? Especially with Ellis and his sons present.

But she had to.

"Did any of you move my necklace out of the trunk?" she asked, trying to keep the anxiety and the other emotions she felt out of her voice.

Clare put down her needlework, an odd expression covering her face. She looked surprised and concerned . . . but something else was there, too.

Shannon saw everyone else in the parlor was also looking at her, with expressions containing some measure of surprise.

Clare cleared her throat. "Maybe you looked in the wrong trunk—or put it somewhere else and forgot about it."

Clare's voice sounded odd, too, Shannon noticed.

She shook her head. "No. It's the right trunk and I didn't take it out."

Shannon saw Clare ease her head to the left and give Ames a covert glance. Ames's handsome young face looked bland, almost unconcerned. He ignored Clare's glance.

Now what did that mean? Shannon wondered.

"Dear, are you *very* sure you didn't take the necklace out of the trunk?" Maud asked anxiously.

Shannon managed a smile for the older woman. She had no suspicions of her. She had no suspicions of *any* of them, but where was her beautiful necklace?

A blend of urgency and sorrow hit her, the urgency stronger.

She couldn't leave here without the pendant!

"I'm very sure."

Shannon's gaze met Clare's again and lingered. Clare's odd expression had turned into a recognizable one. Guilt.

Had Clare taken the necklace out to look at and admire, perhaps to wear in her room, then not gotten around to returning it yet? Was there some way to find out without embarrassing the girl in front of these other people who weren't really family, no matter how they pretended?

Clare dropped her gaze from Shannon's and squirmed in her seat.

"Does anyone know about Shannon's pendant?" Gareth's deep voice seemed to fill the small room. His gaze was on Clare.

The girl swallowed visibly.

"I—I wore it yesterday," she said in a small voice.

Every head in the room turned toward her. Maud gave a shocked gasp. Gwenny frowned in disapproval.

"But I put it back! I wrapped it in the cloth and slipped it down to the bottom of the trunk where I found it."

She lifted her gaze to Shannon's.

"I—I'm very sorry. I shouldn't have taken it. But I *did* put it back."

The same blend of emotions she'd felt since she'd discovered the pendant was missing still held Shannon in its grip

The shock of loss. Anxiety because without the pendant she couldn't carry out her plan.

Relief that without the pendant she *couldn't* leave here.

If she was going to be honest, she had to admit she wanted to stay. This family seemed like her family now, and she couldn't stand the thought of leaving them.

And thinking about leaving Gareth caused her so much pain it was almost unbearable.

But that didn't change the fact she had to go.

She wasn't surprised that Clare had admitted taking and wearing the necklace. But if Clare had put it back, then where was it?

"Are you sure you returned it?" she asked the younger woman.

Clare nodded vigorously, her face and neck red with embarrassment. "Yes! I've said that three times now."

She turned her head and looked at Ames again, and Shannon saw her lips tighten.

"Ames was watching when I put it back! And he—he wanted it. I could tell!"

Shocked gasps followed her impassioned words, and now everyone's gaze turned on Ames.

The young man's eyes widened with what appeared to be astonishment. "I don't have any idea what she's talking about."

Ellis got to his feet. "I believe that Miss Clare owes my sons and me an apology," he said stiffly.

"No, I don't! What I said was the truth. If you search Ames and the room he's occupying, I'm certain you'll find the necklace!"

For long moments silence filled the room. Finally, Gareth, who was also now standing, turned toward his cousins.

"My sister is young and has faults, but lying and stealing have never been among them." His voice was firm and his gaze steady on the three men.

Did Ames really take the pendant? Shannon stared at his face, which still wore only a shocked expression.

Ellis loudly cleared his throat. "It would be an insult to search my son and the room where he sleeps."

A shiver went down Shannon's spine. Ellis's voice held a false note—as if he was putting on an act.

She glanced at Gareth. He was giving Ellis a speculative look. "I believe we'll have to search the entire house."

Ellis drew himself up as tall as possible. But Shannon thought the gesture seemed false, too. "I cannot believe that my sons and I are being subjected to such treatment. And from members of our own family."

Gareth's gaze stayed steadily on the other man. "Shall we start the search?"

Ellis's face blanched. He gave each son a quick look. "Come. We'll pack our things and leave this house where we are being treated so shabbily."

He turned and headed for the front stairs, Ames and Randall following closely at his heels.

Shannon blinked in astonishment. Gareth could move very quickly for such a big man—and one with a limp besides. He stood, blocking the stairs, his hands busily emptying his trouser pockets.

"We'll start with me," he said, putting the meager contents on a small table: a pen knife, a handkerchief, a bent nail, a small coil of rope. He wore no jacket, just a clean shirt he'd put on for the evening.

"I'll have no part of this, nor will my sons," Ellis blustered. "This is outrageous!"

Gareth turned toward Ames. "Will you empty your pockets for me?"

Ames's face paled a little. "Of course." He slowly turned out his trouser pockets, putting their contents on the table a handkerchief, but this one monogrammed linen, an ivory-handled pen knife, some coins.

He glanced up at Gareth. "Will that do?"

"I'm afraid not. Let's see what's in your vest."

Fear filled Ames's face. He backed off, quickly glancing around as if assessing his chances of escape. But before he could act on it, Gareth had pinned him against the wall and quickly patted his vest pockets.

Gareth's fingers stilled; then he reached inside the unbuttoned vest and pulled out the sapphire and diamond necklace.

"I suppose you have an explanation for this?"

All the bluster had left Ellis. He and Randall stood silently, their mouths thinned, as Gareth handed the pendant to Shannon.

Ames glared at Gareth. "Do you mind unhanding me?"

"I'm afraid I do. Clare, get me some rope to keep these three 'gentlemen' secured until I can send Josh for the sheriff."

"That won't be necessary," Randall said quickly. "Surely, you don't intend to press charges against members of your own family!"

Yes, this was an awkward situation, Shannon thought, watching Gareth give Randall another straight look.

"Do you have a satisfactory explanation for your brother's possession of the necklace?"

"Of course! Ames only borrowed it—just as your sister admitted she did. He had every intention of returning it."

"Is that right, Ames?" Gareth asked. "Were you just carrying the necklace around because you liked the feel of it in your pocket?"

Ames jerked his arms in a futile attempt to free himself. The mask of civility was wiped from his face, leaving a sullen, almost feral expression.

"Yes," he mumbled. "Naturally."

"Why do I have a hard time believing that? A very hard time."

"I'm not going to any jail!" Ames cried, futilely struggling again. "Do something," he said to his father. "Don't let them treat me like this!"

Ellis backed away from his younger son, an expression of shocked horror on his face. "I wash my hands of you. To think that a son of mine could be a thief!"

To Shannon, these new actions from Ellis were as fake as his earlier ones.

"You aren't a bit surprised that Ames took the necklace," she said, unable to stay quiet. "You're all in this together, and now you're ready to throw your son to the wolves to get out of it yourself!"

Ellis glared at her. "How dare you accuse me! I knew nothing about this."

Confusion swept over Shannon. This last statement rang with truth. None of this made sense . . . unless. . . .

"Maybe you didn't know about the necklace, but Ames has done it before, hasn't he? That's why this didn't surprise you."

Satisfaction filled her as she saw the truth of her accusation in his eyes, saw his face change despite his attempts to pretend not to understand.

"I have no idea what you're talking about, Miss Shannon. My family has always held a position of the highest respectability in our community. I would never harbor a thief to my bosom!"

An animallike snarl came from Ames. "If you think I'm going to jail and you're getting out of this scot-free, you're wrong as hell."

He jerked his head up to look at Gareth. "He's fooled the lot of you. We don't have a lot of money. That was just an act to wear you down so you'd sell this farm to him. That talk of building a mansion, all of us living here together, was all lies! He was going to sell the farm as soon as he got his hands on it—then buy another and so on."

Shannon heard Clare gasp behind her.

Ellis raised his arm and savagely backhanded Ames across the face. His son staggered and would have fallen if Gareth hadn't still been holding him.

"You stupid fool! Couldn't keep your sticky fingers to yourself, could you? Another week and Colby would have sold this place to me for a third of its worth. And on my terms, too."

"Father! Control yourself." Randall stepped up behind

the older man and held his arms in much the same grip as Gareth still held his brother.

Ellis turned his red-faced glare on his older son. "Everything's ruined!"

He tried to hit Ames again, but Randall stopped him.

Ellis sagged suddenly, his fight gone. "And all because your brother has never been able to keep his fingers off things that don't belong to him. I should have left him in Maryland."

"But then, Father, you wouldn't have had me to pretend to court Clare while you convinced Gareth he'd never be able to hold on to his farm," Ames said coldly.

Clare gasped, her hand flying to her mouth. "You . . . you cad! How could you?"

Ames gave her a sour look. "It wasn't all that hard. You're pretty enough, even if you are a silly, foolish girl. But having to go so far as to pretend I wanted to marry you was a bit too much."

Gareth scowled and pushed Ames against the wall again. "That's enough out of you. You're in enough trouble. You'd better shut up."

Clare burst into tears and headed toward the kitchen.

Gwenny started after Clare, but Maud stopped her. "Leave her alone. She'll be all right. She has to come to terms with her own part in all this."

Maud's firm, sure voice made Gwenny turn to her with a surprised, respectful look. In a moment Gwenny gave Randall a glance as straight as Gareth's had been.

"I suppose that's what you were trying to do with me and Shannon?"

Randall had the grace to look shamefaced. He shrugged. "We were trying to make Gareth believe we'd be one big, happy family if he sold to Father."

"Did you think me such a fool?" Gareth asked, his face and voice hard. "If I don't press charges, what's to keep you from lying, stealing and tricking another family in the valley?"

Ellis's mouth twisted. "Lack of money. I planned to offer

you a very small down payment and low yearly installments."

Gareth's expression changed to amazement. "You actually believed I'd accept, my family would accept, such terms?"

"You seemed to be getting closer to it. And none of your family was objecting to the idea of selling."

"We'd *never* have sold!" Gwenny said.

"No, never," Maud echoed.

Gareth gave them a surprised but grateful look. "We should have talked this over long before."

His lip curled as he turned back to Ellis. "I feel sorry for your family, having such men as you three to depend on."

He paused, then went on. "You and your sons get your things together and get out of here. Out of the Valley. None of our friends and neighbors will be taken in by your schemes."

Shannon watched the unfolding scene with stunned disbelief. Absently, she rubbed the necklace she held curved into one palm. Her flesh had warmed the stones, just as it had that other time, when her mother had given it to her. . . .

A hazy picture began forming in her mind. Her mother was lying in a big bed, with a high, carved headboard.

Her face was white and bloodless. She was dying. As hard as Shannon tried to deny this, she knew she had to accept it. Because her mother needed to talk to her.

"Your stepfather is a good man, honey. He'll treat you kindly, as your own father did. Obey him as if you were his daughter, as indeed he thinks of you. You'll always have a home with him."

Her mother took the pendant from around her nec and laid it in Shannon's palm. "As you know, this belonge to my great-grandmother. It's always been passed down t the eldest daughter."

She smiled wanly. "Since you're the only daughte there'll be no one to dispute your claim or covet it . . .'

No, don't go, please, Mama, don't go . . .

But the picture faded away into the mists of her lost past.

A huge faceless man, wearing a gray jacket and dark trousers, took its place. Fear gripped Shannon, weakening her knees. His upraised hand, as always, held the knife, dripping blood.

A scream rose from deep inside Shannon, and only by the greatest effort of will could she keep it from erupting into this equally horrible scene.

No, not *equally* horrible. Nothing could compare to the vision of the knife-bearing man. And she'd found out something else this time.

He not only wanted her; he wanted the necklace.

He coveted it with an intensity that sent shivers of fear through her.

She must not carry it on her person. Because if—*when*—he found her, he wouldn't kill her until he'd found the pendant.

Sickness invaded her. She had to get out of here! "Excuse me," she muttered.

Clamping a hand over her mouth Shannon ran from the hall, and the house.

Chapter Seventeen

"I'm glad you decided not to run away," Josh said, his voice relieved. He threw another forkful of soiled straw on the heap outside the stall.

Shannon lifted her head from Sugar's warm flank and forced a smile. "I didn't have a very good plan worked out."

"You didn't have *any* kind of plan. Don't you know how dangerous it would be for you to take off like that?"

No more dangerous than staying here and waiting for someone to come after me, dreading the day he finds me. Maybe tells me something I don't want to know about myself.

Before he kills me.

"Yes, of course," she said aloud.

"Since you say your mind won't let you do it, you've got to let me tell Mr. Colby about the man who's after you."

Shannon sighed, returning to her milking. "Please don't start haranguing me about that again."

"I'm not haranguing," Josh said doggedly. "I'm just trying to talk some sense into you."

What was sense? She hardly knew anymore.

Ellis and his sons had taken their hurried departure a

few days ago. It was a wonderful relief, everyone said, to have them gone.

Of course it was. For some reason the whole family seemed to have taken fresh heart about the prospects of being able to keep the farm, despite the raised taxes and the continued drought.

But Clare moped around the house, her normal high spirits gone, only speaking when asked a direct question.

She'd apologized profusely to Shannon, in private, for taking the necklace. Shannon didn't think that small peccadillo was the cause of her gloom.

No, it must have to do with Ames, and how taken in she'd been by him. More to the point—it had caused a serious rift between her and Josh.

"I haven't seen you talking to Clare lately," Shannon ventured.

Silence greeted her remark. She glanced over at Josh. He pitched a forkful of straw with unnecessary force, a dark scowl on his face.

"Josh?" she questioned again.

"I don't want to talk about Clare! She's proved to me how little her promises mean. She's a heartless flirt!"

Shannon continued milking, trying to think what to tell him. "Clare *is* a flirt," she finally said. "But I don't think she's heartless. She—she just hasn't grown up yet. Give her time."

"I'm tired of giving her time! She's no child. Look how she acted when she thought you were a lad—and then with that, that *Ames*. I'm finished with her. She can go flirt with all the men in Page County for all I care."

"I believe she's very sorry for—"

Shannon broke off at a sound from the doorway. She turned to see Gareth standing there. Just the sight of him sent awareness all through her body. His handsome face looked very serious.

Foreboding hit Shannon when his gaze focused on her.

"I just got back from Luray. The storekeeper told me

man was in there a few weeks ago asking about a young woman. The description sounded like you."

She swallowed a sudden lump in her throat.

Did every crisis have to happen in this barn? Thank God she'd already milked Rosie. Shannon finished stripping Sugar with a few deft movements. She got up, moved the stool aside, then again faced Gareth.

She didn't dare face the other, forbidden feelings crowding up in her, clamoring for recognition. How she wanted to push back that lock of black hair that was forever falling down on Gareth's forehead. How she wanted to feel his arms around her again, his warm mouth covering her own. . . .

His expression had deepened from serious to grim.

"He also left posters at a few places around town, with a drawing of the woman and an address where he could be reached if anyone had information. Do you remember anything about a heavyset, dark-haired man in his forties?

Posters! Fear slammed into her, taking her breath away. Oh, God! Right this minute, he could know she was here, be watching her. . . .

Be watching *all* of them.

She had to make some kind of response. "I—I don't know anything about that. Who it is, or why he'd be looking for me."

Shannon avoided Josh's accusing stare at her evasive answer. "Did you see one of the posters?"

"No. Orville said it offered a reward, and the ones around town have already disappeared."

A reward. The fear twisted a knot in her stomach. Why hadn't she thought of this? It was the obvious thing for the man to do.

"Did the storekeeper remember the name and address on the posters?"

Josh's voice startled her, gave her momentary hope.

Gareth shook his head. "No." He took a deep breath, then let it out. "Orville didn't like the man's looks. I just wish he'd thought to get the name and address."

Gareth's gray gaze, steely now, bored into hers, probing, questioning.

Shannon forced her own gaze to remain steady, although her knees were trembling, and she felt as if her whole body would start shaking any second.

Was she still forbidden to tell Gareth about her visions of the knife-wielding man? Or would her mind now allow it?

Instantly, her throat closed, just as it had that other time. She couldn't swallow and felt as if she could barely breathe.

Desperately, she fought the panic surging through her. She couldn't fight this. She had to go along with her mind's dictates, no matter how much she wanted to tell Gareth.

"I have no idea why someone would search for me," she said again, hoping he didn't pick up on her panic. "None of my memory flashes have told me anything like this."

That was the truth—just not all of it. But all she was allowed to tell him.

God, if only she *did* know the answer to that question, knew all the other hidden things about her past still locked somewhere in her memory!

Gareth's gaze stayed locked with hers for more endless seconds. Finally, he lowered it. "All right. I believe you."

And he did. Her last statement had held the sharp ring of truth. But under that layer had been another, as if the truth were concealing something else. . . .

He believed she didn't know who the man was or why he was searching for her. But she feared him. That was evident from her heightened color, the unsteady note in her voice.

As he'd thought from the first time he saw her, Shannon still withheld something. He cursed silently, wishing he knew what it was, why she was doing it.

Another kind of awareness insisted on presenting itself. The unusual pinkness in Shannon's cheeks made her even more appealing, made him want to cross the few feet between them and take her into his arms, kiss away the fears that haunted her.

Gareth fisted his hands, held his feet tight to the barn floor. He wouldn't do either of those things—and not only because Josh was present. He'd leave her alone, as she'd begged him to do only a week or so ago in this very barn.

But he wouldn't allow this situation to continue with nothing done about it.

"I know I promised not to take you to the sheriff for a while—to give your memory a chance to return. But this has changed things. We have to go tomorrow and tell him about this man."

Shannon's face paled even more as she stared at him. "All right," she finally said, an odd, almost rusty tone to her voice.

Her quick agreement surprised him. He'd been ready to insist. "Good. We'll leave early in the morning."

"All right," she said again.

He frowned, something about her manner bothering him despite her unexpected capitulation. Telling himself not to be an idiot, he turned and left.

Shannon stood still for long seconds after Gareth disappeared from view, willing her heartbeat to slow, her knees to stop their shaking.

"Why didn't you tell him the truth?" Josh demanded angrily. "I almost did. I didn't think I could stop myself."

"I did," she countered. "I *don't* know why that man is after me."

"Yes, but you know he wants to kill you! You know you're in danger!"

Yes, she knew that. She also knew she had to get out of here. Before Gareth took her to the sheriff tomorrow.

Before her unknown past brought danger down on this household. Now that the man offered a reward, it made that possibility much more likely.

Turning to Josh, she forced another smile. "I tried to tell him, but just like before my throat closed. I couldn't even swallow."

He gave her a fierce frown. "Then you should have let me! Let me go after him and tell him now."

She shook her head. "Think about it, Josh. What can I say that he hasn't already found out—except that the man I see in the flashes has a knife."

"That changes everything and you know it! Let me—"

She forced a smile. "No, Josh. I—I'll take care of all this very soon. Remember, Gareth plans to take me to the sheriff tomorrow."

And tomorrow she'd be gone, but she couldn't tell Josh that or he'd try to stop her. At the least she knew he'd tell Gareth what she planned to do.

His face cleared. "So you're going to be sensible and not balk at it tomorrow?"

"No, Josh, I won't balk at it tomorrow," she assured him.

I'll be out of here tonight, so that this household can get back to its normal life and forget I was here, disrupting everything.

Sadness mingled with her fear. She could never forget this place, though. She could never forget Gareth. Shannon pushed down the reminder that it was possible she carried a part of Gareth inside her this very minute.

She couldn't worry about that fear now. She had to deal with far more urgent ones.

Exhausted and chilled to the bone, Shannon trudged along the side of the country road. The bundle of cloth-wrapped food tied to the suspenders that held up the shabby trousers she wore felt heavier with every minute that passed, every foot of ground she covered.

Clouds intermittently covered the moon, making the night dark most of the time. She shivered and sneezed. The late September night had turned unexpectedly cold. She hoped she didn't also come down with a head cold or worse before she reached her destination.

Her destination.

Where was that going to be? She'd walked for hours and

reckoned she must be nearly to Luray. She'd slip through the town before dawn and hide in some woods beyond, sleeping during the day.

Then what? She would run out of food in another day or two. She had no money. The sapphire and diamond necklace weighing down her food bundle was her only possession of value.

She swallowed the lump that rose in her throat at the thought of giving up the necklace. Survival. That was what she had to concentrate on now. She'd have to stop in some town to try to barter. Maybe she should do that in Luray. . . .

No, she dismissed the idea. It was too close to the Colby farm, and she might very well be recognized from the posters. She couldn't chance it.

Where was the next town? She couldn't remember. And where in *any* small town could she hope to dispose of the jewel without questions?

Another, scarier thought struck her. Probably the man she feared had given out the posters in *all* the towns in the area.

What if there were no safe places?

She quickly buried that thought before she could dwell on it. She sneezed again. Why hadn't she planned this more carefully before she left? Because she hadn't had time, she answered herself.

This evening had been so awful!

The women had talked about the man who had left the posters. As Gareth had, they had asked her if she remembered anything about him, or why he wanted to find her. Again she'd dissembled, unable to look anyone in the face, knowing she'd have to slip out after everyone was asleep, knowing she'd never see any of them again.

Knowing she'd never see *Gareth* again.

He'd spent the evening in the barn, mending harnesses. She'd been torn between relief she didn't have to face him and longing to be in the same room with him this last evening.

Bedtime had been the hardest. Saying good nights to

everyone which were really goodbyes. Telling Gareth she'd be ready to go to the sheriff with him early the next morning.

Then, changing into the trousers and shirt she'd worn before her masquerade was discovered, slipping out of her room and down to the kitchen where she packed corn bread and a slab of ham into her pack.

She'd had a bad moment when Duke insisted on coming with her. She'd led him around the house and distracted him with a broken-off chunk of the ham, then run out of the yard and toward the road. . . .

Shannon was jolted out of her musings by a noise behind her on the road and stopped to listen.

Horse's hooves.

Alarm went through her. So far she'd had the road to herself. Could this be Gareth hunting for her?

Of course not, she assured herself. There was no reason to think he'd already discovered her absence. He hadn't come into her attic room since that one time, all those weeks ago.

No, it was undoubtedly only another night traveler. She'd better get out of sight, though. Whoever it was might very well stop and ask if she needed help, or even offer a ride.

Shannon slipped into the bushes along the road, finding one big enough to conceal herself behind—or at least mostly.

The clipping of the hooves drew nearer, and she held her breath as the moon came out from behind the clouds, weakly illuminating the landscape.

How well was she concealed?

The horse and rider approached her hiding place, then were past in a flurry of hooves. Shannon stared after them, but another cloud covered the moon and blotted out the terrain. She waited and listened as the sounds grew fainter in the distance, then ended.

She crawled out from behind the bush and onto the road again, knowing she should feel relieved that she'd remained undiscovered. But she was too tired to feel anything that positive.

The bag at her waist dragged downward, making her side ache. She was so tired and sleepy. Maybe she should stop and find a comfortable spot in the woods now, instead of waiting until dawn.

Comfortable? Where would that be? On the ground under a tree? Perhaps she could find a bed of moss . . . that wouldn't be too bad. . . .

Without warning, a tall figure loomed up on the road ahead of her, a darker shadow among the shadows. She stopped dead, her heart slamming against her ribs.

For a terror-filled moment, she was sure it was the man from her nightmare visions.

"Shannon! My God, is that you?"

Gareth's worried, angry voice erupted into the dark night. Her heart slammed again, and now she couldn't deny the relief she felt, even as she turned and made a dive for the woods.

"Come back here, you little idiot!" he shouted as he came crashing along through the underbrush in pursuit.

It was very dark in the woods, and more than once she encountered fallen branches and nearly fell. But she couldn't stop now. She'd entangled Gareth and his family in a maze of danger, and she wouldn't let it go any farther.

But how much farther could she go? Gareth had to be gaining on her. He was much taller and his stride was longer. It was getting harder to draw in breaths, and a sharp pain stabbed at her side with each running step she took.

Then a huge tree rose up straight ahead, its outline barely discernible in the darkness. Shannon dodged around it, the pain in her side making her stagger, almost bringing her to her knees.

Before she could regain her balance, her foot tangled in a vine, and she sprawled on the forest floor, the breath knocked out of her.

Gareth came down beside her, his heavy leg pinning

her to the ground. She struggled wildly for a few moments, then realized its uselessness. Gareth was so much bigger and stronger it was like fighting with the tree she'd almost run into.

Finally, she lay still, offering no more resistance.

Gripping her arm, Gareth gave a satisfied grunt. "About time you settled down, you little wildcat. What in hell do you think you're doing out here?"

He relaxed his grip but didn't let go. She rolled over and sat up. His big form was still only a darker shadow in the woods' darkness.

"What does it look like? I'm . . . leaving."

No, she wouldn't say running away. She wasn't doing that. She was trying to remove herself from their household. "I've caused you and your family enough trouble."

He snorted. "So your solution is to steal out in the middle of the night without a word to anyone?"

"How did you know I was gone?" she asked instead of answering.

"Duke's whining woke me, and when I came down and opened the door, he ran in and straight up to your room and scratched on the door. When I opened it you . . . weren't there."

He reached out and grabbed her shoulders and gave her a little shake.

"Why did you do this? Don't try to make me believe it's just because you've caused us trouble. You're still keeping secrets. I know you're afraid of something . . . the man who's looking for you?"

She tensed, trying to gather her defenses, to think of something to say that would allay his suspicions. And found she couldn't. The long, wearying night, added to the fear and tension she'd been under all these months, finally overwhelmed her.

I can't go on like this any longer. I have to tell him, she told her mind. She waited to be forbidden, for her throat to close, for the whole terrifying sequence.

Nothing happened. Cautiously, she tried to swallow, and

was able to. Had her mind, as well as her body and emotions, reached its limit, too? Was she at last to be allowed to reveal this final secret?

Lifting her head, she faced Gareth's dim outline. "Yes," she said rapidly. "I *am* afraid of that man. I—I'm certain he plans to kill me. I've had memory flashes about him coming after me with a knife."

The moment the last words were out of her mouth, exquisite relief filled her, and she slumped against his broad chest.

It felt so good. She could stay here forever, listening to Gareth's strong and steady heartbeat, feeling his arms holding her protectively close.

"You little fool," Gareth growled. Her admission stunned him; then he wondered why. Orville hadn't liked the man's looks, and Shannon's fear had been plain when he'd told her about the posters.

But still, he hadn't thought she was running for her life. . . .

And this was a secret she hadn't needed to keep. Anger overrode the pleasure brought by having her in his arms. "Why didn't you tell any of us about this? Didn't you trust us?"

He felt her take a quick breath. "Yes, I trusted you. It had nothing to do with that. My . . . mind wouldn't let me tell you until a moment ago."

Gareth frowned. "Why was that?"

She grimaced. "It kept warning me you'd insist on going to the sheriff to try to find out who the man was. And you did—just tonight."

He felt like shaking her. "Naturally. That's only sensible. I've wanted to take you to the sheriff since I found out about your amnesia."

His conscience gave him a nudge, reminding him he *had* gone to the sheriff. And found out nothing. But he had something to go on now.

She pulled back, tried to free herself, but Gareth kept his grip tight. He'd have no more wild chases tonight.

"I . . . can't do that. Something inside is still telling me not to."

He heard the real fear in her voice, but had to continue. "Maybe you should be wondering if your mind is steering you wrong. Do you think running away was a good solution?"

"Maybe not for me, but if I'm gone, it will keep your family from whatever danger I may be in."

He didn't like how she'd phrased that, and he knew what it meant. She hadn't given up her plan to leave the farm.

"How can you be sure that man wants to kill you?"

"How can I be *sure* of anything? The man with the bloody knife was the first and the strongest memory flash. I . . . feel it must be real and true."

Beneath his hands, her slender arms were trembling with cold and fatigue. They couldn't keep on crouching like animals in these woods.

No, because if they did, in another few moments he'd pull Shannon into his arms and kiss her.

And then kiss her again . . . do more than kiss. And she'd be just as ardent, just as eager, as he. The heat that thought generated in his body got him to his feet.

He pulled her up with him. "We're going home. Can I trust you not to try to run away again if I let go?"

He heard her shaky laugh. "I'm too tired to run anywhere. And I wouldn't have told you all that if I still planned to leave . . . now . . . *if* you promise me something."

Gareth had a premonition he wouldn't like what she was going to say. "What?" he asked, his tension growing.

"That you won't go to the sheriff and tell him any of this. That you won't insist on taking me."

Heaving a sigh, he said, "I can't promise you that."

She sighed, too. "Then I can't promise you I won't leave again tomorrow night or the next."

His hands had released her. Now he instinctively reached for her again. This time he did give her a little shake.

knowing his action was a blend of exasperation and a burning need to touch her.

"I've never seen such an obstinate woman in my life! Don't you have any common sense?"

"Yes! Plenty. I didn't say I wouldn't try to find out who the man is. I just don't want *him* to discover me first. Surely, you can understand that. Now, let go of me! You're hurting my arms."

Gareth dropped his hands, and they made their way back to the road. He thought about what she'd just said, grudgingly admitting it had a certain kind of logic.

"All right, I'll agree to what you want—for a little while. But only because I have to get some sleep, not stay awake every night wondering if you're going to try running away again."

"I'm a woman who always keeps her word," she said, then paused. He saw her shadow move as she looked up at him. "Or anyway, I think I am . . . and was—when it's possible."

A sudden flash of insight hit him, and he understood the bitter, unsure note in her voice. He reached out, found her cheek and stroked his fingers down it.

Her skin, although cold, felt satin smooth. A strong urge hit him to gather her into his arms and carry her back to the oak whose dubious shelter they had just left and make love to her the remainder of this nearly finished night.

"You've been going through hell," he said softly. "But now that you've told me this, we have to make certain you don't have family. Someone else who's looking for you."

Her laugh was as bitter as her words a minute ago. "I'm not holding out on anything else. I know I just said I couldn't be sure of anything—but I have no family left, I'm sure of that."

The silence stretched out as they gained the road, and Gareth led her to where he'd tied his horse and helped her on. He got up in front of her, and she slipped her hands around his waist, pulling herself against him to keep from falling.

"As you know, there *is* someone looking for me," she finally said, her voice a whisper of weariness. "But he's not family and I can't let him find me."

All the questions and doubts fell away, and Gareth realized on this point she'd convinced him of the danger she was in.

"*I* won't let him find you," he promised, and felt her relax fractionally at the forceful tone of his voice, his changing of her "I" to mean himself.

Surprise snaked through his tired body and mind. Somehow, he'd let this girl-woman get under his defenses. He'd let her come to mean something to him, something deeper than the strong physical pull between them.

Was it possible that he could come to love this woman?

As he'd once loved Dorinda?

Cold not due to the chilly night washed over him at that unwelcome thought. He didn't want any duplication of how he'd felt then. How devastated he'd been when she'd rejected him.

He'd lived near Dorinda all his life. He'd thought he knew her as well as he knew himself. But obviously he hadn't known her at all.

So how on earth could he believe that he knew Shannon, this sprite who had come into his life so stormily only a few months ago?

He couldn't. She'd proved that tonight when she'd run away without a word. He'd had no inkling she planned anything so drastic.

He knew nothing about how she thought, how she felt. Hell, she didn't even know herself, or who she really was. This wasn't a woman he needed to get involved with. Not at all.

Aren't you forgetting something? his mind asked him. *You're already involved with her in the most intimate way. If she's carrying your child. . . .*

A small cold lump settled in his stomach. If that did turn out to be the case, then of course he'd do the honorable thing and marry her.

But that would be as far as it went, he promised himself. Their physical cravings for each other were too strong for him to convince himself they wouldn't share a bed in every sense of the word.

But that's all they would share.

His deepest feelings, his heart, were still locked safely away where no woman could ever again hurt them.

And that's where they would stay.

Chapter Eighteen

Gareth hadn't bothered with a saddle, only a blanket, and the horse's back was hard and bony. Shannon felt every jolt all the way to her cold feet. The moon kept on playing hide and go seek with the clouds, making it difficult to stay on the road.

Her hands, tightly grasping Gareth's middle, didn't seem to feel the chill. Neither did her torso, also pressed snugly against his broad back. No, all those portions of her anatomy were comfortably warm.

Comfortably? No, that wasn't the word to describe her feelings. She was most decidedly uncomfortable, and not only because of her weary state and the horse's bony back.

From her nipples to the pit of her stomach to where her thighs began, Shannon tingled most disturbingly. She squirmed, trying to move herself back while at the same time keeping her secure grip around Gareth's waist.

It didn't work, and she felt herself slipping sideways. For a moment she thought she was going to slide onto the ground.

Gareth abruptly reined in the horse. "What's the problem? Do you want to change positions?"

Change positions? "What do you mean?"

He huffed out a tired sigh. "Get in front of me. Let me hold on to you."

Her mind provided a vivid picture of Gareth pressed snugly against her bottom, and her body reacted to that vision by developing a throb in its nether regions.

"No!" she said quickly. "I'm fine. I just slipped a little. I'll be more careful."

"See that you do," he said gruffly. "We've had enough trouble for one night."

Embarrassment washed over Shannon.

She straightened, lifting her chin and pressing her lips together, relieved he hadn't realized her true problem.

But gradually, as before, she had to relax her posture. Finally the long day and night caught up with her, and she nodded, her head falling against Gareth's back.

A dog's excited bark jolted her awake.

"Hush, Duke, don't wake up the whole family," Gareth admonished.

Thank God they were home!

Home. The thought jolted her even more than the horse had. An intense longing for that to be true swept over her. This place had been a haven for her. But it wasn't her home. It could never be that.

Gareth quickly dismounted and helped her down. She swayed on her feet, touched by Duke's eager whines and licks of greeting. Gareth gave her a look made up of exhaustion, irritation and concern.

"Go on inside. I have to tend to Molly."

"All right," she said, still stung by his earlier words, determined to cause him no more trouble this night.

"Build up the hearth fire. There's plenty of wood inside."

"All right," she said again, managed a smile and after patting Duke went inside, while Gareth walked Molly to the barn.

She paused just inside the door, listening. All was quiet

she noted with relief. Evidently Duke's barking hadn't roused the household.

The kitchen seemed to fold welcoming arms around her. The hearth fire's coals still glowed, but needed replenishment. She saw that Gareth had not only left a fire burning, but also brought down her nightdress, robe, and a quilt, hastily tumbled onto a chair.

He'd been very sure he'd be bringing her back here tonight.

Annoyance at his arrogance warred with the warm feeling that thought gave her. The annoyance won. He didn't want her because he cared for her. He only felt responsibility toward her because of what had happened between them. He'd do a similar thing for his sisters or mother, out of simple kindness.

Now that she no longer had Gareth's body warmth, she shook from cold. After putting another log on the fire, she peeled off her clothes with trembling hands and left them in a heap on the hearthstones. She fumbled into the nightdress and robe, drew the quilt around her, and pulled up a chair before the fire.

She couldn't seem to lose the deep chill. She was still shivering when Gareth came back into the house and walked over to her.

He gave her a frowning, concerned glance. "You've got to get warm. You'll get pneumonia."

"It's not the time of year for that," she told him, striving for a light tone, but her voice came out quivery, just like the rest of her felt.

"It could be."

Gareth added a second log to the fire and stirred it with the poker, sending up a shower of sparks and a flare of heat.

His nearness created its usual havoc inside her.

"Feel any better?"

Not looking at him, Shannon nodded, although that wasn't true. She was warmer. But it was heat caused by Gareth's closeness. . . .

He didn't move away, and at last she had to glance up. His eyes were a soft shade of gray tonight, and when their glances met, neither seemed able to look away.

"Your face is flushed," he finally said. He leaned over her, placing his palm against her forehead, reminding her of when he'd had the fever and she'd done this same thing to him. His palm, rough and callused from heavy farm work, felt wonderful against her skin.

"You may have a fever," he finally said, taking his hand away. "I'm no expert at this. I'd better wake Mama."

"No! Don't do that. I'm not sick." She forced a sureness into her voice she didn't feel. "I'm just cold."

He stood still, watching her, and she saw his gaze was on her neck . . . or farther down. Instinctively, she moved her hand to that area, discovering the quilt had slipped.

She also discovered something else. She'd neglected to fasten the top buttons of her nightdress, and it was gaping open.

Did he think she'd done that on purpose to tempt him? She felt herself reddening as she fumbled with the buttons.

"No wonder," he said gruffly, pulling the quilt up around her again before she could finish. His fingers grazed her throat, and she felt a flare of heat from that small contact. His hand stayed where it was, the curve of his knuckles against her throbbing pulse.

Neither moved or spoke for what seemed interminable moments. Pictures formed in Shannon's mind's eye, both memories and wishes of what could be between them . . if only things were different.

"Shannon," he finally said, his voice husky with desire just as it had been those other times. . . .

Like those other times, she found herself unable to resist the call in that one word, that soft saying of her name. . .

She lifted her head, knowing what she'd see in his eyes knowing what he must see in her own. Her lips parted involuntarily as she looked at his firm mouth, remembered the ardent pleasure they had found together.

Gareth groaned and sank to his knees beside her chair

He slid his hand around her neck and buried his face in her breasts.

His face was burning hot, but she didn't think it was from fever. Not this time. Gareth's mouth found her bare skin, his lips moved across it, and the flare of heat spread within her.

She drew a shaky breath, knowing she should stop him before this went any farther. Also knowing she wouldn't do that. She wanted this as much as he, despite her brain's reminder that she yearned for more than a physical joining.

And Gareth did not.

But that didn't matter now, here beside this crackling fire, deep in this strange, endless night. All that mattered was touching and being touched, recreating those wonderful feelings. . . .

"Gareth." She breathed his name, her voice only a whisper of sound. She shrugged off the quilt, freed her arms to go around him, held him tightly to her.

He pulled her sideways in the chair, the quilt slipping farther down. He found her mouth, and his own closed over it, taking possession, as if she truly belonged to him.

Her trembling now wasn't from cold. No, that had gone with the quilt, replaced by this all-enveloping heat that increased by the moment.

His lips moved over hers, in that remembered, familiar way, and she tentatively touched her tongue to his, curling it against his, her movements innocently seductive, at once as if she'd never touched him before, and as if they had done this a thousand times.

He groaned against her mouth, and his fingers fumbled with the buttons, loosening her nightdress, pulling it apart. The first touch of his lips on her nipple made her gasp with pleasure. While his mouth covered it, his tongue made slow, circling movements that inflamed her senses with delight.

Gareth left the first breast to find the other and dispense the same intoxicating pleasure. He lifted his head for a moment, and she could see the same passion on his face that must be on hers.

"Shannon, we need to move," he said, "there isn't room here—"

"The back stairway door creaked open, and both of them froze. Footsteps came down the last steps and into the kitchen.

"I thought I heard someone down here," Maud's anxious voice said. "What's wrong?"

For an instant they stared at each other, heated desire fading into startled shock at their predicament. Gareth recovered first. He swiftly pulled the fallen quilt back up, tucking it around Shannon's neck, then rose to face his mother.

"Everything's all right," he said, and Shannon marveled at how normal his voice sounded, only a bit rough-edged. But then, he didn't have as much to recover from as she.

Only physical wanting.

While she had to come down from that high cloud of not only wanting Gareth, but of loving him.

"Is that Shannon?" Maud asked. "What happened—did she take sick?"

"No, she just got a bit cold."

"Cold? How could she get cold? What has happened?" Maud asked again, her voice anxious, walking across to them.

Gareth's gaze met Shannon's. His jaw was set, revealing his discomfiture, but his eyes also held a question. Did she want to tell his mother what she'd told him earlier tonight—or did she want him to?

If there was a trace of something else in his look, regret maybe, she ignored it. She nodded, giving him leave to go ahead.

"Mama, Shannon is sure the man who put out the posters means to harm her. Her memory flashes have told her that."

Thank God he'd been so vague and hadn't told his

mother the man carried a knife he wanted to bury to its hilt in Shannon's body.

Shannon suppressed a shudder and glanced at the other woman. Maud's distressed look had deepened.

"So that's what's been troubling you all this while, child. I knew something was." Maud glanced at the sodden heap of clothes still on the hearth, then back at Shannon.

"Why were you running away from us?"

Guilt hit Shannon at the other woman's hurt tone. "I— I was afraid I'd bring danger to your family. After all you've done for me, I couldn't bear to take that chance."

"Shannon doesn't want the authorities involved. That's why she didn't tell us before."

Gareth's accepting words and tone surprised Shannon. He seemed at last to be truly willing to go along with her wishes.

"You thought he would track you here." Maud nodded, as if fully understanding Shannon's thought processes.

Maud smiled at both of them. "I'm going to build up the kitchen fire and make a pot of tea."

Tea. That would be so good! Shannon turned away from Gareth and leaned her head back against the chair. She felt much better. Her chill hadn't returned after Gareth left her. No, how could it? He'd raised her temperature, heated her body in only a few minutes.

She wouldn't think of that. She would turn it off, just as Gareth seemed to be so easily capable of doing. There were other things she had to worry about.

Other things she had to do.

Shannon lifted her head again to find Gareth's eyes on her.

"I'll go to Luray tomorrow and ask around," he said. "I should be able to locate one of the posters."

Shannon sucked in her breath at his unexpected words. Maybe by tomorrow evening she'd know the name of the man who hunted her, and where he lived. Surely, that knowledge would trigger her memory so that all the missing pieces of her life would fall into place.

Maybe she'd remember what had happened to make her flee for her life. To make the man with the knife want her blood. Want her *dead*. Know if she had done something wrong.

She forced her eyes to stay steadily on his. "I'm going with you."

Her voice was as steady as her gaze, challenging him to disagree.

Gareth's jaw clenched a little tighter. He looked as if he planned to argue with her, then thought better of it. "All right. Now, I'm going to try to get some sleep."

He headed for the stairs.

"You need to get to bed, too," Maud said. "Do you want to wait until morning for the tea?"

Holding the quilt tightly around her, Shannon rose. "Yes. I've warmed up now."

Somehow, Shannon felt that Maud's gaze could see through the concealing quilt, to the nightdress unbuttoned to her waist. And knew why her chill had fled.

The knowledge didn't bother Maud a whit.

"Good night," Shannon said, hoping she wasn't blushing. "I'm sorry for causing all this upheaval. Thank you for being so understanding."

"I don't want to lose you." Maud's smile was as warm as her words. "Gareth needs you, even if he doesn't know it yet. Besides, you're part of the family now."

The words made tears prickle behind Shannon's eyelids. Clutching the quilt, she gave Maud an awkward hug, which the other woman affectionately returned.

She was a fool for doing that, a fool for letting the other woman's words make a flare of hope go through her.

Because the truth was Gareth didn't need her and never would.

Chapter Nineteen

"I still say you should have stayed home and let me do this."

Shannon glanced at Gareth, who was expertly handling the horse and buggy—his jaw set, of course. They'd had variations on this argument since they left the farm right after daybreak, and now they were nearly to Luray.

She wondered if most of it wasn't to keep both of them from remembering last night. How once again they hadn't been able to stay out of each other's arms.

And to keep that from happening again. Her mind's eye presented her with a scene of the buggy pulled off the road, under some trees, and Gareth holding her, kissing her. . . .

Quickly, she blocked out the picture, moving away from him a little on the buggy seat.

"I have to see this man for myself. I believe it's the only thing that will bring back my memory. Nothing else has."

And she was going because she couldn't bear the thought of Gareth being in danger because of her, but she couldn't tell him that.

"That's precisely what worries me most about this. In order for you to see him, he's apt to see you."

He looked over at her, his frown deepening as his glance went over her trousers and shirt, the hair she'd newly cropped last night before she'd left the farm. Her bound breasts.

At least she hadn't caught a cold from last night's adventure, Shannon mused. How could she have, with Gareth warming her so expertly there by the fire. . . .

Again she squelched those tormenting thoughts.

"Not if we're careful. He's looking for a woman, not a lad," she said again, for perhaps the dozenth time.

But was this true? *He* could have been the one who left her for dead beside the road, although that didn't seem likely since he now searched for her.

Gareth pulled alongside the mercantile and halted the horses. After tying the reins, he glanced at her. "If no one's in there, I'll come back and get my visiting *cousin.*"

She nodded at their prearranged plan. "All right."

"Remember, there's a pistol under the seat."

Shannon nodded. "I know." Gareth had showed her how to use it, and she thought she could if it was necessary. That would only happen if the man from her nightmares actually accosted her while she waited here.

Which of course was a remote possibility.

Wasn't it?

Gareth got out and went inside the old frame building. Shannon made sure she could grab the pistol if she had to, then squeezed back in the corner where she wouldn't be easily seen by any passersby.

She looked at the storefront. It brought no spark of recognition to her mind. Disappointed, she realized that neither had anything else on the way here, or the buildings they had passed in the town.

Did that mean she'd never been to this town? Or did it only indicate that like so many other things, she couldn't remember it? What if she'd lived here?

The familiar frustration built in her. Resolutely, she forced it down.

In a few moments, Gareth walked rapidly back out and opened the door.

"Come on, no one there but Orville."

Her heart in her throat, she followed him inside. This was the first time since Gareth had rescued her she'd been in a town, been anywhere away from the farm except for that one visit to the neighbors'. She felt as if unseen eyes observed her every move.

An old man stood behind the scarred wooden counter. His sharp eyes looked her over carefully. "Good morning." He extended his hand. "Orville Wister at your service."

"Good morning, Mr. Wister. I'm Shannon Brown," she said, remembering to lower her voice to approximate a young man's. "Gareth's cousin from Maryland."

"Orville, would you tell us again what that missing girl on those posters looked like? My cousin thought it sounded like a girl who's missing from around where he lives."

Shannon gritted her teeth. How she hated these lies! Last night she'd thought she was finished with the deceptions. She might as well accept the fact that until she knew who the man was, until her memory returned, they would have to use such means.

Orville frowned in recollection. "Pretty girl. Darkish hair. Believe the man said she had blue eyes."

Did Orville notice her coloring was similar to his description? Shannon hoped she looked only suitably concerned for an acquaintance. "I guess that would describe a lot of girls," she said.

Orville nodded. "Yep, 'fraid so. Was it a friend of your family's who's missing?"

Shannon swallowed. More lies. "A neighbor," she evaded. "I—wondered if the man was a relative searching for her."

"I wouldn't want a relative like him, but he said he was cousin. No, sir. Didn't like him atall. He had dark hair, swarthy skin. Big, heavy feller. Maybe in his early forties. That sound like her cousin?''

A cousin. Her stomach turned at the thought she might be related to him. But likely it was only a story to make his search seem plausible.

Frustration rose again. The description triggered nothing in her mind.

''I don't think so. This must be someone else.'' Grasping at straws, hoping this might prompt something in Orville's memory, she fabricated, ''The man I'm thinking about had a scar on his forehead.''

Orville shook his head. ''Nope. I didn't notice anything like that.''

''Well, I hope she's soon found.'' Shannon fought a losing battle with her disappointment at this dead end.

''Orville, Mama and Gwenny need a few things.'' Gareth handed a slip of paper across the counter.

This was part of their plan to provide a reason for the store visit, but Shannon wanted to be out of here. It would look odd if she left now, though. She looked around the big room with its many barrels and boxes. If anyone came in, she could conceal herself.

The storekeeper studied the list. ''Sugar, coffee, a lamp chimney and an ounce of nutmeg. Got all that. Need anything else?''

''A pound of horseshoe nails and a curry comb. Guess that's it.''

''Have all that ready in a minute.'' He bustled off to get the items.

The door opened and closed with a tinkle of its bell. Shannon stiffened, suddenly anxious despite the disguise that had fooled Gareth's family for weeks, and Orville, too, just now.

She moved so that a barrel partly blocked her from whoever had entered.

Glancing at Gareth she saw him looking her way, frowning. Then he turned toward the new arrival, his expression none too friendly.

"Hello there, Mr. Colby," an oily voice said.

A voice that sent a splinter of fear and loathing shooting down Shannon's spine. Her knees suddenly felt weak. With an effort of will she stiffened them.

Was this the man who had haunted her dreams and waking hours all these weeks?

"Good morning, *Mr.* Blakeston," Gareth said stiffly. He again glanced toward Shannon, a tiny shake of his head signaling her to remain where she was.

She heard footsteps walking across the wooden floor, and in a moment a man came into view. He stopped before the counter. Keeping herself rigidly still, Shannon gave him a sideways peek.

Bile rose in her throat as memories flooded her mind. The stoop-backed, slightly built man standing before the counter wasn't the man with the knife.

But she knew him all too well.

Absolute certainty filled her mind. She'd been walking along the road and accepted his offer of a ride in his wagon . . . where? She strained to remember, but it did no good.

He'd tried to rape her.

He was a peddler, and he'd told her to get in the back of his wagon among his wares. That's where she'd found he men's clothing, the scissors with which she'd cut her nair.

Anger filled her veins, mingling with the fear. Her hands lenched into fists, she took an involuntary half step forward before caution overtook her fury.

She couldn't have a confrontation with him now. He might well have seen the posters. And a man like him vould jump at the chance to make a hundred dollars.

"Hey, Orville!" Blakeston called toward the back of the tore, where the owner was rummaging on a shelf. "I brung whole wagon load of new goods today."

"I'll take a look at it, but you skunked me the last time ou was here. Them matches won't strike. People been ringing 'em back to me right and left."

Blakeston's chuckle was as oily as his voice. "Now, you

know how that goes. Ye can't hold me liable for all the goods I sell."

"No, but you'll take back that lot o' matches or I won't buy anything else from you."

"Course I'll make that good." Blakeston's voice was trying to be hearty, but Shannon heard the sourness in it.

Orville came back and plunked several bags and bundles down on the countertop. He frowned at Blakeston, then turned to Gareth.

"Here you are. Want me to put this on your account?"

"Yes, go ahead," Gareth said, hating to say the words. Before the war their household had run on a cash basis. But now, like most of the farmers in the Valley, they ran up accounts until the fall harvests. If crops were good, they paid them off. If not, only paid them down.

Because the taxes came first. Everyone had this yearly burden of fear hanging over their heads.

He again glanced toward Shannon, wishing he'd insiste she stay in the buggy. This man was no threat, but he wa a nosy bastard. Gareth wanted to get them outside withou attracting his attention.

Now that he knew Shannon to be female, he wondere how he and his family had ever been fooled for all thos weeks. But Orville had seemed to be completely taken i by her disguise.

Why was she standing so still, and why did a white lin bracket her mouth? Fright? Partly, he decided, but ange was mixed in with it.

At Blakeston? Did she know him? He couldn't be th man she feared. The description didn't match at all. Garet picked up his parcels and started toward the door.

Shannon sauntered over, then walked beside him. Sh was close enough the sleeve of her man's jacket brushe his own sleeve.

Just that light touch made those moments by the fi last night come to sudden life in his memory.

Half turning to close the heavy door behind him, h

saw Blakeston glancing their way; then an odd, startled expression came over the man's face.

An uneasy feeling swept over Gareth, effectively banishing the erotic memories.

"Come *on!*" Shannon urged, walking so fast he had to hurry to catch up with her.

"What's wrong? Do you know Blakeston?" Gareth got into the buggy, set his packages on the floor and clucked at the horse.

"Just *go!*" she said, her voice trembling.

With the store building dwindling from sight behind them, Gareth gave her a sideways glance. She was still rigid with strain.

"All right, tell me," he commanded.

"He's the man who offered me a ride on his wagon—and who attacked me. That was a true memory."

Gareth's hands clenched on the reins. "Damn! Why didn't you tell me? I'd have throttled the bastard."

"I'd like to see you do that—I wanted to do it myself. But this isn't the time to deal with him."

"He's a slimy, cheating son of a bitch. We should go straight to the sheriff."

"You know we can't do that now. Not until we find the man who's after me."

After a moment Gareth said, "I think Blakeston may have recognized you as we left. He looked at you like you were a ghost."

He heard her indrawn breath. "Do you think he saw one of the posters?"

Gareth knew his expression was grim. "Who knows? If so—"

"He'll contact the man," she finished, her voice flat. "What do we do now?"

Gareth fought with his anxiety and anger. "I should take you straight to the sheriff," he said again. "Tell him all of this."

"No! What good would that do? How could he protect me even if he knows everything?"

He pushed his hair back from his forehead with roug
fingers, hating to admit she was right—there was no sa
haven now.

"He couldn't," he conceded, "unless he locks you u
in a cell, and even that wouldn't satisfy me. It's not sa
at the farm, either, since Blakeston knows me and has bee
there, peddling his wares. We've got to find one of th
posters and get the name and address on it. We've got
find that man before Blakeston can. We can't take a chan
on whether he recognized you."

He paused, then went on. "There is one other thing w
could try. We could go to the sheriff and press charg
against Blakeston."

"Would that work? Would they lock him up?"

"Maybe not. To my knowledge, he's never done an
thing against the law, and the farmers and storekeepe
rely on him. It would be your word against his."

"The word of a woman with amnesia, disguised as a la
who doesn't even know her own name or where she lives

Gareth silently swore at the bleakness in her voice.

"You're right—it would be a long shot. If it failed,
Blakeston didn't recognize you at the store, he would kno
it all and would be after you."

"So we shouldn't do it."

"No, we shouldn't."

After a moment, Shannon asked, "Where are you goi
now?"

"To the tavern. I didn't go there the other day. If anyo
has a poster, it'll be Jed. He never gets rid of anythin
And this time you're staying in the buggy."

"Yes."

Fear and anxiety had extinguished her anger. Gare
wished she'd managed to hang on to it. He hated seei
her fearful.

But fear might keep her safe. Might even save her li
And Blakeston wouldn't get away with what he'd don
After they solved the mystery of the man with the kni
he'd take care of the blackguard.

When they reached the tavern at the edge of town, Gareth pulled the buggy up under a tree far enough away no one would be likely to notice Shannon sitting inside.

"I'll be right back. Don't go anywhere."

She gave him a wry smile. "Where do you think I'd go?"

His answering smile echoed hers. "I don't know, but if you had a place in mind, I have no doubt you'd leave."

Their glances locked and held. Again memories of last night filled his mind. When he'd held her in his arms, kissed her.

If his mother hadn't come downstairs, he'd have carried her up to his bed and made love to her. With no thought of the consequences, no thought of anything but how much he wanted her.

His body hardened. He silently cursed it for its senseless reactions to his erotic thoughts and went inside the tavern.

It was still too early for many patrons. One old man was slumped over a mug of beer at the end of the bar. When he asked the owner about the posters, the man's mouth turned down.

"He's the same one who was in here afore that, askin' about a young woman. *Said* it was his cousin and she'd run away from home."

"I take it you didn't believe him?" Gareth asked, making his voice sound casual.

The man shook his head. "Wouldn't have believed anything that one told me on a stack of Bibles."

So far, no one seemed to have a high opinion of the man Shannon feared. That made the likelihood of his intentions being evil all the higher.

Jed picked up a sheet of paper from the end of the bar. "This what you're talking about?"

Gareth hoped he didn't seem too eager as he accepted the sheet. A drawing of a young woman took up most of the page. The picture looked enough like Shannon that she could be recognized. The major difference was the girl in the drawing had long hair, pulled back into an abundant knot.

Had Blakeston seen this poster? If so, how long would it take him to realize he'd pushed this girl off his wagon.

And just encountered her again in Orville's store?

It was more likely he already had.

Urgency beat in Gareth's pulse, made him want to hurry out of here, push Molly as hard as he could, take Shannon somewhere she'd be safe . . . but where would that be?

No, she was right. They had to see this through. They had to find the man. And then what? Shoot him? He could do that—with the pistol stowed in the buggy. He'd love to do that. His violent feelings startled him, but he couldn't deny them.

"Seen this female, have you? Interested in the reward?"

Gareth took a deep breath, trying to calm himself. He'd do whatever it took to keep Shannon safe.

"One Hundred Dollars Reward For Information!" was printed in very dark letters under the picture, and under that was a name. *Frank Smith, General Delivery, Redmond, Virginia.*

That was a fake name if he'd ever seen one. Gareth shrugged, hoping it looked genuine.

"No, just heard people talking about it. That rewarc money would come in handy to pay the taxes, though."

He forced a grin, hoping he'd thrown the man off track and held out the poster.

The owner tilted his head. "Keep it. I've got anothe one. A hundred dollars would come in handy in a lot o ways."

Gareth's nerves tightened. Jed was a decent man. Bu he probably wouldn't hesitate to try to collect this rewar if he could.

As would any number of decent men. Or women. Ho many people here in town knew a young woman was stayin at their farm? He'd not told anyone—but they had visite the Northrups that day. They could have mentioned it. S could Josh or any one of his family.

What about Ellis and his sons?

The urgency was like a drumbeat in Gareth's blood no

"Yes, wouldn't it? Thanks, Jed." Gareth waved a casual hand and forced himself to stroll out of the tavern.

Once outside, his heart stopped for an instant. Shannon was gone. He hurried to the buggy and jerked open the door. Relief filled him when he saw her crouched low in the seat.

"What's wrong? Did someone see you?"

She straightened up. "I don't think so. I just wanted to make sure no one did."

Once again, her fear was blended with anger. She sounded annoyed as hell at having to do this. Whatever kind of life she'd lived, she'd been no shrinking violet.

Admiration for her spunk filled him, followed a moment later by a rush of compassion. What a lot she'd gone through these last months.

And it wasn't over yet.

"Did you find out anything?"

Her voice sounded dull, as if she expected no good news. He was glad to be able to give her some—even if he had doubts about the validity of the name.

"Yes." He handed her the poster, wincing as her face paled when she saw her likeness reproduced on the page.

She glanced up, her eyes steady on his. "Frank Smith. That name doesn't sound at all familiar to me."

She was trying to force her voice to be steady, too, but couldn't quite make it. Another surge of mixed admiration and sympathy hit Gareth.

He seated himself and started the horses again. "I doubt that's his real name, or that he lives in Redmond. If he plans to do you harm, he wouldn't let his identity be known."

"Yes, you're right. I hadn't thought of that. Where are we going now?"

Gareth shot her a glance, deliberately keeping his expression bland, so as not to alarm her further. "Why, to Redmond, of course. We should be able to make it by late afternoon."

"Then what?" she asked.

"Then we find the store that has the post office in it. They should be able to give us some information about him. Maybe enough to make you remember who he is."

He saw her throat move as she swallowed. "Yes. But I hate to take you away from the farm."

"A couple of days aren't going to matter. If this drought keeps up, we'll not have much in the way of fall crops anyway."

"Maybe it'll rain today. It's getting very cloudy."

"It's done this before and we didn't get a drop."

Yes, she knew that, and she couldn't think of anything else to say to reassure him.

The shock and anger of seeing the man who had attacked her hadn't worn off yet. And Gareth's suggestion that she soon might remember the identity of the man who stalked her, even before she saw him, triggered another apprehension.

She also might remember other things.

What if in reality she was a thief—or worse? What if "Frank Smith" had good reason to want to do her harm?

Her nerves were strung up so tight she sat on the edge of the buggy seat the entire way to Redmond.

That was probably a good thing, she told herself. At least it kept her mind off other matters—such as the fact she was alone with Gareth in the carriage. Not two feet away from him.

Was he thinking the same things? No, of course not. His attraction to her, although admittedly strong, was purely physical. She doubted if thoughts of her kept him awake nights, tormented his waking hours, as they did her.

Half an hour into their journey, a hard rain began falling.

"Thank God," Gareth said, his face momentarily lightening.

The rain slowed them down, but finally, in late afternoon, they reached the outskirts of the town. It was bigger than Luray, but not large. Few people were about because of the rain, and those who were hurried toward shelter.

Shannon turned toward Gareth. "There's not much chance of my being recognized, and nothing seems familiar to me here, either. But that could mean nothing. Where do we start searching?"

His glance met hers, his eyes that softer gray that she loved. "At the nearest general store."

"If you have no luck there?"

He smiled. "I'll ask where the post office is."

She waited while, his coat over his head, Gareth dashed through the rain inside the first store they came to. Her nerves were still strung tight; she *hated* the suspense of waiting.

Gareth was back in the buggy in five minutes, clothes damp, shaking his head.

"The post office is in Harmon's Mercantile, on the other side of town." He picked up the reins and urged the horses forward again.

"Oh." Disappointment filled her, mixed with a relief she tried to deny. She *had* to find him, but she feared it, too. And she was tired of fear. She'd had enough of it to last her a lifetime.

Gareth came back from the second store, wetter, with a different look on his face.

"You found out something."

He nodded. "Yes. A man answering the description was in earlier today. Making his every-other-day visit to pick up his mail. We missed him by a couple of hours."

The same mixed emotions again streaked through her. "Does the storekeeper know him?"

"No, and he doesn't think he lives here. If so, he's a new arrival. There are some Smiths in town, but the storekeeper doesn't think they're related. That pretty well proves he's using a false name—and doesn't live here."

Shannon let out her breath. "That means he could be named anything and live anywhere not too far away. We can't do anything more today, can we?"

"No." He gave a frustrated sigh. "We'll have to come back day after tomorrow. Early in the day. At least we know

Blakeston can't contact him before then either. So you should be safe."

"Yes," she agreed, relief filling her at his words.

"Now we have to decide where to stay. Good thing we brought a change of clothes and told Mama we might not be back tonight."

Shannon moistened her lips, another kind of tension springing to life inside her. "Yes, isn't it?"

"Molly needs a rest and so do we. We didn't get enough sleep last night."

No, they hadn't, and his words made the memory of last night's events flood over her. Resolutely, she pushed them down.

"The storekeeper recommended Johnson's boardinghouse. He said it's clean and they serve good food."

Shannon's stomach rumbled at the thought of food. The meat pie they had shared at noon seemed a long time ago.

"That's fine with me."

She gave Gareth a smile, but the thought of staying overnight with him in a boardinghouse, although of course they wouldn't share a room, made shivers slide down her spine.

"Then that's settled," Gareth said in a relieved tone.

Piqued, she realized he didn't seem to share her feelings, then tried to convince herself she should be glad.

A few minutes later, they pulled up before a big, white frame building. JOHNSON'S BOARDINGHOUSE was painted on a small sign attached to the front gate.

It looked a little shabby, but perfectly respectable, Shannon decided.

"Let's go see about rooms; then I'll take Molly and the buggy to a livery stable." Gareth picked up the small bag under the seat and again put his coat over his head.

Shannon grabbed her own jacket and put it over her head. Together they dashed through the rain up the walk onto the porch.

A sign on the front door invited them to walk in. Inside

was a wide hall, its flowered carpet worn but clean. To the left was a big sitting room; to the right, an equally large dining room, holding two long tables.

A plump, gray-haired woman, wearing an apron, came out of a room adjoining the dining room.

"You folks needin' a room out of the wet? My, this rain is some welcome, ain't it?" she asked, her round face beaming.

"Yes, it is and we are, just for the night," Gareth answered. "In fact, my brother and I need—"

"You're in luck," she interrupted. "Got one room left. It ain't very big, but it's clean and the bed's comfortable."

Shannon froze. Oh, lord. Of course the woman would think sharing a room would be no problem.

But the thought of leaving here, going back out into the pouring rain and the gathering dusk trying to find another place to stay, daunted her.

She was so tired. Besides, another place would think it strange if they didn't share a room. She shot a look at Gareth. The expression on his face mirrored her feelings.

One of them could sleep on the floor. There must be extra bedding in the room. They could work out something. She gave Gareth a nod. "That sounds all right to me."

"Me, too." He looked relieved, but surprised at her quick acceptance of the situation.

"You folks come along with me and I'll show you the room."

They followed the landlady up the stairs and down a narrow hall. She stopped before a closed door, flung it open, then stood back. "Here we are."

Gareth let Shannon enter first. As the woman had said, the small room was clean. The wide bed was covered with a cheerful quilt, and a washstand held a pitcher and bowl. A small chest and two chairs completed the furnishings.

"Supper's in a half hour. Just come on down."

"We'll do that," Gareth said. "Is there a livery stable close by?"

"Next street over. Can't miss it. I'll leave you now, Mr.—?

"Colby." He gave her an affable smile. "Gareth Colby. And my brother's Shannon."

Mrs. Johnson gave a friendly nod and left, closing the door behind her.

Leaving the two of them still staring at each other. Gareth's smile slowly faded, and she saw the exhaustion in his face.

"What else could I have told her?" he asked, anticipating her protests.

Shannon swallowed as the full realization of what they had gotten into swept over her. She and Gareth, who couldn't seem to stay out of each other's arms any time they were alone together, were going to share this room tonight.

All night.

She glanced at the bed. No extra quilts were folded at its foot. Nor anywhere else in the room.

The floor was bare boards except for a strip of worn carpet alongside the bed.

He was more tired than she. He'd driven the buggy all day. She couldn't let him sleep on that hard floor. All right, then, *she'd* sleep there.

"You couldn't have told her anything else," she finally answered.

"Good. I'm glad there's nothing we have to argue about tonight. I'm too damned tired to care about anything except a meal and sleep."

Did he truly mean that? Wasn't his glance lingering on her a little longer than necessary? And didn't she find looking at him an altogether pleasant thing?

"Yes," she agreed, giving him an amiable smile. "I feel the same way."

"I'll take the buggy to the stable. Do you want to wait for me up here or meet me downstairs in the dining room?"

Facing a group of people, fending off their probable

questions, wasn't something she looked forward to. Or planned to do alone.

"Neither one. I'm going with you. It would look odd for your *brother* to stay snug and dry while you take care of the horse and buggy."

Gareth nodded. "You're probably right, and I don't like this any better than you do. But it can't be helped unless you want to try to find another place."

"No. We're both too tired for that." She headed for the door, turning her near flounce into a young man's gait, and he followed closely behind.

He was so close his warm breath tickled the back of her neck. She shivered, knowing the temperature of the room had nothing to do with her physical reaction.

Shannon felt a light touch on that already sensitized spot and froze. She turned to see Gareth removing his hand, an odd look on his face.

"Then, let's go. I'm starving."

So was she. And not only for food.

She gave a small gasp at that thought, opened the door, and they went out into the hall.

It was going to be a long night.

A *very* long night.

Chapter Twenty

Gareth followed Shannon inside the room and closed the door. After a moment's hesitation, he twisted the key in the lock. That small sound made her head quickly turn. She looked nervous—almost afraid—he saw, swearing inwardly.

No reason for her to feel that way. If he had to sleep out in the hall, nothing was going to happen between them tonight.

"At least we didn't have to answer a bunch of questions at supper," she said, still standing in the middle of the room.

He could see she was trying to make casual conversation so he wouldn't realize how she felt. He'd go along with that.

"Good thing, too, because I'm so tired I hardly remember my own name."

The moment the thoughtless words were out of his mouth, Gareth regretted them. Shannon needed no reminders that her true name was one of the things they were trying to discover.

"No one looked at me oddly, and no one looked familiar to me. Surely I can't have lived in this town."

Her tired voice held a question, as if she needed reassurance. Again, he was smitten by how vulnerable she was—how uncertain about everything and everyone. Especially as this was the first time since he'd found her she'd been in any towns and, except for the neighbors that once and Ellis and his sons, met new people.

Hell, he didn't know anything about memory loss. He supposed it was possible she'd lived here and forgotten it. But she didn't need to hear that tonight.

"No, I don't think so," he answered, keeping his doubts from his voice.

He turned up the wick of the lamp they had left burning when they went to eat, brightening the room. After sitting down in one of the two chairs, he started taking off his boots.

"The food was good, wasn't it?" she asked a moment later, and he knew she was talking just to keep silence from settling.

"Yes. But I was hungry enough to eat shoe leather." He glanced over at Shannon, to find her gaze riveted on his feet and hands. He took off the second boot, sighed wearily, and stood.

"You don't need to stand there as if you expect me to grab you and throw you onto the bed."

He waved at the piece of furniture in question. "Go ahead and get in. I'll sleep on the floor. But first check to see if there's another quilt, will you?"

Her cheeks had reddened. He couldn't blame her. His conduct around her so far had given her no reason to believe he'd leave her alone tonight.

She walked quickly to the bed and pulled the quilt back to reveal only top and bottom sheets. Her back stiffened. She turned toward him, face closed.

"I'll sleep on the floor. You've been driving the buggy all day. I'm sure you're far more tired than I. Besides, you're doing this for me. I should be the one to—"

"*I* will sleep on the floor," he interrupted, making his voice very firm.

Her bound chest rose and fell as she took a deep breath, and unbidden, a memory of her white breasts under him on the orchard grass filled his mind. Of her unbuttoned nightdress last night.

"I'm as stubborn as you. If you won't take the bed, then neither will I."

Gareth sighed, trying to ignore the pictures in his mind. "We're too tired for this nonsense. We'll share the bed. It's plenty big enough for two."

Shannon's eyes widened and she swallowed. "You're right. We're behaving stupidly."

She walked past him to a chair, sat down and began unlacing her boots.

Gareth looked at her bent head, then shrugged. Dammit, he wasn't going to sleep in his clothes. He cleared his throat.

"You undress first and get in bed. I'll wait."

"I have no intention of getting undressed," she said frostily.

"Suit yourself. But you'd be a sight more comfortable."

He walked to the curtained window, its blind drawn against the dark and the rain, and stood facing it. After a silence he heard rustling sounds, cloth sliding against cloth, quick footsteps, more rustles.

"I'm settled. You can come to bed, too."

Her voice faltered a little on the last words, and he felt his breath quicken.

Come to bed, she'd said, as if urging a husband to his slumbers.

Or other activities.

Gareth slowly turned. Shannon lay on the far right side of the bed, quilt drawn up to her chin, turned on her side away from him, one arm shielding her face.

In spite of his exhaustion, a grin curved his mouth.

She was taking no chances he'd mistake her willingness to share the bed for any other kind of willingness.

After extinguishing the lamp, thereby plunging th
room into darkness, Gareth sat down on his side of th
bed, his weight making the mattress tilt toward him. H
felt Shannon roll a few inches closer before she checke
the movement and slid back to her edge.

He removed his shirt and trousers, put them on a chair
leaving him in his underdrawers, then slid under th
covers.

Thank God he was too tired to care that Shannon'
tempting body lay only a few feet away.

Too tired to speculate on whether, despite her signal
to the contrary, if he moved toward her, touched her, she'
come into his arms, as she had those other times.

To wonder if she'd give him kiss for kiss, her passion a
hot as his own.

That way lies nothing but trouble, he reminded himself.

But despite his fatigue, his body began to stir and harder

You don't want to marry her. You don't want to marry anyon
If you leave well enough alone, you'll soon discover where th
female belongs, and she'll be out of your life for good.

He wouldn't think about the possibility it was alread
too late for that. He wouldn't think about anything, h
told himself resolutely. He would go to sleep.

He turned away toward the far left edge of the bed an
pulled the quilt up to his own chin.

"No . . . No . . . no-oo." Shannon thrashed on the be
flinging back the quilt and sheet.

The grinning peddler held her down on the wagon be
and the man with the knife knelt beside her, the knife ti
against her throat.

"Where's the necklace?" he growled, moving the kni
just enough to draw blood. "If you tell me, I'll let you go.

She knew he lied, knew revealing the pendant's hidir
place would only prolong her life a few more minutes, b
maybe . . . if she told him. . . .

"I don't know," she gasped out. "I can't remember . .

The knife tip pushed harder. She could feel blood trickling down her neck. Terror choked her. "No . . . no . . . stop . . ."

A warm hand was on her shoulder, shaking her gently. "Wake up. It's all right. You just had a bad dream."

Gasping with fright, she turned toward the voice, the comforting touch, pushing herself against the equally warm body. "Don't let them hurt me!"

"Shhhh. It's all right," the voice said again. "No one's going to hurt you. You're safe with me."

Slowly, Shannon came back to herself, became aware she was pressed tightly against Gareth's warm chest.

His warm, *bare* chest. Her legs were twined with his own, and her lower body was also pressed close to his.

She gasped, feeling the hard ridge of his arousal against her thigh. That portion of him had certainly recovered from its exhaustion. She knew she should pull back, return to her side of the bed, and turn away from him.

Yes, that was certainly what she should do. At once.

But he was so warm and solid and comforting. And the horrible dream wouldn't reappear as long as she stayed here, like this.

It wouldn't hurt to do that . . . for just a few more minutes . . until she was certain the dream was gone for the ıight. . . .

Gareth showed no signs of wanting her to move away. *He* wasn't withdrawing. Quite the contrary. His hand noved from her waist down to her bottom, curving around ıer, pulling her close against his increasing hardness.

This felt so good. *He* felt so good. Their bodies seemed nade for each other, fitting together perfectly . . . just as hey had in the orchard.

How could this be wrong when it felt so completely ight?

He smelled so good, too. A warm, sensual, completely nale scent enveloped her, made her intensely aware she as a woman.

And he a man.

As if she needed any reminders. His curls of chest hair tickled her cheek, making her want to touch him in a different way. She turned her head, and her tongue flicked around a curl, then delved beneath it to his warm flesh.

She felt his indrawn breath, the sudden thump of his heart, and smiled at this evidence of her effect on him. She lifted her head, sliding her body up his until their heads were level. He was only a darker shadow in the darkness of the room.

She couldn't see his gray eyes, watch how his mobile face reflected his changing feelings. . . .

"Shannon . . . ?"

Gareth heard the tremble in his voice as he said her name, heard the question in it. He knew she heard it, too and understood what it meant.

He slid an arm around her shoulders, drawing her close His lips slanted over hers, finding them unerringly, as i he'd done this a hundred times before. She eagerly opene her mouth to him, welcomed the forays of his tongue, me them with her own explorations.

There was nothing between their upper bodies excep her thin undervest. Finding its hem, he lifted it over he head and discarded it on the bed. The softness of he breasts against his chest felt so wonderful he just hel her there for long moments, not moving.

Her hair smelled clean and sweet, the very essence c womanhood. He hadn't known a woman could smell th good, feel this good. . . .

Her face was against his neck, her lips giving him sc little kisses, while her hand moved across his chest, findir one of his male nipples, circling it until he felt it stiffe beneath her touch. For long moments, he enjoyed tl sweet agony.

Finally, he groaned and turned. In one swift moveme she was under him and his mouth was on her breasts, l tongue making the same circling movements her finge had caressed him with moments ago.

His mind supplied the pictures he couldn't see: t

satiny white mounds of her breasts, crowned with the rosy pink tips that he could feel contracting and hardening beneath his lips and tongue . . . her blue eyes darkening with passion, the rosy flush across her high cheekbones. . . .

His mouth left her breasts, kissed its way lower, his tongue curling itself into the small indentation of her navel. Her body convulsed beneath him.

"Gareth," Shannon whispered, hearing her voice breathe his name . . . but there was no fear in it, no question. Only an affirmation.

Her body seemed to have taken on a life of its own. She felt herself arch against him again as he quested lower until he reached her woman's mound and his tongue delved within.

Again and yet again. She felt her breath coming faster, her heart pounding. She squirmed beneath him, her body building to that inner completion. . . .

With one swift movement, he slid upward, his mouth reclaiming hers, making it his. She felt his manhood against her upper thigh, hot and throbbing. Wildness seized her. She couldn't wait for this fulfillment

She slid her thighs apart, and Gareth guided himself into her, slowly . . . slowly until he was tight against her, and they were joined in the way men and women had oined themselves since the beginning of time.

I love you!

The words came unbidden, but this time she kept herself rom uttering them aloud. Forget love, just enjoy this pasion, make the most of it. It was all she'd ever have from im.

Shannon moved upward, inviting Gareth's answering novement, exulting in his trembling body pressing her ownward, pressing into her again and again, until they oth reached that moment of completion that gave a pleasre beyond compare . . . beyond anything she'd ever expeenced or ever would.

He collapsed upon her, breathing hard. In a few moments, he rolled to his side, taking her with him, so that they lay closely together. Her fingers found his face in the darkness, traced the lines of his features.

One of his hands came up, grasped hers, squeezed it, then released it. He buried his face in her breasts, and in a few moments she heard his slow, even breathing and knew he was asleep.

Deep inside her, she felt all the unanswered questions, the unsolved problems, beginning to stir to life. Firmly, she pushed them down, denying them entry into her consciousness.

Tomorrow could take care of itself.

She curled herself more comfortably around Gareth's warm body and went contentedly to sleep.

Gareth came awake instantly, at his usual rising time Seeing the light square of the window, he was disoriented That window wasn't in the right place . . . it should be o the other wall. . . .

He sat bolt upright and looked around him. His eye fell on the small mound of Shannon's body close besid him, and last night's events flooded back into his mind.

Damn it all to hell! he swore silently.

He pushed away the covers and slid out of bed, n looking back at her, forcing down the urges trying to su face, telling him to stay in the warm bed, to reach for th warm and willing woman sleeping beside him.

That would be an even more stupid thing to do tha what he'd done last night. Besides, he couldn't be su that in the cold light of dawn Shannon would still be willi and eager.

As she'd been last night.

Forget about last night!

He savagely jerked on his trousers, sat down in a ch and pulled on his stockings and boots. Once again, he let the desires of his body overwhelm his good sense. On again, he'd taken the woman he didn't want to get involv with.

He wanted Shannon out of his life as soon as possible. He had nothing to offer her, and if she hadn't lost her memory, if she wasn't in such a vulnerable position, she'd realize that.

She didn't need him. Didn't *want* him. She'd only turned to him out of her temporary need and fear. She might even resent him for taking advantage of that situation.

His jaw tightened. Shannon was a beautiful woman—just as Dorinda had been. Still was, he supposed. Her beauty and intelligence would find her a husband soon enough.

Dorinda certainly hadn't had any trouble finding someone else to marry after she'd rejected him. No trouble at all.

Neither would Shannon. When this mess was cleared up—when she'd regained her memory and they had found the man who threatened her and dealt with him—she could go on with her life.

And leave him with his. Such as it was. His mouth twisted. A farm he was in danger of losing, a family totally dependent on him for their support. A body that was no longer whole.

Shannon stirred a little, made a small noise in her throat.

Gareth stiffened. He couldn't be here when she awakened. He couldn't face her as he had that other time when she'd told him she loved him.

Which she'd quickly denied.

He didn't want to know how she thought she felt because t made no difference. The only thing that could was if he were to be with child.

Last night had doubled the chances of that possibility.

Again he swore at himself, his stupidity. He should have ooked ahead, not let this situation develop.

He wouldn't, couldn't, make that mistake again.

When he returned to Redmond to try to find the man hannon feared, he'd leave her at the farm.

No, she wouldn't allow that, he admitted after a noment's reflection. All right, he'd have to bring her, but he'd make sure they started early, didn't have to spend the night here.

The store list was still in his pocket. He found a stub of pencil on top of the chest and quickly scribbled a note on its back side, then left the room.

Shannon awakened slowly, stretching, wondering why a feeling of well-being filled her, why a satisfied smile curved her mouth upward. . . .

She sat up and for a few moments was disoriented. Then she remembered and glanced across the bed. Gareth's side was empty, and he was gone from the room.

The warm, delicious feelings evaporated. Coldness rushed in to fill the void.

She admitted she'd thought last night's lovemaking would make a difference. Would make him see that he cared for her as she did for him.

Again she'd been wrong. Again, she'd been a fool.

If his feelings had changed, he wouldn't have left her here alone. He'd have awakened her with kisses . . . which would have led to other things. . . .

Stop it! she told herself. Anger, both at herself and at Gareth, swept over her, dispelling her weaker emotions. She got out of bed and swiftly dressed, washed and rearranged her hair.

Only as she was leaving did she see the scrap of pape on top of the chest.

Her heart lightened. Gareth hadn't left without a wor He'd written a note. Something must have happened th he had to tend to and he didn't want to wake her. Hop surging through her, she picked up the paper.

I'm getting the horse and buggy. Dress. I'll be back soon a we'll eat and leave.

Gare

She stared at the few words for long moments, then cru pled the paper and threw it on the floor.

Not a word of caring, not a hint of what last night had meant to him.

"Because it *didn't* mean anything, you idiot," she said aloud, then swept out of the room.

She met him at the foot of the stairs. The smile he gave her was forced. His gray eyes had that remote, steely expression.

"Good. You're up and ready to go. We can get an early start home. It's still raining, so the trip will take longer."

Shannon gave him an even look. "I'm quite ready to go," she said coolly. "After breakfast. I'm famished."

That was as far from the truth as possible. But she'd never let him know how he'd affected her. She'd manage to eat something.

She walked on toward the dining room, leaving him to follow or catch up with her, not caring which.

Chapter Twenty-One

"Mr. Colby, you and your brother be sure to stop here the next time you're in Redmond." Mrs. Johnson beamed at Gareth.

"Thank you. We've enjoyed our stay."

Gareth managed a smile, wishing he'd used different words. What he'd said sounded a little odd to describe an overnight stay for two "brothers" at a boardinghouse.

Although he couldn't deny he'd enjoyed what had happened between him and Shannon last night, he doubted if she'd want any reminders. Not that he did, either.

He'd done a stupid thing—again.

He glanced at Shannon, standing rigidly beside him, her smile stiff, too. She was furious with him. She'd made that perfectly clear since she'd met him at the foot of the stairs, and all through breakfast.

He knew why, too, of course.

But leaving before she woke and writing that cold note had seemed the best thing to do.

Damn it, it had been the best thing! Talking with her would only have made matters worse, as it had that first time in the orchard. He had no reassuring words of love to give her. Not then. Not now.

Bleakness shot through him at the thought of living the rest of his life without a woman's love.

Without *Shannon's* love.

He tried to push these disturbing feelings and thoughts far back in his mind.

"Goodbye, Mrs. Johnson," Shannon said. She'd pitched her voice low, and the soft breasts he'd taken such pleasure in fondling last night weren't in evidence under her man's shirt and coat.

But he could never mistake her for a male again. He wondered how anyone could.

She glanced up at him, her gaze still remote. "We'd better get started. It's a long drive ho—back."

He caught her small slip and wondered what it meant. Did she not want to think of the farm as home or was it just the opposite?

"Yes," he agreed. "And it's raining harder."

They hurried to the buggy waiting out front, and he helped Shannon inside, then got in himself. He saw a small puddle on the floor.

"Watch your feet," he warned. "The buggy is starting to leak. At least the rain is coming straight down now, and most of it should stay outside."

She didn't answer, just did as he said and settled herself on her side of the buggy seat.

Gareth settled himself and clucked to the horse, trying to concentrate on the weather and not the withdrawn silent woman beside him.

The drought-breaking rain was welcome of course, bu traveling in it wasn't going to be pleasant.

Pleasant. Did he really think any part of this trip hom would be enjoyable? Did Shannon know how much h dreaded it? How he wished it were over?

How he wished last night had never happened?

You don't really wish that, his mind told him. *No matt how much you're protesting now.*

He tried to ignore the thoughts, but found it impossible. His mind kept replaying those moments when he'd held Shannon in his arms. Holding her, loving her, had seemed so right. Sleeping with her curled up beside him afterward had, too.

But it wasn't right. He shouldn't have let it happen, he kept repeating silently, trying to disregard the desperate quality of his denials.

Shannon was as silent as he during the wet, miserable drive. The rain grew heavier the nearer they came to the river and the farm, and Gareth began worrying about the possibility of flood.

He tried to dismiss it. After the drought the ground could soak up a lot of water, and the Shenandoah wasn't prone to flood.

The narrow country road leading to the farm was a muddy, rutted mess, almost impossible to navigate. When at last they reached the turnoff to the farm, Gareth heaved a sigh of relief. "Thank God we're home."

Shannon's mouth tightened. Did he have to make it so painfully clear how glad he was to be soon rid of her presence? She'd stayed as far to her side of the narrow seat as she could, so that he'd get the message that she felt the same way.

Which was a lie.

How she wished she could dislike being with him, dislike *him*. That would make his rejection so much easier to bear.

What was wrong with her? Was she so love-starved that she had to grasp at every crumb he threw her way? Had no one ever shown her any affection?

Her mother's smiling face appeared in Shannon's mind's eye, and a rush of feeling went through her. No, she knew better than that. She'd had love, plenty of it.

But she'd lost all the people who had given her that affection.

And she was a person who couldn't live a loveless existence. She might not remember much of her previous life, but she knew that.

"I'll tend to Molly," Gareth said at the back entrance.

"Yes." She glanced over at him. "Thank you for doing this for me," she told him, not able to force a smile or keep the stiffness from her voice. "I appreciate it."

Neither did he smile at her. "I'll help you any way I can."

Shannon got out of the buggy and hurried onto the porch. Of course he would help her. The sooner all her problems were solved, the sooner she'd be out of his life.

And do you think what happened last night helped solve your problems?

Her mouth twisted at that absurd thought. Once again she and Gareth had made love. No, she corrected herself. They had shared the delights of the body. It had only been love on her part.

Never mind what you call it, her mind mocked. *The fact remains you've increased the risk of conceiving a child.*

A child that Gareth would want no part of.

Even if she might.

She drew in her breath. Of course she didn't want that! She wasn't an entire fool yet, was she?

The kitchen door swung open, and Gwenny stood outlined in the doorway. "Come in out of the rain!" she called, anxiety in her voice. "We've been so worried about both of you."

Shannon hurried to the house, pulling her jacket's collar up around her neck. At the door, Gwenny enfolded her in an embrace, then stood back.

"You look so funny in that men's garb. Get out of those wet clothes at once," she directed.

Clare looked up from where she was setting the supper table, her hands full of cutlery. She dropped the utensils with a clatter and ran over to hug Shannon. "I'm so glad you and Gareth are home!"

Maud, a worried smile on her face, hurried from the stove. "So am I. We were afraid the roads might be washing out with all the rain. Did you find out anything?"

The warm welcome partially dispelled Shannon's blea

mood. Briefly, she recounted their experiences, omitting the fact she and Gareth had shared a room and the rest of last night's events.

Despite that disaster, she still had love in her life. She could bask in this family affection for a while longer.

Until two days from now, when, if luck was with them, she'd find the man who searched for her.

Somehow she'd manage to get a glimpse of him without putting herself in danger, without him seeing her.

And when she looked at his face, surely her memory would return, and she'd know who he was, why he wanted her dead. She'd know if her memory flashes had been real, and the man actually was the menace she believed him to be.

And if any of this was her fault, due to some wrongdoing.

All the mystery would be resolved. She'd leave here, this time never to return. Firmly, she pushed down the houghts nibbling at the fringes.

Where would she go? What would she do?

Shannon hurried upstairs to her room and changed out of her wet shirt and trousers, gratefully donning Clare's old blue gown, then returned to the kitchen.

On the bottom step she stopped, her heart contracting.

Gareth had come back from the barn. He stood just nside the door, dripping onto the floor, drenched to the kin.

Just the sight of him brought back a flood of memories om last night.

"Josh says the river is about over the banks down by the ornfields, and the corn is still in the shocks!" Clare told im. "He's so worried!"

Gareth's face looked grim as he struggled out of his coat nd hung it on a wall hook, then grabbed the towel Gwenny anded him. "So am I."

He glanced around at all of them, his gaze quickly mov-g on when it reached Shannon. "In the morning we'll ove as much as we can from down here to the upstairs."

Clare gasped. "Do you really think the house will flood?"

"I hope not, but we'll be prepared. The barn's high enough the animals should be all right."

Fear went through Shannon at his words.

She hadn't thought that far ahead; she hadn't realized the river could actually threaten this house. What a terrible thought that was!

"Maybe we should start moving upstairs tonight," Maud said, her voice calm and even.

Gareth nodded. "Let's do that. If it's worse by morning we'll leave."

Maud looked alarmed. "I'm sure it won't come to that!"

Gareth's smile looked forced. "I hope you're right. Bu I'm not taking chances with our lives."

His glance crossed Shannon's and lingered for a moment.

Do you really care what happens to me? she asked him silently then was at once ashamed of herself. He wouldn't hav bothered coming after her that night she'd tried to ru away if he didn't care.

He wouldn't have insisted they marry after their on night together.

Something he hadn't done this morning.

After their second night together.

The thought slipped into her mind unbidden an unwanted. She swallowed a sudden lump in her throa Why should he? She'd earlier refused him in no uncertai terms.

If he asked her again, she'd give him the same answe Of course she would. She'd not marry a man who didr love her.

Not unless it was absolutely necessary.

What if it is? her mind asked. *What if you have concei and you leave here before you know? What then?*

Then she'd worry about it when she must. Now, the were other things to be concerned about.

Supper was a quick affair, with the rain drumming do relentlessly. Afterward, while the women made short wc of the cleanup, Gareth moved furniture to the second floor, using the wider front stairs.

The women soon joined him. Sharing this hurried preparation, this sense of danger, Shannon felt even more a part of the family. Brushing by Gareth with a chair, Shannon's hand touched his. He quickly drew away, not letting his eyes meet hers.

Shannon stared at him, her mouth tightening with anger, her earlier intentions not to concern herself with how things stood between them forgotten.

She'd like to kick him where it would do the most good!

Why was he avoiding her to the extent it would soon be noticeable to everyone else?

A thought occurred to her. Could he think that she'd *planned* last night's events? That she'd decided she'd be better off wed to him?

She caught Maud's sympathetic gaze. That made her even angrier. Gareth's mother still believed she and Gareth belonged together. Still thought in time Gareth would feel that way, too.

How wrong she was! Gareth didn't want anyone—except the woman he'd lost years ago. He'd sealed his feelings off when Dorinda had jilted him.

Only his physical cravings remained alive. And he fought giving in to them.

She didn't want him, either. She didn't want anyone who could deny his need for love as Gareth did.

What a bleak marriage that would be.

"Excuse me," she told him coolly, her chin raised. "I didn't mean to bump you."

Her blue eyes were snapping. Gareth realized she was still furious with him. Now, too late, he knew how wrong he'd been this morning. He shouldn't have left her before they had talked.

He should have again insisted they marry—and this time made her agree.

Belatedly, he understood her anger, knew how she must have interpreted his actions. She thought he was trying to evade her, evade his responsibility, and last night had meant nothing to him except their physical joining. She thought he now regretted even that.

His mouth tightened. What he should have done was resist the pull of his desire for her last night. Gotten out of the bed. Spent the rest of the night on the floor.

But he hadn't.

"My fault," he finally answered. He forced a smile, then wished he hadn't because she could *see* it was forced, could sense his tension. And was putting the wrong interpretation on that, too.

The turmoil inside him came to a head. He finally let himself admit something he'd been pushing down all day trying to deny.

Last night had touched his soul. Their physical joining had sparked something else deep inside him, something he'd thought long dead and buried.

Buried, yes; dead, no.

Fear struck him at this admission. He was in danger of falling in love with Shannon, with this woman who had come into his life so unexpectedly and had created turmoil ever since her arrival.

He didn't want to love another woman. Never again did he want to consider the possibility of going through that pain and hell of loss.

That possibility was very real with Shannon. Her past life was full of shadows and mystery.

He knew there was no lover she couldn't remember—that night in the orchard had proved she'd never before been with a man.

But what if she was promised to another? That possibility couldn't be ignored, since her past was still unknown.

Next week, if all went well, Shannon would see the man she feared—which could trigger the return of her memory.

She could walk away from him—just like Dorinda had.

What if she did that, and she was carrying his babe inside h

All the more reason, once the threat of a flood was over, to insist they marry. If they married now, it wouldn matter if a man later turned up, claiming to be Shannon's intended.

Shannon would be protected from any consequences of their rash lovemaking. Her reputation would be saved, even if she was getting a sorry bargain in acquiring him for a husband.

But what about his own protection?

Gareth pushed that aside. He was the man—he should have resisted her allure. He began to sweat. Yes, they must marry, but he couldn't give her his heart.

If they were married, he couldn't lose her as he'd lost Dorinda. But what if she discovered she'd loved another man—and still loved him? And was tied to Gareth irrevocably?

To hell with that scenario! Marriage was the best solution—so as soon as the flood threat was over, he'd get her to agree even if he had to tie her up and drag her to a preacher!

With the ominous drumbeat of the rain accompanying them, by midnight they were finished. Exhausted, they all went to bed for a few hours' sleep.

By daybreak everyone was up. The rain was still coming down in torrents.

"Stay in the house," Gareth told the women, after they nad eaten a hasty breakfast.

"What are you going to do?" Maud asked.

Gareth struggled into his oilskins and boots. "Check on he animals and see if the river's still rising."

"Be careful," Maud warned, her voice shaking.

He managed a smile for his mother. "Don't worry. I von't do anything witless."

A few minutes later, he stood in knee-deep water that only yesterday had been his cornfield. Rain pounding at im, taking his breath away, he swore at himself for understimating the danger, for not believing the placid Shenanoah River could rise this far, this fast.

Could threaten everything he loved, everything he'd orked so hard for all these years.

Even the very lives of his family. "Damn your cocksure belief that this Valley could never harm you or yours!" he raged, raising a clenched fist.

It was too late now to even get his family to higher ground. The water had risen so far since last night it completely covered the road, blocking that escape.

Fear knotted his gut for his womenfolk. Thank God they had supplies of food and water on the upper floor. Surely, the water wouldn't rise that far—or the current become so swift it would take the house off its foundations.

"Mr. Colby? Is that you?"

Gareth recognized Josh's agitated voice just as the boy's figure loomed before him in the gray early morning light.

"Yes, Josh. What's wrong?"

"Some of the sheep got out! I'm afraid they'll get in the river. You know how sheep are."

Gareth swore under his breath. Yes, he knew how dumb and silly sheep could be. He also knew how the loss of a few sheep would affect Josh's family. They were in as precarious a position as the Colbys.

"Let's check. You take the section over by your place and I'll look around here." He gave the boy a stern look. "If you see any in the river, don't try to get them out. The current is too swift. You'd never make it."

Josh nodded, his young face creased with worry. "I know. I won't."

Frowning, Gareth watched him lope off. He wasn't at all sure Josh would heed his warning. Not with what was at stake for his family.

"I *won't* stay cooped up here any longer! Gareth may need us—or be in danger. Josh and his family, too." Clare stood in the kitchen doorway, looking out through the pouring rain.

Shannon heard the tremble in the girl's voice when she said Josh's name. Although Clare and Josh hadn't spoken to each other since before the debacle with the Bartons, it was obvious Clare still cared for him.

"You'll have to. Going out in this won't help anybody. There's nothing we can do except have hot food and coffee ready for them," Gwenny said.

"How do you know Gareth and . . . everyone are all right? Gareth left an hour ago and we haven't seen him since!"

The fear Shannon had tried to repress broke through. Yes, why hadn't Gareth returned to the house? What could he be doing?

"I'm not staying here another second!" Clare said. "I'll find out what's going on."

Before anyone could react, she slipped out the door and disappeared.

"Clare! Come back here!" Maud hurried after her daughter, but Shannon slipped in front of her.

"You stay here, Mrs. Colby. I'll bring her back."

"She won't pay any attention to you," Maud protested. "You know how she gets."

"Yes, we do, Mother," Gwenny said. "So either Shannon or I will go."

"Let me." Before Gwenny could move, Shannon hurried outside, the full force of the rain hitting her as she ran toward the barn in only her day dress, not even a shawl to help protect her.

She was soaked to the skin by the time she reached the building, but was relieved to see the big main door still tightly barred, no frightened animals outside.

There was no sign of Gareth or Clare. A shout from the direction of the river sent her hurrying that way. Soon she was in knee-deep water. She stopped several yards from what used to be the shore, her heart hammering against her ribs.

Josh bobbed in the torrent that had been the peaceful Shenandoah so short a time before. He clung desperately to a sheep whose terrified bleats could be heard above the sound of the storm and the current.

But that wasn't the worst.

Clare stood on a partly submerged rock, screaming at Josh. Her foot slipped, and then she was also in the water, sinking beneath the surface.

Without thinking, Shannon flung herself into the river.

That was when she discovered she knew how to swim.

Thank God someone had taught her that skill, she thought as she struggled to the place where Clare had gone down.

But of course she wasn't still there.

Farther down, Clare's head popped up for a few moments. She was gasping for breath, and Shannon knew there wasn't much time left.

Fear giving her strength, she battled the current and her clothes, which were trying to pull her under, too. One last desperate stroke gave her purchase on Clare's sleeve, then her arm.

Josh was long gone, swept down out of sight. No help there. Where was Gareth? Had he, too, been swept away?

Terror for his life mingled with her fear for hers and Clare's. Wildly, Shannon looked around. If she could just get them a little closer to some overhanging tree branches pull them up. . . .

Clare was fighting her, the girl's fear making her frenzied. "Stop it! You'll have us both drowned!"

Shannon's desperate words floated back to Gareth, who was sloshing through the water in their direction.

He recognized Shannon's voice, and a stab of dread shot through him. He struggled to increase his speed.

What could she be doing down here? Why wasn't she safely inside with the other women? When he saw the two thrashing figures in the water, his heart stopped for a moment.

Not only was Shannon fighting that treacherous current but also Clare!

And they were losing the fight.

As he watched, Clare grabbed Shannon's head, and pulled her under the water.

Chapter Twenty-Two

When Shannon bobbed up seconds later, Gareth was in the water, stroking strongly toward them, fear propelling the movements of his arms and legs.

The current was moving them too fast for him to catch up. Gritting his teeth, Gareth forced a speed and strength from himself he wouldn't have thought possible only moments ago.

In what seemed an agonizingly long time, he saw he was gaining.

Shannon had seen him and now used her strength to try to stay where she was until he reached them. Finally, he grasped her arm. Clare's head lolled on Shannon's shoulder, her eyes closed.

"Is she . . . ," he shouted above the water's noise as the current swept them onward, hard rain still coming down.

"No! She's breathing."

He swallowed in momentary relief. "Keep your grip on Clare! I'll tow you both."

If he could. But he wouldn't voice that doubt.

"No! Take Clare. I'll be all right."

"I won't! Come on, do as—"

Shannon shoved the unconscious girl into his grasp, and the current moved her away as she struggled toward shore.

She'd left him no choice. Gareth struck out for shore, too, trying to keep an eye on Shannon.

She was tiring, her movements slowing. His fear increased. He saw a tree ahead, low branches hanging over the turbulent water.

He grasped a branch and somehow managed to pull himself and Clare out of the river. His breath heaving, he carried her to a raised spot and laid her down.

Clare was still breathing. Relief flooded over him.

"Oh, Gareth!"

Clare suddenly bent over and began heaving up river water, crying and gasping.

Gareth held her steady, wiping her face with his shirt while rain at once covered it again. Urgency beat in him as seconds ticked by. He had to get back to Shannon!

In a few moments he was sure she'd be all right. "Stay here, Shannon's still in the water."

Fear widened her eyes. "Go get her!"

"I will." He ran back to the river.

Shannon was nowhere in sight. How could she be, with such a current tugging at her? Where was she? Had she drowned?

A fear such as he'd never known gripped him, mixed with a terrible regret.

She'd saved his sister, and in so doing had she given her own life to the river?

He loved her! God, he loved her more than his own life. More than he'd ever loved another human.

And he'd never told her. If she'd died, she'd left this life believing he cared nothing for her. He couldn't stand the thought. Tears fell, washed away in an instant by the pouring rain.

He plunged into the torrent and propelled himself down the river, trying to catch a glimpse of a bobbing dark head, the flash of deep blue eyes.

Nothing greeted his sight except the churning, mudd

current, pulling him inexorably farther along. Gareth fought the sickening defeat trying to engulf him, fought his fatigue, fought the pain in his crippled leg.

He wouldn't give up. He *wouldn't.* She had to be alive. She couldn't be dead. Not now, when he'd finally realized how much he loved her.

He rounded a bend, and saw something in the water ahead of him. A dark blob. His heart lurched, and he forced another burst of speed into his aching limbs, his heaving chest.

When he drew alongside, sickening disappointment shot through him.

It wasn't Shannon—only a floating piece of what had once been a chair.

That could only mean homesteads were flooding, their contents washed out into this seething mess.

It meant the river was still rising.

New urgency stuck him. He had to find Shannon and get her and Clare safely back to the house, to the upper floors.

Letting the current help him along, Gareth passed by tree limbs, half-submerged logs, other bits of furniture. Two people, a man and woman, clung to pieces of timber. He hailed them, but passed on by, knowing he was unable to help. He was weakening himself. He couldn't go much farther.

Yes he could! He *would* find her. He'd follow this accursed river that he'd loved since boyhood, and which now had become his mortal enemy, to Hades and back if that were necessary to find Shannon.

A new burst of energy followed that resolution, and he began stroking strongly again, fighting the despair trying to defeat him.

But his vigor was short-lived. Soon the ache in his limbs was back, his chest burned as if a fire raged inside, and his mind approached exhaustion. He shook his head to clear away the film that kept forming before his eyes.

And then he saw her.

Just ahead, where the river bent, prone on a pile of debris that had lodged against trees in the bend. Her head was down, her eyes closed.

New, sharper fear knifed into him. He pushed it down. She had to still be alive if she'd managed to climb onto the drift.

Just then, Shannon lifted her head, and those amazing eyes looked into his. Wild elation surged through Gareth. He felt a silly grin curving his mouth upward.

"Hang on!" he called. "I'm almost there." How secure was the drift? Would it hold or break up any moment, casting Shannon back into the river?

She managed a tired smile and pushed herself up.

At last Gareth reached the drift and cautiously pulled himself onto it, relieved to feel its solidity beneath them.

He drew Shannon's cold, wet body into his arms. Her dress was torn in a dozen places, one shoulder bare, and her skin scratched and bruised.

How nearly he'd come to losing her!

He crushed her to him so tightly she gasped.

"I love you," he said, his voice trembling with feeling. "I feared you were gone and I'd never be able to tell you that!"

She stared up at him, her eyes widening as if she thought he'd gone mad.

"I've been a fool, but then you knew that all along."

A flood of mixed emotions to rival the river's rampage filled Shannon.

He loved her. Gareth loved her.

They clung together, Shannon savoring Gareth's words Then the ordeal she'd undergone caught up with her.

She drooped against him, feeling limp and boneless, s tired she could never move again. She heard his intake c breath, sensed his sudden fear, and forced her head u to give him a wavering smile.

"I'm all right," she reassured him.

He sagged with relief. "Thank God."

"Do you think we can get off this drift into the trees it's caught on?"

He looked at the trees, then nodded. "The drift is deep, and looks well wedged. But it could break up anytime. We can crawl back along it and grab that overhanging branch and pull ourselves out as I did with Clare."

Shannon shot him a worried look. "How is she?"

"She's fine. Probably worried to death about us."

"Thank God! But Josh was in the river, too, trying to save a sheep. That's how Clare fell in. She was standing on a rock, calling to him, and she slipped."

Gareth swallowed. Finally he said, "Josh will be all right. He'll survive if anyone can."

He sounded as if he were trying to convince himself, Shannon thought, forcing down her own anxiety.

"Are you rested enough to try to get ashore?" Gareth asked.

"Yes."

Carefully they crawled across the drift toward an overhanging branch. Shannon shuddered as they passed by a curled-up pile of snakes also taking refuge. At the tree, Gareth boosted Shannon up, and she grasped the branch. Just as she started to heave herself over it, she heard a loud snap, and the branch broke off and fell.

As did she.

Gareth caught her; but her weight made him stumble, and they both fell with a hard thump into the drift. It shifted beneath them, creaking ominously.

The noise disturbed the serpents. One raised its head and hissed in their direction.

Shannon closed her eyes, willing herself not to panic. They didn't move, hardly breathed, for long moments.

Finally, the drift settled again, without any of it breaking away.

Gareth let out his breath in relief. "Up to trying that again?"

Ignoring her fear, Shannon nodded. She opened her

eyes and glanced toward the snakes. They had calmed; no wicked-looking head was raised.

Gareth found another branch low enough to grasp. Once more he lifted her on his shoulders, and she pulled herself onto the branch, fearful of it snapping as the other had.

But this one held. Once she was secure, Gareth pulled himself up. They scooted along the limb's rough surface to the tree trunk, then got onto another branch on the opposite side, swinging from it onto solid ground again.

"I feel like kissing the earth," Shannon said. "Now I know how people feel after a long ocean voyage."

"Me, too," Gareth agreed. "But we've got a long walk ahead of us."

Staying well away from the river's ever-widening edge, they fought their way back. Debris of all types was still being swept along by the current. Thankfully, they saw no more people helpless in the water.

"A flood like this has never happened before in the Valley's history. It's hard for me to believe what I'm seeing," Gareth said, his voice grim.

"Yes," Shannon agreed, feeling sick at the devastation, knowing lives had been lost.

But deep inside her a tiny flame glowed. Gareth loved her. She had to hang on to that knowledge.

More than an hour later, so exhausted it was all either of them could do to lift one foot and then put it down, the chill rain still relentlessly pelting them, they got back to where Gareth had left his sister.

They had expected Clare to be pacing the riverbank, wringing her hands.

But she was gone.

"Where is she?" Shannon burst out. "You don't think she somehow got back into the river?"

"No. She's at the house," Gareth reassured her. "Come on, at least there's no danger of it being flooded so far."

But Clare wasn't there, and neither was Gwenny or Maud. They searched the house, from kitchen to attic.

In the kitchen again, bare except for the still-warm kitchen range, Gareth huffed out a tired sigh.

"I should have known they wouldn't stay here when we didn't come back. No doubt they're searching for us."

"How could we have missed them? Surely they wouldn't go upstream."

"I don't know." Gareth's face was taut with anxiety and weariness. He looked at Shannon, shivering in her soaked clothes. "You're about to drop on your feet."

He grabbed a cup, poured coffee from the pot on the stove and thrust it into her hands. "Here, drink this." He poured himself coffee, gulped it down, then set the cup on a windowsill.

Their eyes met and the glance held. She smiled at him; then the smile faltered.

"Did you mean what you said in the river? Or was that just a reaction to fearing me dead?"

He covered the space between them, took her cup from her nerveless fingers and placed it beside his, then folded her into his arms.

"I meant every word of it. I thought I'd lost you and I couldn't bear it."

Shannon lifted her head, and Gareth covered her cold, wet mouth with his own. Fire leaped between them despite their fatigue, and hunger of a different kind began to build.

Gareth regretfully dropped his arms and moved away. "Go on upstairs, get into dry clothes and rest. I'm going to look for the family."

"No, I'm going with you!"

The door opened on a rush of wind and rain.

Maud stood framed in the opening, soaked, her hair straggling about her wet face. Gwenny was behind her and someone else, half-hidden.

Clare! Thank God.

"You're all right!" Maud's tired face lightened. "We were so worried about you!"

They came inside, and Shannon saw it wasn't Clare

behind Gwenny. It was a boy of perhaps eight, blood running down the side of his face, now that the rain wasn't washing it away.

"This is Nathan Adams," Maud said. "His family lives upstream. We heard him crying when we were out looking for you. He'd been washed ashore and hurt his head."

"Where is Clare?" Gwenny asked. "Upstairs?"

Shannon tried to keep the stricken look from her face. "We thought she was with you."

Fear swept across Maud's features; then she controlled it. "We haven't seen her. Where could she be?"

Gareth quickly explained about Josh and the sheep, Clare's tumble into the river and the rest of it, then headed for the door. "I'm going to search for her."

"I'll go with you," Maud declared.

"So will I," added Shannon.

"No, Mama." Gwenny grasped her sleeve. "You're too tired. So are you, Shannon. You both stay here and tend Nathan. I'll go with Gareth."

Shannon shakily moved forward, and Gareth put a hand on her shoulder. "You're so tired you'll be a hindrance not a help. Stay here."

Realizing he was right, Shannon subsided.

Maud stood, undecided, then finally nodded. "All right, but if you're not back in half an hour, I'm coming after you."

Gareth and Gwenny left, and Maud washed and bandaged Nathan's cut, which turned out to be minor. Shannon brought down cold corn bread and ham from the store of food upstairs and settled the boy down on a rug by the heat of the cookstove.

Maud poured herself coffee and quickly drank it, then turned to Shannon, sagging on one of the kitchen chair they had brought back downstairs a few minutes ago afte changing into dry clothes.

She motioned to Shannon to follow, and they move out into the front hall.

"I fear the boy's family is gone," she said in low tone

"He said their house was swept away and he didn't see his parents or his sisters after that."

A sudden thought made bile rise in Shannon's throat. *What if the couple she'd seen clinging to the boards were Nathan's parents?* She fought back the sickness.

She'd never know, and she could have done nothing to help them.

Maud's eyes were deep pools in her pale face. "There are going to be many terrible happenings due to this flood."

Shannon saw she was nearly frantic with anxiety over Clare. She reached out and touched the older woman's hand.

"Yes. But I'm sure Clare's all right. She may be flighty, but she knows how to take care of herself."

"I keep telling myself that, but none of us has ever gone through anything like this. Not even during the war." She turned away. "We'd better go back to Nathan. He's a mighty scared little boy."

Nathan had finished his food and was fast asleep, curled up on the hearth rug. Shannon looked down at his innocent sleeping face, and tears came to her eyes. "I hope somehow his family escaped."

"It's possible. When nature goes on a rampage like this, all kinds of strange things can happen."

Shannon could see Maud didn't have much hope of this, though. She also realized they were talking to keep from falling into a silence during which they would have to face another terrible possibility.

Maybe Clare would never be found alive.

Shannon gathered up the used dishes and put them in the dishpan on the back of the stove, then washed them to keep her hands busy, her mind occupied.

"I'll dry."

Maud plucked a towel from the wall peg. She glanced at Shannon. "Something happened between you and Garth," she said rather than asked. "I could see it in the way you looked at each other when he left."

"Yes." Shannon kept her eyes on the dish she held. "We've . . . come to an understanding."

"Thank God. I've prayed for this to happen. Gareth needs you—and you need him."

"Yes," Shannon said again. She smiled at Maud, and the other woman smiled back.

His knees trembling, legs about to collapse, Josh grimly pushed the protesting sheep ahead of him toward the barn door.

He'd saved the dumb beast; he wasn't going to give up now. The Colbys' barn was closer than his family's. The sheep could stay here until tomorrow, until it recovered from its ordeal.

Josh reached for the heavy wooden latch, then realized the door stood ajar a few inches.

He frowned. Who had done this? And why? He pushed the door farther open, enough to let the still-protesting sheep enter.

Clare lay on her side in the middle of the big open area, her eyes closed, her clothes torn and muddy.

"Clare!" Josh forgot the sheep, forgot everything except that the woman he loved with all his heart was injured—maybe badly.

He stumbled to her, fell to his knees beside her. Frantically, he felt for a pulse in her wrist, relieved when he found it strongly beating.

She sighed and moaned, then rolled over on her back. Her eyes fluttered open. For a few moments, her blue gaze was unfocused, then it sharpened. She jerked herself to a sitting position.

"Josh! I was so afraid you'd drowned!" She reached for him, her arms and hands scratched, one sleeve of her gown ripped and hanging loose.

Josh folded her into his trembling arms. "Thank God you're all right. What in the world are you doing out here? Why aren't you safe in the house with the other women?

Her smile was shaky. "I went to look for you—I saw you eing swept away holding on to a sheep. Didn't you see ie standing on the rock at the river's edge—hear me elling?"

"Of course I didn't!"

"I fell in, and I'd have drowned if Shannon and Gareth adn't saved me!"

She hugged him tighter, lifted her face for his kiss, voring the solid feel of him. She'd been so afraid she'd ever be able to again.

His cold, wet lips covered her own, reassured her of his ve despite all that had happened between them.

Finally, reluctantly, he moved back a little. "What are ou doing here?"

Clare explained what had happened. "I couldn't just and there waiting for Gareth and Shannon. I knew he'd ve her. I—I had to try to find you."

She gave him a wan smile. "I wasn't thinking straight. —I guess when I got here I was so tired I went to sleep."

"Then you don't know if Gareth and Shannon are all ght?"

Her eyes widened, delayed worry hitting her afresh. Gareth wouldn't let Shannon drown," she said, struggling her feet.

She swayed, and Josh caught her. "I love you so much, lare," he said. "I couldn't have lived without you!"

Clare raised her head, her face radiant. "I love you, too, osh! I've been such an idiot! Can you ever forgive me?"

"Yes," he said simply. "I can and do. Now let's get to ie house."

Leaving the sheep in the barn, Josh carefully latched ie door behind them. They supported each other during ie walk to the house.

Halfway there, they encountered Gareth and Gwenny.

The kitchen door swung open. Shannon quickly turned. osh entered, carrying Clare, Gwenny and Gareth behind him. Clare's eyes were closed, and fear leaped through Shannon.

"My baby!" Maud dropped her towel on the floor and hurried to the group.

"She's all right, Mrs. Colby," Josh said. "She's just worn clear out."

"Where did you find her? Bring her upstairs and let me put her to bed."

Gareth explained. "That's why none of us saw her earlier," he finished.

Shannon's eyes met his for a brief moment, and they exchanged a silent message. *Our time will come later.* She stayed with Nathan while Josh took Clare to her bedroom, Maud and Gwenny following.

Gareth also stayed in the kitchen.

"She was searching for Josh, wasn't she?" Shannon asked.

He nodded. "Yes."

"Thank God he's all right!"

"We've all been very lucky." He dropped heavily into a kitchen chair.

"What about Josh's family?"

"Their house is on as high a ground as this one. Gwenny and Mama went over there before they found the little boy. They were all right. But I'll go back with Josh."

She ached to tell him to wait, he was dead on his feet but stopped herself. Of course he had to see Josh safely home. He'd looked almost at the end of his rope.

But, oh, how she wanted to be with Gareth! "I love you," she told him, thrilling to the sound of the words. The same words she'd said to him those weeks ago.

How different things were now between them.

His face and eyes softened for a moment. "I love you too."

Josh came back downstairs, lines of exhaustion etched in his young face, but smiling happily.

"Clare's just worn out."

Gareth nodded. "I'll walk to your place with you."

"You don't have to do that," Josh protested. "I'm fine."

Gareth grinned. "You're about as fine as we all are. Come on, don't argue."

"All right," Josh finally agreed.

Shannon walked with them to the door, and not caring that Josh saw, they exchanged a brief, sweet kiss before the two men left.

Something seemed different.

Then she realized no wind and rain had blown in when Gareth opened the door. The rain had stopped. She listened. The silence felt strange after the last two days of unrelenting downpour.

She opened the door again. Duke came out from wherever he'd retreated and grinned at her, then offered his paw. She took it, then looked at the sky.

A weak, watery sun tried to penetrate the still-present storm clouds. While she watched, it succeeded, and a ray of sunshine laid a streak across the porch.

Oh, let the rain be over! Let the floodwaters recede!

Just as suddenly as it arose, the lightened mood fled, leaving her bleak and tense. Swept up in the excitement and danger of the last day and night, her personal problems had been all but forgotten. Now everything rushed back, flooding her mind, her emotions, as the Shenandoah had flooded this land.

How could she have felt, even for an instant, that Gareth declaring his love for her made everything right between them?

Nothing could be right until she remembered the secrets from her past. Until she knew her identity, and what had caused the flight from her home. Or if she even *had* a home—and where it was.

Knew why a shadowy, faceless man wanted her blood on his knife.

She and Gareth could never find happiness together until she found out if she *deserved* a life with him.

It was still very possible she didn't merit the happiness that now seemed almost within her grasp.

Chapter Twenty-Three

Vance tried to keep his excitement from showing.

"Are you positive the girl you saw in the store was the one on the poster?"

The other man sitting in the buggy seat eagerly nodded. 'Yessir. I'm as sure about that as I am of my own name."

Vance gave the peddler such a piercing glance the other nan shrank back a little. "That's not much reassurance. Iow do I know you gave me your right name?"

"Why shouldn't I? Not ashamed of me name. Jimmy 3lakeston's as good a one as any."

"You say she was with this Gareth Colby—who lives on farm near Luray?"

Jimmy nodded again. "That's right. They went out ogether and got into his buggy and drove off. Toward edmond, they went."

Alarm shot through Vance. He leaned closer to Jimmy, is stance menacing. "What's that you say? Toward Redond?"

Jimmy shrank back a little more. His sharp features grew ary. "Yes. But that ain't where he lives, I just said, e—"

"Shut up!" Vance commanded. "Let me think."

If this idiot was right, it could mean the girl and this Colby fellow were trying to find him from the address on the poster.

But why would they be doing that? Shannon knew where he lived. Hell, she'd lived there, too.

Of course it could mean something else. This Blakeston could be mistaken—or lying. Just after the money. God knew others had tried that since he'd offered the reward. It still seemed likely she was dead. Otherwise, why hadn't she gone to the authorities long before now?

But he couldn't take any chances. This was the best lead he'd had. He had to check it out. "Can you tell me exactly how to get to the Colby farm?"

"Sure can. Been out that way many a time."

"Tell me now."

Jimmy did, then gave Vance a sly, calculating look. "Why are you so interested in finding that gal? She's a purt piece. Even with her hair cut and them boy's clothes on. Looked the same in the store, t'other day, too; that's how I knew—" His voice broke off, his glance darting to Vance' again.

Vance's heavy features hardened. "What are you talkin about? Did you see this girl before?"

Jimmy swallowed, his eyes narrowing warily. "No, cours not."

Vance reached under the seat and brought out a pist which he leveled at the other man. "Tell me the trut you fool!"

Fear came into Jimmy's weasellike features. He swa lowed, edging away on the buggy seat. "I already did. Nev seen her before two weeks ago in the store in Luray."

Vance steadied the pistol with his other hand and cock it. "I'll give you a minute longer."

"All right," Jimmy gabbled, sweat popping out on h forehead, his rump now against the side of the bugg "Picked her up in my wagon a few months ago. Look like she was runnin' from the devil hisself. Told her to g in the back and next thing I know she's cut off her hair and put on some of my clothes I keep back there."

Vance wobbled the pistol a little. "What happened? Did she tell you why she was running away? Who from?"

"No, nothin' like that. I—she . . . fell off the wagon. Hit her head. Looked like she might be dead."

"And?" The pistol bobbed again.

"I drove off."

"You left her there? Not knowing if she was alive or dead?"

"Couldn't do nothin' else," Jimmy protested. "She'd have told on me—" His voice broke off again, and his face grew even more weasellike.

"Tell on you for what? Did you try something with her?"

Jimmy shrugged, but now sweat was running down his face. "Weren't no call for her to act like a wildcat. I wouldn't a' hurt her."

"I'm sure of that. No more than I plan to hurt her." Triumph filled Vance. This story made all the pieces fit. It had to be Shannon. Finally, he'd found her!

Something in Vance's voice seemed to alert Jimmy. His gaze sharpened.

"She was runnin' away from *you,* wasn't she?" he burst out. "That's why she was so skeered."

This fool knew too much. He had to get rid of him. But why waste a bullet, risk drawing someone's attention, even if they were off the main roads and almost into the woods.

Vance placed the gun under the seat again.

"None of that's your business," he told Jimmy.

"I just might *make* it my business," Jimmy said, his courage returning with the gun now out of sight. "I think that hundred dollars ain't quite enough. I believe maybe I need about two hund—"

Vance's hands shot around the little man's neck, choking off his last words.

Grunting, Vance squeezed. Jimmy clawed at him, scratching the backs of Vance's hands, guttural sounds coming from his throat.

Finally he quit his frantic fighting for life and grew limp, his head slumping to the side.

"I guess you won't have to worry about spending any reward money," Vance said.

He pushed the man down on the floor of the buggy, then started the horse again, looking for a likely spot. Plenty of woods around here to dump a body in. With nobody to find it but wild animals.

By tonight he'd be at the Colby farm.

"Oh, God . . . please . . . no . . . !"

The last word was almost a scream. Shannon sat bolt upright in bed, her heart pounding, her breathing labored. The nightmare visions were still so vivid in her mind, still so real, that she glanced wildly around the room.

The moon was almost full, the wind rising, making shadows from the big oak tree outside her window writhe across the room, advancing and retreating.

Shannon trembled so hard she pulled her knees against her body, trying to quiet her fears, calm herself.

She'd dreamed about the man with the knife.

Again she hadn't seen his face, although his mocking laughter still rang in her head so insistently she finally clamped her hands over her ears as if that would stop the ghostly sounds.

At last her trembling slowed enough that she could release her legs from their cramped position. But she knew sleep wouldn't come again for a long time. She didn't wan it to.

One nightmare such as she'd just experienced wa enough for tonight.

She swung her legs over the side of the bed and stood reaching for her robe.

Clare's robe. Her mouth twisted into a grimace as sh pulled it on. Nothing she wore, nothing here, belonge to her. As her life didn't belong to her, but was lost i dimness and shadows.

A thought hit her. Yes, there was one object in this house that was hers alone. Or at least she believed so. A sudden longing to hold the sapphire necklace assailed her.

Quietly she let herself out of her room, tiptoeing up the attic stairs to the cubicle, and retrieved the jewel.

She held it for a few moments, absorbing some comfort from the feel of it against her palm. But she wanted more tonight. She wanted to feel it against her skin where it was designed to be.

Shannon put the gold chain around her neck and fastened the clasp. The jewel's cool heaviness slid down her neck, under the robe and nightdress, settling between her breasts.

A sensation of absolute rightness went over her. It belonged there. How could she have stolen this? Her memory *must* be a true one. Her mother had given this to her as she lay dying.

Sadness enveloped her, lightening a little as she passed Gareth's room on the lower floor. She paused before his closed door, aching to open it, to go to his bed, take comfort from his arms.

But she couldn't do that. Not yet. Although they were promised to each other, no wedding date had been set.

Nor would it be, until she recovered her memory.

She and Gareth had argued long about that. He wanted their marriage now, but no longer because she could be carrying his babe. A few days ago that possibility had been done away with, and she was illogically disappointed.

But he wanted her in his bed. He wanted her for his wife.

Why was it so hard for him to understand that she couldn't wed him until she knew who she was? Remembered everything, good and bad?

He didn't care about any of that. She'd proved her courage, her essential goodness. He refused to believe she could have done anything wrong.

How she wished she could be that sure. But she couldn't, and the flood had effectively delayed their efforts to discover the identity of the man who hunted for her. Or anything about her past. Of course, the flood would also have delayed any plans Blakeston might have along that line.

In the last few days they had all labored beside Gareth, in a desperate effort to save what they could of the crops. The corn crop was gone, meaning a double loss—no money from its sale and, moreover, they would have to buy corn for the farm animals this winter.

It had been by far the Shenandoah's worst flood in Valley history, taking out all the bridges in the Valley, and many homes and businesses. Several people had died, and more were still unaccounted for.

Clare was with Josh every possible moment, and it seemed her fickle, flirtatious ways had gone. The girl had at last grown up.

No trace of little Nathan's family had been found, and he knew of no other relatives. So he'd settled into the Colby household. Maud and Gwenny fussed over him like mother hens. Although his grief still overcame him at times, it was plain he was growing to love these people.

Unless relatives appeared to claim him, or some miracle occurred and his family had survived, it seemed likely he'd stay on here.

Now the flood waters had receded, and roads were once again passable. They had done all they could to salvage the crops. Gareth could leave the farm for a day or two.

Tomorrow, she and Gareth would go back to Redmond, stay overnight in the boardinghouse and, early the next morning, be at the store waiting for the man she feared to collect his mail.

Her stomach clenched at the thought, with anticipation and dread. She'd wear the masculine disguise and wait in a shadowy corner of the store.

Surely, surely, when she finally saw that face she'd remember everything!

By tomorrow night she could look forward to a bright future with Gareth.

Or maybe not.

Her stomach rolled again.

She wouldn't think of that possibility. She'd cling to her hope that she was a good person, that she'd done nothing to deserve the torture she'd gone through these last months.

Shannon reached the kitchen and quietly walked onto the porch. The wind still gusted, making the clouds flirt with the moon, now plunging the landscape into darkness, then lifting to expose a dazzling silvered world, mysterious and strange.

She caught a glimpse of Massanutten's bulk before the moon hid itself again. Its brooding presence made her remember that other night she'd come outside like this, when the moon had been beautiful, and walked to the orchard.

And Gareth had found her there. The magic of those moments in his arms swept over her. It had been so wonderful!

Then, so terrible, afterward.

But all that was behind them now. Gareth loved her as much as she loved him. They would have a happy future together. They *would!*

A sudden strong desire to walk to the orchard again seized her. Maybe she could find comfort under the old apple tree.

Maybe she should wake Gareth and persuade him to go with her.

No, she decided in a moment. They had vowed they would wait until marriage to make love again. Their first child would come no earlier than nine months from their wedding.

And that vow would be impossible to keep if she led him to the orchard.

She'd take Duke.

But Duke wasn't in his usual place, sleeping as close to the back door as possible. He was probably off after a rabbit or some other wild creature.

Why hadn't she heard him bark? Duke always began his night prowls with that announcement of his intentions.

Of course she hadn't heard him. She'd been entangled with nightmare horrors.

Shannon stood a few moments longer, undecided. "You're being silly," she scolded herself out loud. "Go on to the orchard. That will make you feel better."

So she would.

She left the porch and walked toward the trees, hurrying while she had the moon to light her way. She'd gotten a good distance when again clouds swallowed the moon, slowing her steps.

She thought she heard a whisper of movement behind and turned. "Duke?" she called, but no eager whine came. She could see nothing, no dark shadow in the blackness.

Uneasiness hit her, and she wished she hadn't left the house. Maybe she'd better go back. Again she thought she heard a tiny sound behind her.

Just as she whirled again the moon showed itself.

Showed the man a few yards behind her.

Her heart stopped, then began a wild dance of fear, as the night brightened.

The moon's rays struck full on the man's face, revealing his dark hair and eyes, his swarthy skin, his heavy features.

"Vance!"

The sound tore out of Shannon's throat, hurting her with its passage.

All the lost memories, all her past, came crashing down.

Their weight made her shoulders slump, her knees sag. Horrified, she knew she was going to fall and he would be upon her.

Desperately, she tried to regain control of her body, tried to run, but he was too fast. Belying his bulk, he ran toward her, his wide mouth stretched in a ferocious grin.

He pounced on her and bore her down, his heavy weight on her back pinning her to the ground. Shannon gasped for breath, sharp pain piercing her. She tried to wriggle free, but it was impossible.

"You may as well save your energies, you hellion," Vance's harsh voice hissed in her ear.

His breath moved the fine hair along her temple. She shivered in disgust and struggled harder. She felt a sharp pain on her cheek and realized he'd slapped her.

"I told you to stop that!" he snarled.

He moved away from her a bit, then grasping her arms, rolled her over and straddled her again. His leering face was just above her, his obsidian eyes staring into hers.

Shannon stifled a scream, knowing he'd only hit her again, and she was too far away from the house for anyone to hear even if they were awake—which was unlikely.

Why hadn't she woken Gareth? *Why* had she come out here alone?

She forced herself to stare defiantly at Vance. She instinctively knew that to allow him to see her terror would only make things worse.

Worse? How could this be any worse? She was looking into the face of her nightmares. And they were all true. The only thing missing was the knife.

Even while she formed the thought, he fumbled in a pocket and brought out a gleaming object.

The moon hid itself again, plunging them back into darkness just as the scream she could withhold no longer burst from her.

She felt the cold steel of the blade against her throat and stopped breathing.

Was it all going to end here in this meadow? Would her life be snuffed out now before she'd even lived?

Shannon felt a tiny nip of pain and knew the blade had cut her. She closed her eyes and waited for the final thrust.

Instead the knife was withdrawn, and she heard a satisfied chuckle.

"Decided to behave yourself, I see. You've led me a merry chase, my girl. I've been waiting out by the barn for three nights, trying to decide how I could get in the house and find you without waking the whole household, and here you come, nice as you please, walking out to meet me."

Vance paused, and once again the moon brightened the night. Shannon swallowed as she saw him looking down at her, saw him lick his thick lips.

"Damned if you aren't dressed for it, too. In your nightie, no less."

She realized her gown was hiked up to her thighs. A new kind of fear swept over her, and she surged upward. With a heavy hand he pushed her down again.

But his gaze wasn't on her face or her body now. It was fixed on her throat. A greedy look came over his heavy features.

"By all that's holy," he whispered, "you're even wearing the necklace."

She cursed her impulse to wear the pendant, cursed her lack of forethought in coming out here alone. Blakeston must have gotten to Vance after all.

"How did you find me?" she asked, trying to hide her desperation. If she could keep him talking, maybe she could get away from him. Maybe someone at the house had heard her scream and would come.

Vance's grin returned. "The peddler saw you in the store and wanted that reward money," he said, confirming her thoughts. "Too bad he got greedy."

He lifted one hand and curved it. "Scrawny little neck he had."

Livid scratches slashed across the back of Vance's hand She pictured the peddler fighting for his life, and a cold knot formed in her stomach.

"You'll never get away with this," she said, forcing her voice to stay firm, her gaze steady. "The whole family here knows everything."

He gave her another evil grin. "Then why haven't I been arrested long before? Why didn't you go to the authorities Did you really believe I'd tell them *you* were the one did it?"

Yes, she remembered that threat. That must have been

why her mind had insisted she not tell anyone. Why it had blanked out all her past.

Her throat felt dry as paper, every word an effort to force out. But she had to keep him talking, someway. *Any way.* It was her only chance.

"What *did* you tell them? Why haven't they been searching for me?"

The grin widened. "No reason for anyone to search for a girl who got burnt up in a fire in the summer kitchen."

Shock hit her. "Everyone thinks I'm dead?"

"And buried. Alongside your mother and stepfather. Likely the murdering robbers will never be found."

The gloating satisfaction in his voice made her stomach turn, made her fears worsen. He'd covered everything very neatly.

"After the legal waiting time, I'll get Parker's property, as I should have to begin with. No reason for him to leave it all to you. You're no blood kin."

Did he realize he was admitting he planned to kill her? Never mind, just keep him talking . . . buy herself more time. . . .

"I told everyone here what you did," she repeated. "You can't get away with this."

"I don't believe you. From what I've heard about Gareth Colby, he'd have dragged you to the sheriff long before now."

He put the knife against her throat again and pressed. "Tell me the truth."

If she admitted she'd only remembered her past a few minutes ago, and that no one here knew his identity, he could very well get away with all his crimes.

Including her murder.

"Tell me!" He pressed harder. She felt the knife point enter her flesh again, a little deeper this time.

Fear swept through her. If she didn't say something, he would kill her here and now.

She had no choice.

"I lost my memory when I hit my head falling out of the

peddler's wagon. I couldn't remember you—or anything about my life."

Astonishment lightened his heavy features. The pressure on her throat eased.

"My God! You mean all these months I was worrying for nothing? Hunting for you, afraid any minute they'd come for me because you'd told them what you saw."

"You killed my stepfather—your own uncle!" she burst out. "You stabbed him a dozen times!"

Instantly, she regretted her impulsive words. They could only inflame him.

But he merely shrugged, as if she were talking about swatting a fly.

"I had to. He'd found out I embezzled all that money. Our blood ties didn't mean enough to keep him from turning me over to the sheriff."

Shannon swallowed. He seemed proud of his crimes, wanted to talk about them, so she'd continue. Try to kee herself alive a little longer.

"You killed that woman who was with you, too. You'r a cold-blooded devil!"

He smiled. "I don't mind being called a devil—but you' soon find out just how hot-blooded I am."

A moonbeam glanced off the blade of the knife again her throat, striking terror to her heart.

"Promise you'll be a good girl and I'll take the kni away."

She knew he lied, knew as soon as he was finished wi her, he'd kill her in the manner she'd feared all the months. He'd already killed three people. What differen did one more make?

But her will to live was strong, her blood beating fast her veins. She *would* live!

Life was too sweet to lose.

Even if she lost Gareth when she had to tell him wh she'd remembered.

Yes, even then.

New strength surged through her. If she had to let h

take her, she would somehow survive. She forced herself to lie still, to look calmly up at him.

"All right. I won't fight you anymore."

A satisfied smile curved his mouth. "You're finally being smart, Shannon." He took the knife away, and with his free hand stroked her cheek. "Poor baby. Did I hurt you? I'm sorry."

Like a snake striking, he slapped her again, hard, on the other cheek this time.

Her face tingling, tears in her eyes, she heard his laughter.

"Now they match. Both your pretty cheeks are nice and red. Just the way I like my women to look."

He raised the knife, bringing it toward her throat, lowering it, and she drew back, sure he'd changed his mind and was going to finish her off now.

But instead he grasped the front of her nightdress and cut it all the way to the bottom, then pulled it apart.

Now she knew how a small animal must feel just before the fox pounced, she thought wildly, watching Vance devour her almost naked body with his eyes.

He reached toward her again, and she shrank back as he felt his hand touch her flesh, curve around one breast, hen squeeze it painfully.

She let out a gasp of pain, and once more he laughed. He released her breast, grasped the necklace and pulled down until it lay flat between her breasts again.

"I have a powerful yen to feel that between us when I ke you," he told her.

Still holding the knife in one hand he moved back and egan working at the buttons on the front of his trousers th his free hand.

Terrible fear hit her anew. No one was coming to save er. This was her last chance to save herself.

"You said you'd lay down the knife if I—if I behaved," e said from between numb lips.

She tried to force a smile, but knew it must be a horrible rody of one. "I—I'm behaving."

His feral eyes gleamed in the moonlight, and she fervently wished clouds would hide the moon again. In the dark maybe she'd have a chance to escape. If not, at least she wouldn't have to see him when he took her.

"Aren't you the meek little girl. Not like the princess old Parker spoiled to death. Shame you had to find out at the end he was no better than me."

Sickness washed over her as she remembered that last scene. But she'd do anything to keep Vance talking and not acting.

"You're right. He was no better. How could he pretend to be such a good man? How could he fool my mother?"

She wasn't only talking to keep Vance from burying himself in her body, she realized. She needed to know this.

How could a man she'd grown to love like her true father have betrayed them as Parker had?

"Your dear mother wanted to be fooled. She'd ha enough of starving and doing without. Parker offered he a good life again. An easy life."

Was that true? Had her mother, too, betrayed her an all they believed in? She forced down that unbearabl thought.

"How could Parker do those horrible things to his ow people?"

Vance gave a sharp bark of laughter. "For money, yo little fool. People will do anything for money. Everybod has his price."

He gazed down at her, a ferocious hunger filling h eyes. "Enough talking," he said roughly. He put his fre hand on her stomach, spread it flat, moved it lower.

Loathing filling her, she twisted sideways and dug h nails into his hand.

"You little bitch!" He raised his bleeding hand ar slapped her again.

Wild barking suddenly filled the air.

Then a snapping, growling dog flung itself upon Vanc leg. Vance let out a startled yell and jerked around.

Dropping his knife upon Shannon's bare stomach.

She made a grab for it just as Duke renewed his attack, upon Vance's other leg this time. Vance howled with pain and rolled off her, searching for the knife.

He kicked at the growling animal. "I thought I'd killed you at the barn, you bastard!" he yelled, as the dog grabbed his ankle.

Shannon scooted backward, moving into a crouching position, holding the knife in her upraised right hand. Her hand was steady, her eyes holding Vance's.

"Don't come near me!" she warned. "I'll kill you!"

Vance sneered. "You haven't got the guts, little girl. Give me the knife." He crawled toward her.

Duke pounced again, this time landing squarely in the middle of Vance's back, tearing at the man's neck.

Unable to keep his balance, Vance fell forward.

Onto the razor-sharp blade of the knife Shannon still held in a death grip.

She heard the terrible sound of steel going into flesh, felt the metal vibrate against her fingers, but grimly held on. Vance's weight fell against her shoulder, tumbling her sideways, wrenching the knife away from her hand.

Missing her by inches, he fell forward onto the ground, the knife under him.

A cloud passed across the moon, turning the night to pitch. Shannon frantically scrambled backward, expecting Vance to come to roaring life.

But he didn't. The seconds ticked by. The cloud drifted on, and the moon shed its light again. Heart pounding, she got up and warily approached the inert body. There was no movement, no sign of life.

She had to be sure. Hands trembling, jaw clenched, she bent and rolled him onto his back, ready to grasp the knife and plunge it into him again if needed.

It wasn't.

Vance's black eyes stared unseeingly at the night sky. The knife was buried to the hilt in his massive chest.

Relief swept over her in a weakening wave. She sank to her knees, then sprawled facedown.

Shannon heard Duke's anxious whine, felt his wet tongue on her face. She managed to raise her head enough to see how badly he was hurt. His head was cut, but the bleeding had almost stopped. She gave him a reassuring smile and pat.

"Thank you, Duke," she whispered.

Then her hand dropped, as did her head, onto the cold ground.

Chapter Twenty-Four

Gareth knocked on Shannon's door. He couldn't sleep for thinking of how much he wanted her in his arms—his bed.

He had to talk to her, hold her and kiss her, no matter how late it was.

No answer came to his knock. He quietly turned the knob and opened the door. "Shannon?" he asked softly.

Again, no sleepy, well-loved voice answered, and an uneasy feeling hit him. He opened the door wider and entered.

Moonlight showed the empty room, bedcovers thrown back. His uneasiness deepened. Where was she? Was it possible . . . no, there were no signs of struggle. No one had abducted her by force from here.

Quickly, he searched the house, finding no disorder. She must have gone outside.

Damn it! He didn't want her out now, even though there was surely no danger. They had agreed it was unlikely Blakeston could have already gotten in contact with the man she feared because of the flood. But still. . . .

He walked out on the porch, and the silvery moonlight

reminded him of that other time she'd gone out . . . to the orchard . . . and he'd followed her.

That must be where she'd gone tonight. Duke was gone from his accustomed place, too.

He decided he'd follow her, although he realized that wasn't a good idea if they were to keep their vow to not make love until after their marriage.

But he didn't want her outside alone. He'd go bring her back.

Halfway there, Duke's barking erupted into the quiet of the night. The frenzied sounds were those the dog made only when real danger threatened.

The moon went behind a cloud.

Fear shot through him.

Why hadn't he grabbed Shannon up and carried her to the minister? If he'd insisted they marry now, she'd have been safe in his bed tonight.

He forced his legs to run faster. The crippled one ached fiercely, and the knee kept trying to buckle.

Go, damn you, he told it. *Don't you dare give out on me now*

The moon was out again. Ahead of him he saw shape moving, saw Duke attacking a large man. Another figur was there, too, half under the person Duke assaulted.

His heart thumped as dread filled him. They had bee wrong.

The man she feared had found her.

The second figure moved backward, and his hear stopped. It was Shannon.

His fear eased a bit when she sat upright. The moo struck a gleam off something in her hand. Duke lunge again. Gareth heard a yell of pain.

The man fell forward, toward Shannon. Gareth drov himself faster. Without warning, his bad leg gave out an he stumbled and sprawled flat.

He jerked his head up. Shannon moved sideways, an the man fell facedown and stayed there.

The night was again plunged into blackness.

Gareth struggled to his feet, cursing.

The cloud moved on. Shannon now stood, close to the man. She rolled him over and stood motionless for endless seconds.

Then she staggered and fell. Duke walked over and licked her face, and she lifted her hand, patted him.

Her hand fell to her side. She lay unmoving.

Terrible fear gripped him, squeezing until he gasped. Limping, his lungs laboring, Gareth at last reached the group.

Shannon lay on her back, as still as the man close by. Her eyes were closed, her face white, except for red patches on her cheeks.

He fell to his knees beside her.

His heart contracted. Her nightdress and robe were ripped down the front. Pitifully, she'd tried to pull them to cover her.

Incongruously, the sapphire and diamond necklace hung on its chain around her neck, blazing deep blue and white fire in the moonlight.

"Shannon, are you all right?" The words emerged as croaks. He laid his face against her breast. Hearing her strong but fast heartbeat, his fear ebbed a little.

When he felt her hand on his neck, relief and joy shot through him. He lifted his head.

Shannon smiled weakly. "I'm—fine. Oh, Gareth! It's over! I remember—I remember everything! My name is Shannon Bradford. And Vance can never harm me or anyone else again."

What had the bastard done to her? He sat up and glanced quickly at the still figure of the man. "He's dead, then—the man who was after you?"

Shannon nodded, then pulled herself up. "Yes. He fell on his own knife. He dropped it and I grabbed it."

She swallowed. "I was ready to kill him. I would have, if he hadn't done it himself."

Gareth's lips compressed. "I'd better make sure."

He felt for a pulse, pulled back the man's eyelids.

Getting to his feet, he glanced at Shannon, his eyes

burning. "Yes, he's dead. And I wish he wasn't, so I could kill him myself!"

"I'm not sorry, but it was *awful!*" She shuddered. "I prayed for you to come, but—"

"But I didn't. Not in time to do anything." His hands clenched at his sides; then he pounded one fist into the other palm.

"Don't blame yourself. It's my fault. I shouldn't have come out here alone. How could you have known? How *did* you know?"

He explained. "God! If anything had happened to you, I'd have killed myself here, too."

Her eyes widened, shocked. "Don't say such terrible things. It's over."

"What if he hadn't fallen on his knife?" His gaze fell to her ripped clothes.

Shannon got to her feet, pulled the torn edges of her garments together, fumbled for the robe's sash and tied it. She hurried to him and threw her arms around his neck.

"But he did—and he's no longer a threat to anyone."

Gareth took her wrists in his hands, gently disengaged her grip, then stepped back a little. "You've regained your memory, you said. So you know why this . . . Vance wanted to kill you?"

He saw her swallow as if the thought of talking abou this was painful. "Yes. I—I was a witness to murder. I'd seen him kill my stepfather—Parker Davis."

Shannon's face tightened as she said the name. She sho a glance at him he couldn't interpret.

"Vance was Parker's bookkeeper, and he'd been embez zling from him for months. Parker discovered it and con fronted Vance in his study. I was reading in the windo seat, behind the curtains—and heard and saw it all. Vanc stabbed him to death—and also his own mistress, who wa with him."

"My God," Gareth said, a world of meaning in the tw words.

"He heard me cry out, found me, and dragged me out." She paused and swallowed again. "I fought him and managed to get away . . ."

She shuddered and swayed a little. Gareth reached out and pulled her into his arms. He had to comfort her, no matter how inadequate he felt for the job.

"And so you ran away, and the peddler gave you a ride on his wagon. Why didn't you go for help, or to the sheriff?"

She hesitated, then went on.

"It was night and I was terrified. We live—lived at the edge of Colfax in an isolated house. And Vance had threatened to tell the authorities *I'd* murdered Parker. Vance was so close behind me I couldn't think straight. I hid in the woods all night. I was frantic to get away from Colfax, away from Vance."

"But Blakeston had other ideas and tried to rape you. God, what a time you've had!" He clutched her fiercely to him.

"There's more." She told him how Vance had set fire to the summer kitchen, with his mistress's body inside, and identified the charred corpse as Shannon's, blamed both murders on robbers, and also killed the peddler.

"Blakeston told him how to get here. He'd been here for several nights, waiting for a chance."

"And tonight he found it." Gareth wanted to keep her safe in his arms forever.

Safe? In *his* arms?

"So your family lives in Colfax?"

"Lived," she corrected, her voice full of pain. "My memories were true ones. My mother, father and brother are all dead. And now so is—Parker, my stepfather."

He heard the hesitation in her voice whenever she mentioned her stepfather. There was still something she didn't want to talk about.

But anything else could wait.

"That's enough for tonight," Gareth said. "You can tell me the rest later."

Shannon glanced up at him, desperately holding on to

her resolve. Trying to summon courage from somewhere deep inside, she stepped out of his embrace.

"No. I—I have to tell you everything now. The necklace truly belongs to me. My mother gave it to me just as I said."

He smiled at her. "I've told you that all along."

"I had to know for myself."

Only a little while ago, she'd believed finding out she'd stolen the jewel was the worst thing she'd have to face.

If only that were true!

She couldn't go on with this. Why would he ever have to know? She could sell the house, give away the money. . . .

You could be a coward. you mean, her mind coldly told her. *Live a lie . . . haven't you had enough of that?*

Yes! She had.

"My stepfather was—a scoundrel. With backing from the North, he lent money to hard-pressed farmers. He—verbally offered such good terms, many didn't read the fine print on the agreements. Didn't know the payments were so high they'd never be able to keep them up."

Gareth stiffened, his face hardened.

She shrank inside herself a little more.

"Then he—he would foreclose, take their farms. He was careful to do business over a wide area—so people wouldn't get together and blacken his name. He remained highly respected until he . . . died."

Shannon's voice thickened, and she faltered. "It was all legal. That's how he got away with it. How he could buy an elegant house for my mother and me. Fill it with fine furnishings, servants—"

The hardness in Gareth's features deepened into shock.

Bile rose in her throat.

"You lived the good life paid for with the sweat and blood of people like myself and my family?"

Guilt swept over her. "Yes," she whispered. "I did."

A cloud sailed in front of the moon, and she was glad she didn't have to look at his accusing face for a few moments.

The silence drew out. Insects and birds cautiously

resumed their night sounds. Her heart ached until she thought it would surely burst.

"How could you do that?"

His disembodied voice out of the darkness startled her. She jumped and shivered.

"I—didn't know about it," she said dully, "until I heard Vance and Parker talking that night. But I . . . I felt uneasy many times. It didn't seem right that we were so prosperous when most of the South was in such poverty."

The cloud passed, and once more the landscape lightened around them. She wished it hadn't.

Gareth's eyes were dark pools, his glance fixed.

She couldn't stand it. "We—we almost starved during the war after my father died early on. We lived in a small town near Richmond. Right after the war, Parker met my mother there, married her and brought her to Colfax, where—"

She broke off her rapid recital, hearing the almost pleading note in her voice. Enough of this. She wouldn't beg. She deserved his scorn.

"I won't hold you to your promise. I can see how you feel. You don't want to have anything else to do with me."

New shock waves rippled through Gareth's body at her last words.

"As you want nothing further to do with me after finding out what a poor excuse for a man I am?"

"What?" She stared. The surprise on her face looked genuine—but how could it be?

"I failed you when you needed me most. You saved yourself from death—you and Duke. While I was limping across the field, my goddammed leg giving out on me."

Her face paled until the red patches on her cheeks stood out like smears of blood.

"You didn't fail me. If I'd stayed at home in bed, this wouldn't have happened."

"And Vance would still be stalking you. And tomorrow night he might have killed you." That thought was unbearable. "God! I couldn't stand to lose you!"

"And I—I couldn't stand to lose you, either."

Her words were soft, her voice trembling, but he understood every syllable.

She lifted her head a little, as if bracing herself for pain. "But I don't expect you to marry me now that you know what kind of person I truly am."

What kind of person she truly was.

"I already knew. You're a kind, loving woman," he heard himself say before he realized he intended to.

But it was the absolute truth. And all that mattered.

Her head jerked. Her eyes fully focused on him.

"But . . . I was a coward. I should have found out what—"

"If you had, would your stepfather have stopped what he was doing?"

After long moments, she shook her head. "No, of course not."

"So you couldn't have done anything about it."

"I . . . I could have left his house."

"And been unable to support yourself."

She bit her lip. "My mother gave piano lessons during the war. I could have done that."

"You just said you almost starved then."

"I . . . could have done something."

"You were trying to survive. Like we all were—and still are."

Her face crumpled. "Parker treated me like his own daughter. I . . . guess that's why I found it so hard to believe he'd do anything wrong."

"You're not perfect. I don't expect you to be." He hadn't known he'd say these words, either.

But they were also true.

The corner of her mouth trembled. "Yet you expect perfection from yourself."

He didn't say anything as the moments ticked on. Finally he heaved a sigh. "I think it's high time we demanded little less from ourselves."

He saw her chest move as she took a breath, then let it out. "I think you're right."

She stepped forward, toward him. "I love you," she said. "And accepting all our imperfections, I want to marry you."

He moved forward, too, and all in one motion pulled her into his arms. "I want to marry you. As soon as possible."

Gareth's hands tightened on Shannon, pulling her close against him. He kissed her hair, her red cheeks, which he now saw bore the imprints of Vance's fingers.

Finally, he claimed her lips, then released her.

"Go on ahead of me with Duke," he said. "I'll . . . take care of this."

"All right."

She called for Duke, and the animal hurried to her, limping.

"Oh, Duke, your leg is hurt!" She knelt beside him. Gareth joined them, examining the animal's swollen back leg, the cut and lump on his head.

"You sweet, wonderful boy. Come on back to the house with me," Shannon crooned. "I'll put some salve on you and find you something to eat."

Gareth watched them walk across the field. At the edge, Shannon stopped, turned, and raised her arm.

She called something to him.

Although he couldn't understand the words, he knew what they were.

He lifted his own arm.

"I love you," he called back.

And heard his life-affirming words float across the distance to her.

Epilogue

"Do be still, Clare. You are the most fidgety girl today ever saw!"

Gwenny, her mouth full of hairpins, hairbrush in hand, tood behind her sister in their mother's bedchamber.

"Of course I'm fidgety. I don't get married every day, ou know."

"Thank God for that," Gwenny muttered. "None of us ould survive."

"I have a bump on the end of my nose!" Clare nnounced in tragic tones.

"Let me see." Maud bustled over to examine her younest child's pretty, rosily flushed face. "It's nothing. No ne can notice it."

"*I* will notice it! I did so want everything to be perfect!"

"And so it shall, child. Stop fussing."

Nathan, splendidly dressed for the occasion in new knee ants and white shirt, his sandy hair slicked back, suddenly peared in the doorway. His brown eyes were round with terest, his hands hidden behind his back. "Can I come ?"

Maud gave him a loving smile. "Of course you may."

He walked across to Clare and thrust forward a pink rose. "Here. This is for your wedding."

Clare's fretful look disappeared. She carefully took the flower he offered. "Thank you, Nathan. It's beautiful. I will wear it on my gown like this."

Smiling, she tucked the end of the stem behind the sash of her white muslin dress, so that the bloom faced forward. "See? Doesn't that look nice?"

Nathan beamed.

From her corner seat, Shannon watched the happy bustle, contentment filling her. Clare was a lovely bride. And she knew Josh, waiting impatiently downstairs, was a handsome groom.

How could things have changed so much for all of them in little more than a year?

Clare had matured into a lovely woman who would make Josh a good wife. Josh had been spending all his spare time, with his family's help, building the small house he and Clare would share. Gwenny kept company with one of the neighbor's sons, and they seemed serious abou each other. Maud was happily engrossed in raising anothe child, and Nathan flourished under all the attention.

The farm was flourishing now, too. The crops looke good, the taxes paid up. . . .

She smiled at that recollection. What an uproar Garet had made when she pawned her necklace, paid the taxe then presented him with the receipt.

The house in Colfax was long sold. The proceeds of th sale, and of the rest of Parker's estate, were now the bas of The Valley Fund, a foundation that lent money to loc farmers at low interest rates.

True low interest rates this time.

As for herself and Gareth. . . .

Maud had given her a sharp look this morning and sa that marriage certainly seemed to agree with her. H cheeks were blooming, and wasn't she putting on a litt needed weight?

As she did a dozen times a day, Shannon slid her ha

across her still-flat abdomen. Another smile curved her lips—a small, secret one.

She glanced up to see Gwenny's intent gaze on her hand. Shannon felt her face redden. Gwenny's eyes widened. Shannon nodded at Gwenny's silent inquiry.

Gwenny's eyes widened more. "My goodness, aren't you the sly one, Shannon Colby! When did you plan to let us know, may I ask?"

"Very soon," Shannon said. "I didn't want to detract from Clare's day in the sun."

Maud's hazel eyes brightened, her smile satisfied, as she realized what they meant. "I suspected. How wonderful!" She went to Shannon's chair and gave her a kiss.

Clare stared at them as if they had lost their senses, Nathan beside her regarding everyone with interest.

"What in the world are all of you babbling about?" Clare demanded.

Gwenny turned to Nathan. "I think you'd better go see f Gareth needs you," she told the boy.

"All right," he said agreeably and left the room. Gareth vas still Nathan's idol and hero, and he never missed an pportunity to be with him.

"Will one of you tell me what is going on?" Clare again sked. Her gaze went from one beaming face to another, nally lighting on Shannon's hand, still on her stomach. Then, her mouth opened, forming a circle. "Shannon! re you really going to have a baby?"

Shannon's smile widened even more. "Yes. I am."

Clare rushed across the room and hugged her. "I'm so ad! You'll make a wonderful mother."

Shannon laughed, returning Clare's hug. "I hope so. ow, that's enough about me. This is your day. And I have present to give you."

Clare straightened, her blue eyes sparkling. "What? I love a surprise!"

The other three women chuckled at Clare's unabashed light in the anticipation of a gift.

Shannon reached into a side pocket of her gown and

brought out a small, tissue-wrapped object, which she placed in Clare's palm. "Here. This will look beautiful with your gown."

Clare carefully peeled back the tissue, gasping as the sapphire and diamond necklace was revealed. Open-mouthed, she jerked her head up and stared at Shannon. "You have it back!"

"Yes."

"But you can't mean that you're giving it to me."

Shannon nodded. "You've always loved it."

"But so do *you,*" Clare protested.

Maud gave Shannon a concerned look. "Child, this was given to you by your mother. It belongs in your family."

Shannon's smile was serene and loving. "And it will remain there. All of you are my family now."

She picked up the pendant. "Clare, let me fasten this around your neck."

Clare's frown smoothed out at Shannon's expression. "All right, if you're sure."

"I'm sure." Clare turned, and Shannon fastened the clasp at the back of her neck, then stood back to see the effect. The necklace looked as if it belonged on the simple gown, giving it an unexpected elegance.

Clare's slim hand caressed the stone; then her frown reappeared. "But, Shannon, this was for you to pass on to your daughter. What if the baby is a girl?"

Shannon shrugged. "It will be a long time before she'd be ready to wear it."

"This is only a loan," Clare said firmly. "I'll return when your daughter wants it. Or when you want to wear it yourself."

"All right," Shannon agreed.

"We'd best be getting downstairs," Gwenny said. "Mama, do you want to stay with Clare until it's time for her to come down?"

"Of course. It will be the last time I'll be alone with her as my little girl."

"Oh, Mama," Clare protested. "I was a little girl far to

long. I'm sure you'll be glad to be rid of me. Not that I'll be very far away."

Shannon followed Gwenny out the door, and halfway down the stairs, they met Gareth, also splendidly attired in a gray coat and black trousers. His black hair was smoother than she'd ever seen it, and his boots shone.

They exchanged loving smiles.

"I'll go on ahead," Gwenny said, "and leave you two alone."

The arch tone of her voice made Gareth raise his dark brows. "What was that all about? Does she know something I don't?"

Shannon tilted her head, and her smile widened, ecame mischievous. "Maybe."

He gave her a mock frown. "What do you mean? Aren't ou going to tell me?"

Shannon sighed. "I suppose I must, since Gwenny lready alerted you." She looked up at him. "I had this l planned out. Tonight, after the wedding was over and l the guests gone, we'd walk out to the orchard and sit nder our apple tree. And then I would tell you."

"Tell me what?" Gareth rumbled. "Why are you being mysterious?"

"Because this special time will never come again, darng," she said. "Not quite like this."

Her voice was soft, her face luminous. Gareth couldn't sist. He bent and kissed her, long and deeply. "Now, tell ."

"You're going to be a father."

Surprise and awe filled him. "Are you sure?" he finally ed.

'Yes. I wanted to tell you first, of course. But your percep family figured it out a few minutes ago."

Shannon took his hand and placed it on her abdomen. gave her a startled look.

She laughed. "No, it's too soon to feel movement. But on't be long before you can."

The awe Gareth felt spread until he felt it in his entire being. Between them, they had created a new life.

"Kiss me, Mama-to-be," he demanded, holding out his arms.

"Gladly, Papa-to-be."

A few minutes later Nathan found them still entwined. He stared, then quietly went back downstairs, shaking his head.

As much as he adored Gareth, he couldn't understand why he wanted to do all that kissing stuff.

AUTHOR'S PAGE

Dear Reader,

I hope you enjoyed THE HEART'S HAVEN. My next istorical romance from Zebra will be out in June 1999.

Hayley Armstrong and her sister are sold as bond ser-ants after their parents die on the voyage to America. Vhen they run away from cruel masters, Conn Merritt escues them—and falls in love with Hayley.

But can their love survive when Conn discovers Hayley's ecrets?

I love to hear from readers. Write me at P.O. Box 63021, ensacola, FL, 32526. If you'd like bookmarks and a news-tter, please include a self-addressed, stamped envelope.

Elizabeth Graham

A GUARDED SECRET...

When Shannon Brown opened her eyes, things were not what she expected. Lying in a wagon with a terrible headache, all that was left of her memory was the hauntin image of a bloody knife. The dark-haired stranger who found her thought she was a boy...and from the looks of he worn trousers and too-big boots, Shannon knew she'd bee hiding from someone. Now, not knowing who to trust, she desperately fought to keep her amnesia a secret from her handsome rescuer...

A LOVE REVEALED...

Ever since his fiancée left him after he returned injured from the war, Gareth Colby had no interest in marriage. H knew no woman in her right mind would see him as a desirable husband. In spite of Shannon's mysterious pas Gareth brought the young boy into his bustling, happy family only to discover that he'd been fooled. He wanted throw Shannon out of his home, but he suddenly found himself irresistibly drawn to the beautiful young woma who stood before him. Now, he would risk anything to keep Shannon safe and help her remember her painfu past, so that she could begin a future filled with the sweet promise of love...

THE HEART'S HAVEN

ZEBRA
U.S. $4.99
CAN $6.50

ISBN 0-8217-5958-2